MW01504357

# The Extraordinary Life and Love of Reginald Fubster

A Novel

Geoffrey Hall

ISBN 979-8-89345-182-5 (paperback)
ISBN 979-8-89345-183-2 (digital)

Copyright © 2024 by Geoffrey Hall

All rights reserved. No part of this publication may be reproduced, distributed, or transmitted in any form or by any means, including photocopying, recording, or other electronic or mechanical methods without the prior written permission of the publisher. For permission requests, solicit the publisher via the address below.

Christian Faith Publishing
832 Park Avenue
Meadville, PA 16335
www.christianfaithpublishing.com

Printed in the United States of America

# The Journey to England

AS THE TIME approached for his fifteenth birthday, Reginald Fubster eagerly awaited the moment his father would confirm his entry into His Majesty's Thirty-Third Infantry Regiment. One night after dinner, Wilfred was smoking his pipe on the verandah of their bungalow when he called Reginald to his side.

'I've been thinking, my boy.'

'About my joining the regiment?' Reginald interjected.

Wilfred lifted his eyebrows. 'You're still set on that, are you?'

'More than anything, sir!'

'I tell you what. You're too intelligent to join the regiment in any other capacity than its commanding officer. As that post is currently occupied by myself, you'll have to find some other means of employment.'

Reginald's face fell.

'I have a relative in England by the name of Merriweather Fubster,' continued Wilfred. 'He's your great-uncle and our last living relative in the old country. He's not the martial type, but a good man nonetheless. I've written to him to ask if he will look after you while you receive your education in England.'

'England!' Reginald exclaimed in horror. 'Why England?'

'That's where you'll get the best training. And when you graduate, you can return to India as a commissioned officer. Why, that's

1

what I did when I was your age, and it'll be good for you to see your native country. It'll broaden your mind.'

Reginald had always considered his father's word as law, but this was going too far. How could he leave behind everything he'd ever loved? He had to protest.

'But, sir, I want to stay in India!'

'Nonsense. I've already decided the matter. You'll sail from Bombay by steamer in a month's time. Your friend, Mr McAuliffe, is going with you. His father persuaded me to let you two travel together.'

Wilfred turned away as if that was all he had to say on the subject.

'Father, please!' Reginald gasped.

Wilfred had expected his son to be disappointed. He was dreading their impending separation himself. But he knew (or at least thought he knew) that it was necessary for his son's growth that he struck out on his own. Only then would the value of the boy's early education be brought to light. From the age of seven, Reginald had been cultivated as the ideal soldier. Wilfred had overseen his training personally. It included not only physical exercises, riding, shooting, and performing drills on the parade ground, but a rigorous study of the classics in Greek and Latin.

When he saw that there was no succour forthcoming, Reginald fought his dismay by burying it. A heavy gloom set in about him. He went through the motions of his days mechanically, with no life inside. The remaining month passed quickly and the dreadful day arrived for his departure. He embraced his mother and saluted his father and, trying his best to curb his emotions, boarded the train for Bombay.

His faithful servant, Narendi Ram, was with him. Though born a Mohammedan, the young Indian had given up the regular practise of his faith upon entering Reginald's service. Now he would be losing his caste by sailing across the sea, but he considered this a small sacrifice to make for fulfilling the life debt he owed.

Also with them was the odious presence of Jack McAuliffe. He and Reginald had been rivals in everything since the McAuliffes had come to Delhi from Peshawar a couple of years ago. Reginald's animosity sprang from their first meeting. He had been on his way to assist his father in directing the movements of the regiment when McAuliffe, obviously amused at the sight of a twelve-year-old in a full dress uniform marching smartly down the road, had burst out laughing at him. Reginald, who had an elevated sense of his own dignity and of the reverence due to soldiers of the British Empire, had never forgiven this slight to his honour.

He tried to find a seat where he could sit and nurse his painful thoughts, but was immediately accosted by McAuliffe, who had a grin on his face from ear to ear.

'Crying, Fubster?' he said mockingly. 'Already miss your mommy and daddy?'

Reginald turned his face away and tried to ignore him.

'My father says we're going to the same school,' McAuliffe continued. 'You may know more useless information, but I'm sure I'll prove the better student. And I'm much superior at athletics. It's too bad you're such a scrawny little thing or you might actually make a decent rival.'

'Not everything is a competition, sir,' replied Reginald.

'Oh, but it is!' exclaimed McAuliffe. 'Your father taught you that, didn't he? He's wrong. *My* father has a much better philosophy.'

Jack's father, Leopold, was an unscrupulous arms dealer and mercenary of a kind whom Wilfred had always been convinced would be the downfall of British India. His rifles tended to wind up in the hands of the Pathan tribesmen of the Northwest Frontier who were the perpetual enemies of the Raj. This had earned him the disapprobation of the Commissioner of the Northwest Provinces and forced the move to Delhi.

McAuliffe's mocking soon became too much to bear. Reginald raised his fist to strike him, but as he did, he met the disapproving eyes of Narendi Ram. They both rebuked and reassured him, and he lowered it again.

McAuliffe sat with a smug smile on his face and then, every now and again, would whistle an irritatingly loud tune in Reginald's ear.

Reginald distracted himself by staring out the window.

Now that he was leaving it, he imagined he saw the land of India for the first time. Some of it was romantic, the storybook Hindustan: gleaming palaces and temples, shimmering rivers, golden fields, and lush jungles. Other parts were horrid. Families living on top of each other in squalid hovels, the poor pressing all around the railroad stations, devastated fields and villages that had been burned to the ground. That such things could exist side by side was quite beyond the boy's comprehension.

At last, they reached the bustling port of Bombay and boarded the steamer. It was to Reginald's deep displeasure that he learned that Master McAuliffe would be his cabin mate for the duration of the voyage. During the day, Reginald strode about on deck, listening to the sailors talk and trying to avoid his adversary, but somehow, McAuliffe always found him.

'I can't take it anymore,' Reginald vented to Narendi Ram when he had a moment of peace. 'I can't stand being around McAuliffe for another minute!'

'Try to be patient with him,' said Narendi Ram soothingly.

'You sound like my father. I'd like to throw the lad overboard.'

'Please, sahib. That would not be behaviour befitting a gentleman like yourself. You must be the better man. Don't let anything he says or does bother you. Ignore him completely if you must.'

Narendi Ram proved wise beyond his years. Reginald heeded his advice, refusing to react to anything McAuliffe did, no matter how irritating. Finding his tactics no longer effective, McAuliffe grew increasingly silent and sullen, a fact that offered Reginald secretly a great deal of pleasure.

\* \* \* \* \*

After a month at sea, the steamer chugged into the harbour at Dover, and Reginald Fubster had his first glimpse of the white cliffs and the shore of his native country. This was a sight which brought much joy to the returning Englishmen. But to him, it was a foreign land and place of exile. The leaden skies over the town served as an ill omen for his arrival.

Reginald and Narendi Ram were met at the dock by Reginald's great uncle, one Merriweather Fubster. Merriweather was an elderly man, of a somewhat corpulent physique and with a red face that hinted of a jolly countenance. He embraced Reginald warmly and even condescended to shake Narendi Ram's hand (against the latter's will).

'Ah, and is this young Master McAuliffe?' he said, regarding that worthy with a twinkling eye. 'I've come ter collect yer as well. Yer uncle Finnegan's me neighbour.'

Merriweather hurried them to the train station with a gait surprisingly swift for someone of his bodily composition, and they were soon bound for the English countryside. It was nearing winter and the fields stretched barren and desolate toward the horizon. It would be hard to imagine a more contrasting landscape from what Reginald was used to in India. There were hardly any people here, and the only buildings were clustered village houses and a church with a tall steeple. After a time, he stopped looking and turned away with a shiver.

'Do yer like it, eh?' asked Merriweather Fubster, catching Reginald's eye.

'I'm not sure that I do, sir,' replied Reginald.

'Yer'll get used ter it, I'll reckon. You can expect it ter be a great deal colder than where you come from, eh?'

Reginald wasn't quite sure whether this last remark was meant as a question or as a comment, so he said nothing and stared at the ground. The train pulled into the station at a little Kentish village called Cottebury-on-Lalley. The 'Lalley' in the name was a trickle of water that wound its way through the centre of town.

'Is this where you live?' Reginald asked, eyeing the dark houses and the sombre church with some trepidation.

'Not here exactly. A little ways off, five miles perhaps. Wake up, little master,' he said, gently stirring McAuliffe. 'We're almost ter yer home.'

They got down from the train and boarded a carriage that lay waiting for them. The driver cracked the whip, and they took off along an empty road bordered by a line of dark leafless oak trees. Beyond the trees, the fields lay grey and fallow; the sky also was grey, casting a spell of dreariness over the countryside. They turned off at the first house they came to, an opulent mansion, and Merriweather motioned for Master McAuliffe to follow him.

'This here's yer uncle Finnegan's house.'

'Well, goodbye, Reginald,' said McAuliffe, grinning at the sight of the grand edifice.

'I'm sure we'll be seeing a lot of each other!' Reginald mumbled under his breath.

Merriweather soon returned, and they drove on. It was drawing on night by the time they reached another mansion, smaller than the first by far and in a state of great age and decay.

'So what do yer think of yer ancestral house?' asked Merriweather, gazing proudly at that ancient domicile.

'I'm sure I'll like it, sir,' replied Reginald, though the expression on his face said otherwise.

With Narendi Ram carrying the bags, Merriweather led Reginald along a yew-lined pathway to the front door. Reginald recognized the Fubster family crest, a lion rampant, carved above it, though the lion was missing its right paw. Merriweather rang the bell, and the door was opened by a stooped butler who looked every bit as old and decrepit as the house itself.

'Welcome home, master,' said the butler in a ghostly voice.

'Thank yer, Mr Beech,' the master returned kindly. 'This here's me great nephew, young Wilfred's boy. He's here ter get himself an education.'

Mr Beech bowed his head to Reginald and then limped away, leaning heavily on his cane.

'Poor ol' fellow,' Merriweather said, shaking his head. 'He's seen better days, no doubtin' that. Come along now, Reginald. Ye be hungry, eh?'

Reginald nodded with vigour.

Merriweather led Reginald and Narendi Ram to the dining hall.

'You can take yer victuals with us, as part of the family,' he said to Narendi. 'Mr Beech, tell Miss Natalie that supper's ready.'

Mr Beech appeared suddenly, bowed his head, and limped off. Merriweather settled down comfortably in his chair and motioned for Reginald to take a place beside him.

'Who is Natalie?' Reginald asked. 'Is she your daughter?'

'Eh? No, she ain't me daughter. I'm a bachelor. She's the daughter of one of me old friends who died when she were but a little girl. I look after her now.'

Just as he finished this comment, Mr Beech escorted the girl into the room, startling Reginald so much that he nearly fell out of his chair. She wore an elegant dress and carried herself in a manner befitting a young lady. Her golden hair was tied behind her in a bow and her cornflower blue eyes shone even in the dim lighting of the dining hall. She was beautiful.

'Natalie, this here's me great-nephew Reginald Fubster. His father Wilfred serves in the army over in India,' Merriweather said by way of introduction.

'How do you do?' said Natalie with a graceful curtsey.

Reginald was rendered temporarily speechless and could only nod in reply. He did not remember much of that first dinner in his ancestral house; his mind was in a strange daze.

When he at last returned to consciousness, he was lying in bed, and it was morning.

# *Natalie*

REGINALD SPENT THE first few days exploring his new home. Fubster Manor might have been past its days of glory, but contained many treasures accumulated over its long history. Reginald had always been fond of study and was delighted to find an extensive library full of dusty manuscripts of all shapes and sizes. The house was crisscrossed by halls and secret passageways that connected room to room. Each room had its own unique style of architecture; in one, Reginald found an ivory chess set, in another, a lance and hauberk that he imagined must have belonged to one of his ancient ancestors. Outside of the house, there was an orchard and formal gardens where Reginald was fond of walking, fascinated by the strange plants and creatures he found there.

The one place in the estate where Reginald did not go was the east wing. That was where Natalie lived, and Reginald was afraid of her. Having been reared in a military society, he had no experience with the female sex besides his own mother and had never before spoken a word to a girl his own age. He only saw Natalie twice a day at lunch and dinner, but that was already too much for him. His face turned red, and his tongue became glued to the roof of his mouth.

Merriweather attributed this awkwardness to homesickness and unfamiliarity with the new surroundings, but Reginald knew better.

To him, Natalie was at once Helen of Troy, the goddess Aphrodite, and an angel in heaven.

When he could not stand the present circumstances any longer, Reginald arranged a private interview with his great uncle.

'Sir, I'd like to know when I will start my education.'

'Eh? Not long now, I daresay. Is that what's been bothering yer lately? Yer don't like being idle fer long?'

'Not exactly,' answered Reginald. 'I'd like to be away from the house.'

Merriweather started in surprise. 'Aren't ye comfortable here? What can I can do fer yer?'

'No, it's not you. I'm sorry! I...I'm just not used to being in one place for long, that's all.'

The great-uncle frowned. 'From what I understand, yer lived in one place in India. Tell me what's really bothering ye, son.'

'It's Natalie,' Reginald admitted, turning scarlet.

'Bless my soul! The girl wouldn't hurt a fly! What do yer have against her?'

'It's not that I have anything against her—'

'Oh, I see now. Yer ain't used ter having womenfolk around. Yer'll get used ter it soon enough, if yer give it the chance.'

'No, that's not it at all,' Reginald protested.

'Then what is it? Come on, my boy, let's have it out!'

'Well,' said Reginald, drawing in a deep breath, 'to be honest with you, sir, I am quite in love with her, so much so that I can scarcely endure being near her.'

'Ahh,' said Merriweather, his eyes twinkling. 'Of course! I should've known! And why shouldn't yer be? She's the best girl in the world and the pertiest too.'

'What should I do?' Reginald gasped.

'Ye know, I was about yer age when I had me first love,' Merriweather said wistfully. 'That was quite some time ago, of course. She was the vicar's daughter. I loved 'er from afar fer many years, but I was always too bashful ter say anythin' ter her, which is part o' the reason I'm still a bachelor ter this day. I don't want ye ter make the same mistakes as I did. Ye should get ter know Miss Natalie before ye decide yer in love with 'er and find out whether ye two can get along as friends.'

'Oh no, sir,' returned Reginald ardently. 'I'm not ready for that.'

'Nonsense,' said Merriweather with a dismissive wave of the hand. 'I'll arrange fer a meeting between ye tomorrow.'

Merriweather showed the protesting Reginald to the door. The boy imagined as he descended the stairs that he could hear the old man's jolly laughter echoing in the hallway.

Reginald could not get to sleep that night. His stomach was tied in a knot, and his breathing came in short bursts. Several times, he imagined that he was suffocating.

When dawn came, he got out of bed and surveyed his haggard face in the mirror. He had by no means a remarkable appearance. His height was somewhat less than average and his build was slight, disguising the wiry strength of his frame. His brown hair was cut short in military style, with not even a hint of a moustache at the age of fifteen, and the only distinguishing facial feature was his eyes, which were green and piercing, hinting at his inner intensity. He dressed himself in his best clothes and slowly, and almost mechanically, feeling the lack of his personal charm, descended the staircase to the dining hall. He tried to force down some breakfast, but upon finding that his stomach was still tied in a horrid knot, he merely stared out of the window. The clock on the wall struck eight when the door creaked open, and Reginald looked up to see the wizened figure of Mr Beech.

'The young lady will see you now,' croaked Beech. 'Follow me.'

Reginald had half a mind to stay where he was, but his better sense prevailed, and he followed the ancient housekeeper as he shuffled toward the east wing. Mr Beech paused on the threshold of a delicately carved oak door and rapped softly.

'Who is it?' came a sweet voice from within.

Reginald's heart almost stopped at the sound of it.

'Mr Beech, madam. Young Mr Fubster is here to see you.'

'Show him in, please.'

Mr Beech swung open the door and stood respectfully to the side. The room Reginald entered, with difficulty, was the loveliest in the house, having been decorated by Natalie herself. There were several large windows that looked out over the orchards and the expanse of the park, where a light snow was falling. Mr Beech closed the door, and the two were alone.

Natalie was seated at her desk wearing a blue dress that matched the colour of her eyes and reminded Reginald of the skies over India. Her golden tresses, which were usually tied in a bow, fell down to her shoulders.

'Master Merriweather said that you wanted to see me,' she said, regarding him inquisitively.

Reginald stood rigidly by the door, too nervous to speak.

'Is anything the matter? Would you like to sit down?'

She motioned to a chair, and Reginald stiffly took a seat.

She looked at him closely, as if noticing him for the first time. Reginald blushed, awed by the beauty of her face and painfully aware of his own deficiency.

Natalie was one of the rare and valuable set of girls who have no idea how attractive they are. As a result, she could only assume that Reginald's reticence must be due to some fault of hers.

'Have I done something to offend you?' she asked.

'No,' said Reginald, finding his voice. 'You have not.'

'Is there anything I can do for you, then?'

'Nothing at all.'

The young girl gave a confused smile, wondering why this appointment had been scheduled in the first place.

'The thing is,' said Reginald, plucking up a bit of courage, 'my great-uncle wanted me to talk with you. He thought it would be good for me to get to know you.'

He figured this would be a better way to start than by immediately declaring his love.

'Oh!' the girl said pleasantly. 'Well then, what would you like to know about me?'

'I...well...I,' stammered Reginald, trying to think of something to say.

'Why don't you tell me about yourself first?' she suggested. 'Is it true that you come from India? I want to hear all about it! I've never been anywhere, and I can only imagine what things are like out there in the world.'

Reginald started slowly, describing his father's regiment, life in the cantonments, and the ancient city of Delhi. His passion for India picked up as he went, and Natalie listened with rapt attention.

'And your servant, when did you meet him?' Natalie asked eagerly.

'Narendi Ram? I...well, it was on a tiger hunt. I went with my father and Major Hawke, his commanding officer. Jack McAuliffe was there too. He was bragging about his new Enfield rifle.'

'Who's he? Is he related to our neighbour, Finnegan McAuliffe?'

'His nephew,' Reginald replied. 'And my worst enemy.'

Natalie tried to hide a smile.

'Anyway, we took the train to Gujarat and hired a couple of *mahouts* (elephant handlers) at the station. Narendi Ram was one of them. I suppose you've never ridden an elephant before, but it really is the best way to travel. You feel like a rajah. We didn't see any tigers the first day. My father shot a blackbuck and Major Hawke a nilgai. Around dusk, I spotted a sloth bear at a termite mound, but I didn't have the heart to shoot it. McAuliffe did, though, and everyone was impressed by him.

'That night, I had trouble sleeping. I thought I heard snarling in the bushes. It turns out I was right. We found tiger tracks near the camp. At midday, when we stopped for water in a *nullah* (ravine), there was a flash of orange as a tiger leapt out of the canebrakes and started mauling one of the mahouts right before our eyes. McAuliffe shot first, but missed. His hands weren't steady. I raised my gun and kept it level, as my father taught me. It was still a lucky shot. I must've hit the tiger's heart because it died immediately. The mahout had his arm torn, but otherwise, he was fine. He came up to me and bowed. "Blessings be upon thee," he said and offered to be my servant. I tried to wave him off. My father thought he would make a good companion for me though, and so we took him back to Delhi with us. He was right. Narendi Ram is the best servant a boy could ask for. He still has the scars on his arms from the tiger, and I'm sure he'd be happy to show you.'

'You've had such an exciting life!' Natalie exclaimed.

'Could you tell me about yourself now?' Reginald asked, interrupting himself.

'Oh no, you wouldn't want to hear about me.' Ahe sighed. 'My life's been dreadfully dull.'

'Oh, but I would!' he returned ardently.

'All right then.'

She told him about her childhood in a castle in the north of England and how her mother and father had died in a terrible fire when she was a little girl. She had come south to live with Master Merriweather who looked after her and treated her as his daughter. She loved him very much, but she was quite lonely because she had never had any friends her own age.

Merriweather had said that when she reached her eighteenth birthday, she would inherit a large fortune with much property besides, and that then, she would be her own mistress and free to marry whoever she chose.

'In the meantime, I'm trying to be a lady,' she concluded. 'But I hope someday, I'll be able to see the world and visit all the places I've read about in books.'

Reginald listened to her with a great deal of amazement, astonished that their upbringings could be so different. His compassion was also aroused that such a pretty and lively young girl should be kept cooped up in this old house without friends or companions. He felt a tremor in his heart—*he* would be her friend and accompany her wherever she wanted to go.

Deciding he had stayed long enough, he stood up to take his leave.

'I must be going, miss,' he said.

'You will come back, won't you? I've had a wonderful time!'

'Yes, of course!' he exclaimed and rushed quickly to the door.

Once he reached his room, he fell into his bed in a state of complete bliss and spent the rest of that day reliving in his mind every word that had passed between him and Natalie.

Merriweather noticed immediately that this first tete-a-tete between his great-nephew and young ward had been successful. At lunch and supper, the two had eyes and ears only for each other, while he sat back and watched them, a smile playing on his jolly face. The boy and girl had more in common than they first supposed. Natalie was a great reader; she and Reginald had many long discussions over their favourite books, invariably agreeing with each other's judgments. Reginald, for his part, thought that she was brilliant. Not only did she have a vast and varied knowledge, but her insightful comments made Reginald think more deeply than he ever had before.

The person Reginald spoke to Natalie about most was his father. It was plain to Natalie that he was Reginald's idol.

'We Fubsters have a long history of military service,' the boy explained.

He and Natalie had been exploring the house and uncovered a suit of armour.

'My father Wilfred is captain of His Majesty's Thirty-Third Infantry Regiment in the Indian Army. His father (my grandfather) Mortimer fought at Sevastopol in Crimea against the Russians. My great-grandfather Alfred was with Wellington in Portugal and at Waterloo. Wilkins, my great-great-grandfather, climbed the cliffs of Quebec under Wolfe, and Philip, his father, routed the French with Marlborough at Blenheim.'

Natalie laughed. 'I had no idea I'd been taken in by such heroes! I'm a lucky girl!'

'We're humble soldiers,' replied Reginald modestly. 'Nowhere close to being worthy of fine ladies like you.'

Natalie blushed. 'Tell me more about your childhood. How do you know so much about everything?'

'Well, I'm not sure I really had a childhood. When I was seven, my father took me out of the nursery. He thought that my mother and the *ayahs* (nursemaids) were spoiling me, so he put me on a strict schedule. At four every morning—'

'Four!' Natalie exclaimed.

'That's actually the best time of day. Everything's cool and quiet. You have no idea how hot India is. By midday, it hurts to even move. Anyway, we would drill for a couple of hours before breakfast at six. After breakfast, I was tutored in Greek and Latin by one of my father's friends. I never really got on with Greek, but I know Latin fairly well by now. Then there was another tutor for mathematics and military strategy. When my father came home from his regimental duties at four o'clock, he expected me to repeat back to him everything I had learned that day. I had an hour's break before supper, then I read classical literature and history until bed at eight o'clock.'

'What did you think about all this? I'd have found it insufferable!'

'A soldier isn't supposed to think. He does what he's told and what's best for his country.'

'And yet you *do* think, Reginald. I can tell. You're always thinking. You also feel much more than you let on.'

Reginald bowed his head. 'My father taught me that duty should always come before personal considerations. Country is everything.'

'But what if the country is wrong?' Natalie asked.

He had no answer. That kind of nuanced thinking had not been a part of his training. Wilfred Fubster's moral lesson to his son was simple. The nation was larger than self and therefore greater than it. Those who disgraced their fatherland (the McAuliffes) were evil, while those who served it were worthy of emulation and respect. With this, Wilfred had instructed Reginald in the importance of controlling his emotions. Fancy must never interfere with doing what was right. Reginald feared that his attachment to Natalie would be looked down upon by his father and viewed as a distraction from matters of real importance.

Reginald was torn between two worlds, one being that of duty, soldierly reserve, and rigour, represented by his father, and the other of emotion and romantic fulfilment in his love for Natalie. He wondered if these could ever be reconciled as he became more invested in Natalie day by day.

The one subject which they did not often talk about was Natalie's fortune. It was an embarrassment for her and the cause, she believed, of her loneliness. She suspected that Merriweather kept her hidden to protect her from the attention of suitors. It was not that she desired to enter the world of elegant society; she only wanted to be loved and treated with respect. Reginald was too young to care about money.

\* \* \* \* \*

After Reginald and Natalie had spent a very merry Christmas in each other's company, Master Merriweather requested a private audience with Reginald.

'What is it, sir?' asked Reginald, standing rigidly inside the master's study.

'Eh? Oh, I just wanted ter let yer know that yer ter start school next week.'

Reginald staggered like a man who has been rudely awakened from a pleasant dream. His mind was so obsessed with Natalie that he had forgotten the reason he had come to England in the first place.

'Very good, sir,' he said.

Did he know then that his entry into school would mark the end of those days of happy innocence and that the bright sky of his future would soon be obscured by dark and threatening clouds? If he did have a presentiment of this sort, he kept it hidden within, determined to spend every waking moment with Natalie while he could.

# Messer's Knubby and Johnstone's Military Academy for Boys

THE ESTABLISHMENT WHERE Reginald Fubster was to be educated in military affairs was located on the outskirts of London. A few days after New Year's 1914, Merriweather drove with him and Narendi Ram in the coach to the train station. Reginald had taken his leave of Natalie earlier in the day, not departing until she had promised to write to him every day and come to visit every week. The two had agreed that after Reginald graduated with his commission, they would embark on a tour of India together. At the train station, he was unhappily reunited with young McAuliffe, who greeted him with a snickering laugh. Merriweather turned to look down at his great-nephew.

'Goodbye, me friend,' he said affectionately. 'I'll make sure that Natalie writes ter ye.'

Reginald waved to him and boarded the train. He found an empty compartment for Narendi Ram and himself to sit, but they were soon joined by McAuliffe.

'Who's Natalie?' McAuliffe sneered shortly after sitting down.

Reginald flushed with anger. Natalie's name was too sacred for a scoundrel like McAuliffe to utter.

'She's an heiress, isn't she?' said McAuliffe, becoming suddenly excited. 'My uncle told me about her. He says she's pretty, too. Do you like her, Fubster? She'd undoubtedly prefer me if she had the choice.'

'You! You're not worthy to kiss the ground she's walked on!' retorted Reginald.

'You're jealous, Fubster!'

'If I hear you so much as mention her name again, McAuliffe, I'll punch your face in.'

'Natalie, Natalie, Natalie! Beautiful Natalie!' chanted the worthy lad gleefully.

Reginald glanced over at Narendi Ram to get his permission to strike. The latter's face remained expressionless, but he gave a very slight, almost imperceptible, shake of the head. He knew how much Reginald cherished Natalie, but he would not allow him to make a fool of himself in public because of her. With much restraint, Reginald turned away to stare out the window.

The train rushed onward until dusk when it pulled into the station on the outskirts of London. As Reginald got down onto the platform, he got his first glimpse of that great city, and he did not like the look of it at all. The smog hung heavy in the air above the grimy buildings, while crowds of people clad in drab clothes huddled against the wind. The place looked as dreary and forbidding as anywhere he'd seen in his life.

'Fubster, McAuliffe!' a voice called.

They turned to see a middle-aged gentleman with grey hair and crooked spectacles pushing his way through the crowd.

'I am Master Silas Knubby. You two are to be pupils at my academy. Well, hurry up, we haven't got all day!'

Master Knubby escorted them through the station, using his cane at intervals to clear the way. Reginald thought it peculiar that he possessed such an article, having no apparent difficulty in walking. They passed through a few narrow alleyways and then, rounding a bend, found themselves in front of a rather squat building which may have once been beautiful, but whose façade was now encrusted with black soot. A sign above the door read: 'Messer's Knubby and Johnstone's Military Academy for Boys.'

'Come on, hurry up,' said Knubby. Looking back, his eyes alighted for the first time on Narendi Ram.

'What is that foreign fellow doing following us?' he snarled.

'Please, sir!' Reginald answered. 'His name is Narendi Ram, and he is my servant. He is going to stay with me.'

'He'll have to sleep on the floor then. We don't have extra beds.'

Here, Reginald had his first impression that something was amiss.

Knubby led them up a rickety staircase to a narrow dormitory.

'Your beds are over there,' he said, pointing out two cots at the end of the room. 'You're to report to dinner at seven o'clock. That is half an hour from now.'

Knubby turned and left them. Narendi Ram helped Reginald unpack his scanty wardrobe and deposit it on the shelf above his bed.

'There's hardly any room for you here,' said Reginald. 'Why don't you take the bed? I'm smaller, and I won't mind sleeping on the floor.'

'No, sahib,' replied Narendi. 'I am used to worse conditions than these, and I will get on all right. Do not worry yourself on my account.'

Reginald heaved a deep sigh. Narendi hadn't seemed himself since they came to England, and Reginald was a little worried about him. The Indian's good nature would never allow him to complain outwardly, so Reginald never had a clear picture of how uncomfortable he felt on the inside.

At seven o'clock, they went down to dinner in a dining room that looked suspiciously like a cramped kitchen. There were twelve pupils seated at the table with Knubby at one end and another gentleman who Reginald presumed was Master Johnstone at the other. Two seats remained open.

'Where is my servant to sit?' asked Reginald.

'Your *servant* is to wait in the dormitory,' replied Knubby unkindly.

'But what will he eat?'

'He can eat whatever scraps you decide to leave for him. Really, you can't expect us to take care of an extra person when we are already quite beyond our capacity.'

'Didn't my great-uncle write to inform you that my servant would be coming along?'

'He did, but did you expect us to take that seriously? A boy of your age with his own personal servant, and a foreign one besides?'

'You'd better wait in the dormitory,' Reginald whispered to Narendi. 'I'll see if there is anything I can do for you.'

Narendi Ram bowed and left the room. Taking his seat, Reginald had the chance to examine his fellow students for the first time. They looked to be of the same age, but they were all extremely scrawny and had their eyes cast down in melancholy. Reginald helped himself to a hearty helping of potatoes, ignoring the disapproving look he received from Master Knubby. A dead silence hovered over the table as he began to eat.

'Well, gentlemen, what are your names and where do you come from?' Reginald said at last in an attempt to start up a conversation to break the awful silence.

'Master Fubster, we do not allow idle chatter at our dinner table,' Knubby said sternly. 'It is not becoming in a military society.'

'But we always had a lively conversation in the soldier's mess hall in India!'

'Master Fubster, I don't care how things are done in India. This is England, and we have our own way of doing things. Now you had better fall in line or I can see your time here being very unpleasant indeed.'

Reginald glanced over at McAuliffe, who was grinning in obvious delight at his discomfiture. He lowered his eyes and spent the remainder of the meal in silence. He made sure that he saved a fair bit for Narendi Ram, which he hurried up to give him. As Narendi sat eating, the rest of the boys filed into the dormitory.

'Well, gentlemen, can I ask you now what your names are and where you come from?'

'You'll learn tomorrow,' one whispered. 'We'd better get to sleep now. It wouldn't be good if Master Knubby heard us talking.'

The light was extinguished, and Reginald lay on his bed wide awake, thinking about this astonishingly disagreeable start to his education and wishing he was back at Fubster Manor with Natalie.

## The First Day of Class

REGINALD WOKE UP at six o'clock the next morning to the jarring sound of a bell. He sleepily followed the other pupils down to breakfast, which was again spent in complete silence. They left the dining room and entered into the classroom, a long, narrow construction with a blackboard at the far end and rows of wooden benches that looked like (and probably were) church pews. Each student had a book of Latin grammar, a notebook, and a dictionary. Reginald took an empty place near the blackboard, which was thankfully well away from Jack McAuliffe.

'It is time for Latin class. Since this is the start of a new term, you have all been given new books,' said Master Knubby, who stood in front of the blackboard. Master Johnstone sat near the window, his face the very image of graveness. 'You will have an hour to translate the first page. When the hour is up, you will stand and present your translation in front of the class.'

Reginald set out about his work eagerly. The text was quite basic, of the sort that his father had him translating when he was nine years old. He had soon finished not only the first page, but the entire first chapter. A casual glance at the student in the desk next to him revealed that he was still working out the opening paragraph.

Glancing up at the clock, Reginald discovered that only half an hour had passed. He paged through the book and discovered that it contained fourteen chapters. *I'll finish this book in no time,* he thought. *This is easy.* Rather pleased with himself, he leaned back and looked out the window.

A sharp rap on his desk from Master Knubby's cane startled him out of his reverie.

'Master Fubster, why aren't you working?'

'I was working, sir, only I've finished.'

'Let's see it then.'

Reginald showed him his complete translation.

'Writing down nonsense words, I see,' said Knubby.

Reginald looked up at him in astonishment.

'We'll evaluate your work when it's your turn to present.'

The clock struck eight, and the students put down their pencils.

'Master Fubster, why don't you present to the class first?' said Knubby with a wry smile.

Reginald stood at the front of the class with his notes and proceeded to provide a flawless translation of the book's first page.

'Very good, Master Fubster,' Knubby said slyly. 'Now, please tell us where you got the translation to copy it?'

'I didn't copy it!' Reginald exclaimed indignantly. 'I translated it myself, not just the first page, but the first chapter. I know Latin quite well. I learned it as a boy in India.'

'That's enough! Take your seat.'

Reginald sat down and watched as his fellow students struggled through their translations. The only one who did tolerably well was Jack McAuliffe, and he was rewarded for his efforts with shower of praise from Master Knubby and even a murmur from Master Johnstone.

'I can see that you are a rather precocious young scholar,' said Knubby.

McAuliffe gave Reginald a smug grin as he returned to his seat.

*I don't understand this at all,* thought Reginald. *Did I do something wrong? Why is this happening to me?*

'It is now nine o'clock,' Knubby informed them. 'It is time for your mathematics lesson.'

He got up and distributed a pile of dusty mathematics textbooks among the students.

'Complete the problems on the first page, and in an hour, you will present them to the class.'

Reginald peered at the problems below him. They were so laughably easy that he thought it scarcely worth his time to write them down. However, a sudden desire for revenge gripped him, and he tore through the problems at such a rapid pace that he had completed the first three chapters in forty-five minutes. He leaned back and once again looked vacantly out of the window. Out of the corner of his eye, he caught sight of Master Knubby approaching, brandishing in his cane, and pretended to be surprised when it came crashing down on his desk.

'Master Fubster, slacking off again, are we?'

'As a matter of fact, I am not, sir. As you can see, I have already completed the problems for this chapter and two more besides.'

Master Knubby looked down at Reginald's neat equations.

'Random numbers, the lot of 'em!'

'If you examine them closely, sir, you will find that the answers are all correct.'

'You're sure of that, are you? We will see. Yes, we will see.'

He returned to the front of the room and waited until the clock had struck ten.

'Master Fubster, why don't you present to the class first?'

'Certainly,' said Reginald, heading to the front of the room with his notes. 'The answer to the first problem is fifty-seven.' (As indeed twenty-three plus thirty-four is.)

'That is incorrect,' said Master Knubby.

'I believe you are mistaken, sir,' replied Fubster. 'Fifty-seven is the correct answer.'

'No, Master Fubster. It is you who is mistaken. The correct answer is fifty-six. Is that not right, class?'

The other pupils nodded, McAuliffe, for his part, moving his head up and down so rapidly that his head threatened to come loose from his neck.

'You see, Master Fubster, you have clearly miscalculated the sum. Please amend the total in your notes. Now, what is the answer to the second question?'

'I did not miscalculate the sum, sir,' said Reginald, almost crying with vexation. He seized a piece of chalk and demonstrated the equation on the blackboard. 'The answer, as you can see, is fifty-seven.'

'I cannot understand why you persist in your obstinance. The entire class has agreed that the answer is fifty-six. That makes it the right answer.'

'The fact that the class agrees does not make the answer fifty-six any more than the class agreeing that you are the Duke of Wellington would make it so!'

'Sit down, Master Fubster. You will soon learn your place. A soldier must never think for himself. An answer is right because he is told it is right. That is the essence of a military education.'

Reginald took his seat, confused by a pedagogical philosophy so completely at variance with everything his father had taught him, and watched as the other students presented and received commendation from Master Knubby when they reported that the answer to the first question was fifty-six. He wanted to cry, but his father's advice to maintain a manly bearing forced him to choke back the tears. The clock struck eleven o'clock, and the time came for their history lesson. Master Knubby opened up an ancient volume and read word for word a lengthy (and unenlightening) history of the city of Birmingham from the years 1621 to 1705.

At midday, they partook in a silent meal before returning again to the classroom. Military tactics were discussed at the one o'clock hour, and any hopes that Reginald had of enjoying this subject were soon dashed. Master Knubby read from a book that described in minute detail the supply trains of the Egyptian and Nubian armies, which had clashed in a 1571 BC battle. For Reginald, the subject was preposterously irrelevant. The piece must have run to a hundred pages because it took Master Knubby three hours to read it.

'We will begin volume 2 tomorrow,' said Knubby upon reaching the last page.

*Thank goodness that's over with*, thought Reginald.

With his hour of free time before dinner, Reginald rushed to the dormitory to see how Narendi Ram was getting along. The poor Indian was famished, but tried his best not to let it show.

'Why don't you go into town and buy yourself something to eat?' said Reginald, offering him a few shillings.

'Oh no, sahib. This is a strange place, and I'm not sure what might happen to me if I went out on my own.'

'I'll go with you, then.'

'No, sahib, you would miss your supper. I will be all right. Do not mind me.'

'We can't stay here if they are going to treat you like this. I have the money my father sent. I'll rent us a place at the inn. I'm sure Master Knubby wouldn't mind one less mouth to feed. And I'll write to my father and tell him about this place. There has to have been some mistake.'

With this new plan in mind, Reginald felt his spirits lift. Not only would they have much better food and accommodation at an inn, but he would also be free of the detestable presence of McAuliffe for at least part of the day. He could handle anything as long as it was temporary. When his father learned of how he was being treated, he would surely be enrolled in a different school. He headed down to dinner, determined to put his plan into action.

After another silent meal, Reginald caught up with Master Knubby before he could retire for the night.

'May I have a word with you, sir?' he asked.

'What is it, Master Fubster?' said Knubby impatiently.

'With your leave, sir, I would like to take up residence in a nearby inn. I will arrive here at six o'clock in the morning precisely and leave at five o'clock in the afternoon. You needn't worry about feeding me anymore.'

'So you refuse my hospitality, do you? Very well, *Master* Fubster. Be warned that this will most certainly affect your marks.'

He swept off.

With this interview having gone better than he expected, Reginald returned to the dormitory. He ignored McAuliffe's taunts and helped Narendi Ram pack up his few belongings. When this task was completed, they set out onto the dark streets of London, where a light snow was falling.

'This ought to do,' Reginald said, catching sight of a cosy-looking establishment.

There was a creaking sign over the door with a painting of a roaring lion. A cheery fire was blazing in the common room where a few men sat back reading the *Times* and puffing their pipes. As Reginald approached the desk, the friendly proprietor saluted him.

'I take it you'll be needing lodging for you and your servant. Can I put you down for one night, or do you wish to stay longer?'

'We are actually intending to stay here for quite some time,' replied Reginald. 'Do you have any places available that are more permanent?'

'I do, as a matter of fact,' said the proprietor with a wink. 'The gentleman who was staying in our guest room left just this morning. He was a rather disagreeable old chap, I'm not sorry to have seen the last of him. That will be five pounds down payment and an additional pound per week.'

Reginald handed over the money in great relief, thanking his father for providing such a large allowance.

'Follow me, then,' rejoined the proprietor.

He led them up several flights of stairs to the top floor and unlocked a blackened door. The room inside was small, but looked comfortable enough with a fireplace, a table, a writing desk, and a bed.

'I'll bring a cot up for your servant,' said the proprietor kindly.

'Thank God!' breathed Reginald, once they were settled.

While Narendi Ram unpacked his master's clothes, Reginald sat down at the desk and wrote a letter to Natalie describing his experiences on the first day of class. He was so tired that he fell asleep partway through.

## School Days

'SAHIB, WAKE UP,' said Narendi Ram giving Reginald a gentle shake. 'It is time for you to go to school.'

Reginald's eyes flew open. He was lying in his bed, the good servant having carried him to it while he was fast asleep.

'Oh, bother!' he cried. 'I really don't want to go back to that place.'

'You must, master, you must. Think of your father.'

'I know. But I have to tell him about the school and the way they've treated you.'

He started to dress himself.

'What are you going to do while I am away?' he asked.

'Nothing, master. Stay here and mind my business.'

'But you can't do nothing all day! You'll be miserable! We have to find you some friends. There has to be Indians somewhere in this city. Why don't you go looking for them?'

'Oh no, master, do not say such a thing! I would get lost and freeze to death.'

Reginald sighed. He didn't want to leave his friend and servant all alone in this strange place, but circumstances were forcing themselves on him more rapidly than he knew how to deal with.

School that day was just as boring, but not quite as uncomfortable as it had been the day before. Reginald was determined not to attract attention to himself. He deliberately made mistakes in his Latin translation and showed such an appalling lack of progress in mathematics that Master Knubby was pleased. At lunchtime, he returned to the inn for a meal with Narendi Ram. For the afternoon's military strategy lesson, he amused himself by writing a letter to his father with the pretext of feverishly taking notes. The clock struck five, and he hurried back to the inn.

*I may not learn anything at school, but at least I'll get through it,* he thought.

A week of classes passed, and it was finally Sunday, his day off.

'Come on, Narendi. We're going on an adventure,' he said, pulling on his overcoat.

Narendi Ram had hardly any winter clothes, so they went first to the tailor's and had him a suit made. From the tailor's, they pressed on deeper into the city until the dome of St. Paul's reared above them.

'What do you think?' asked Reginald.

'I do not know, sahib, I do not know. This is a strange place.'

They ate lunch in a nice restaurant before turning back through Hyde Park. The lake was frozen, and there were a few couples ice-skating. They looked so happy that Reginald was suddenly jealous and lonely. He still had not received a letter from Natalie and was worried she had forgotten him. When they had returned to the inn, he wrote asking if she still loved him and why she hadn't bothered to reply to any of his letters (he had written an average of three per day).

The next day as school ended, Master Knubby approached him with a letter.

'This came for you in the mail.'

Reginald immediately recognized Natalie's neat handwriting. He was so anxious to read it that he tore it open as he walked and started on the first line. Unfortunately, on his way back to the Black Lion, he had to pass through the dormitory. And in the dormitory, McAuliffe was waiting for him.

'What's this?' he said, snatching the letter out of Reginald's hands. 'Dear Reginald, I have missed you very much,' he read, then his eyes flashed to the bottom. 'Yours affectionately, Natalie. So you love her, do you? And you think she loves you back? Admit it or I'll tear this letter apart!'

'If you don't give me the letter this instant, you'll wish you'd never been born!'

'I'd like to meet this girl,' McAuliffe cackled. 'Why don't you arrange it for me? Then I can tell her the truth about you, you arrogant, self-important little bastard!'

Reginald's right fist caught McAuliffe squarely on the cheek and knocked him up against the bed. The left collided with his gut, violently forcing the wind out of him and preventing him from crying out. Snatching the letter, Reginald administered a few more well-aimed punches to McAuliffe's face and was about to make his break for the door when one of the other students noticed what was happening and cried out for Master Knubby in a shrill voice.

Reginald heard the pounding of Master Knubby's cane on the staircase and the sound of the door being thrust open.

'What is going on here?' Knubby snarled. 'Master Fubster, what have you done?'

McAuliffe was lying on the floor, his face bruised, and tears running down his cheeks.

'Explain yourself at once!' cried Knubby.

'He stole my letter and insulted me, and I punished him for it,' said Reginald, looking down at McAuliffe with contempt. 'He received exactly what he deserved.'

'I ought to have you expelled!' fumed Knubby. 'Beating a pupil to death under my roof? I would never have imagined such a thing!'

Knubby gave Reginald such a ferocious glare that the poor lad almost wilted where he stood.

'As it is, I will write to your great-uncle and your father explaining what you have done and asking for their opinion whether you shall remain enrolled in my establishment. Give me the letter.'

With a trembling hand, Reginald handed it over and watched in horror as Master Knubby tore it up.

'You are to receive no more letters. Tomorrow, you will write out a written apology to Master McAuliffe and his family.'

'But, sir!' Reginald gasped.

'Don't you dare say another word,' warned Master Knubby. 'Turn around.'

He raised his cane and struck Reginald across the back. Reginald took the blow without a flinch. Unnerved by this cool determination, Knubby faltered, lowered the cane, and swept out of the room.

On his way to the Black Lion, Reginald reflected on his changed circumstances. His one hope had been dashed. How could he survive without hearing from Natalie? A white-hot fury burned in his mind against McAuliffe.

*I wish I'd killed him*, he thought. His conscience reproached him a moment later: *Thou shalt not kill*, a precept his father had taught him. *I can't do this*, he thought. *I have to get out of here!*

Narendi Ram immediately noticed his agony and made Reginald lie down while he bathed the boy's bruised back with a warm towel. The whole story spilled out. The Indian listened silently, but his dark eyes shone with compassion.

At last, he spoke. 'Master, Mr Knubby may be able to prevent you from receiving letters sent to the school, but he can't stop the letters that are sent directly here.'

Reginald hadn't thought of this.

'Oh, he'll probably find some way to do that too,' he said despairingly.

'Do not give up hope, sahib,' said Narendi Ram.

'What am I even doing here?' Reginald exclaimed. 'The only thing I want is to be with Natalie. I love her, Narendi, and I don't care about anything else.'

'Yes, I understand,' said the servant. 'But this is how you prove your love, that you do not allow circumstances to drive you to despair. You must remain strong for her.'

Reginald gazed in wonder at the young man, who'd been by his side constantly for two years and yet remained an enigma. How had he acquired such wisdom? Reginald's heart was strengthened. He pulled himself to his desk and wrote a letter to Natalie that she should address her correspondence to the Black Lion inn.

Sure enough, two days later, he received the following:

Dearest Reginald,

It makes me quite miserable to hear of all the ways you are being mistreated at Messer's Knubby and Johnstone's Military Academy for Boys. I have been pleading with your great-uncle to have you transferred to another school. We are coming to see you this Sunday. Until then, you must find a way to endure your persecutions. I wish I could do more for you, but I feel so powerless!

Yours affectionately,
Natalie

Reginald sat down at his desk and scrawled a few lines.

Dearest Natalie,

I can hardly wait to see you this Sunday! I will be all right; you needn't worry yourself on my account. If my great-uncle receives a letter in the mail from Master Knubby, tell him it is nothing but lies.

Yours,
Reginald

In the meantime, at school, Reginald had to stand up in front of the class to give a speech apologising to Jack McAuliffe and begging humbly for his forgiveness. His oration was so convincingly sincere that even Master Knubby was satisfied. As he took his seat, he struggled to conceal a grin, then laid back and listened to Master Knubby's meaningless verbiage.

The next few days were some of the longest of his life. His time at school was excruciatingly boring, and while at the inn, he had nothing better to do than stare out the window and think about Natalie.

At last, the awaited day arrived. There was a knock on the door, and the friendly proprietor poked his face inside the room

'A gentleman and young lady to see you, sir.'

Reginald leapt out of his bed. 'Come on, Narendi, it's them!'

He raced after the proprietor to the lower parlour and nearly burst into tears at the sight of Master Merriweather and Miss Natalie. Narendi Ram was likewise visibly cheered. It was as though a light had dawned over a dark and brooding landscape.

'Have yer eaten yet, Master Fubster?' Merriweather asked.

Reginald shook his head.

'Master innkeeper, we'll take the finest victuals that money ken buy.'

'Aye, aye sir,' saluted the innkeeper and hurried about his work.

In the meantime, they sat down at a table near the fireplace.

'I've read every letter yer wrote,' said Merriweather. 'Both me and Miss Natalie agree that yer shouldn't stay in that place any longer. But the matter must be left up ter yer father. I'll write ter him to get his opinion.'

Reginald's face fell. A reply from India could take a month. He looked over at Natalie.

She reached out, took hold of his hand, and gave it a slight squeeze.

'What's all this about yer getting into a scuffle with young Master McAuliffe?' asked Merriweather, a slight smile tugging at the corners of his mouth as he unfolded Master Knubby's letter and laid it on the table.

'The young rascal's lucky he didn't receive a worse thrashing!'

'What did he do?' Natalie asked, her eyes wide.

'He stole your letter and insulted me.'

'And you fought him?'

'Of course I did!' replied Reginald with bravado. 'I gave him a fist to the face and another to the stomach and three more for good measure!'

'Really now, Reginald,' Natalie said, blushing. 'You shouldn't have been so hard on him.'

'I would do the same thing this very minute. He deserved everything he got and a great deal more.'

'Master Reginald, if yer ter be a gentleman, yer will have ter learn ter master yer temper.'

'But, Great-Uncle, Natalie's honour was at stake, as was my own. I had to do something!'

Master Merriweather's eyes twinkled. 'Spoken like a true Fubster. It's in the blood, I'd reckon.'

The proprietor arrived with their food, laying out a full English breakfast for all of them. As they ate, Natalie gave an account of everything that had happened at Fubster Manor since he had been gone. Soon, they were pleasantly full and ready to go on an outing into London. Natalie was bursting with excitement to finally be out and about. Merriweather knew a great deal about the city and pointed out many things that Reginald had never noticed before. They saw Westminster Abbey and the Houses of Parliament, crossed the Tower Bridge, and stopped inside one of Sir Christopher Wren's soaring churches. By the time they got back to the Black Lion, they were exhausted and it was the late afternoon. Even Narendi Ram had enjoyed himself.

'We had best be off, Master Fubster,' said Merriweather. 'I will write ter yer father as soon as I get back.'

'Thank you,' said Reginald. 'Will you come to visit again next week?'

'I think we will,' replied Merriweather, looking over at Natalie, who had declared several times in the course of their outing that this was the best day of her life.

Reginald waved and looked after Natalie until her graceful form had disappeared into the crowd. He waited a little longer until some snow started to fall and turned with a shiver back to the inn.

## Wilfred's Letter

THE NEXT FEW weeks passed by extremely slowly as Reginald waited for his father's reply. The lone source of comfort was the Sunday visits of Merriweather and Natalie. Then, in the blink of an eye, they were gone, and he was forced to endure another week of drudgery.

One day, the students were treated to a special lecture delivered by Master Johnstone himself entitled 'On Our Asian Dominions.'

'The lands of South Asia are populated by a barbaric, teeming race of men whose culture is so crude and debauched that it is entirely unworthy of study,' the great scholar began. 'Its true history begins with the establishment of the Honourable East India Company in the year of our Lord 1600. The Company brought order and progress to a country benighted with mediaeval squalor. Peaceful commerce was established between the Company and the various states, while the natives were given the blessings of railroads, bridges, canals, irrigation, and the other miracles of civilised society. The ungrateful Indians rose in 1857 in a rebellion known to history as the Sepoy Mutiny. The cowardly mutineers were soon routed by the British Army, and the rule of the subcontinent was transferred from the Company to the Crown. The Crown has heaped immense blessings on these savages, and yet there are still pockets of rebellion even to this day. The Indian must be taught that he is by nature inferior and exists only to serve the purposes of the White man.'

As Reginald listened, his brow grew more furrowed. His political beliefs had been influenced by his father, who, though a patriot, believed in the principle of the brotherhood of man. Johnstone's lecture smacked of the unreflective bigotry Wilfred had so often denounced. That the British were technologically superior to the Indians was undeniable, but equating mechanical sophistication with moral superiority was a dangerous error. Wilfred had taught his son that the strong must serve the weak; it was their duty to God and country. Johnstone was arguing precisely the opposite.

At last, Reginald could stand it no longer, and his hand shot into the air.

'Master Fubster?' Johnstone said, looking up. 'This is highly irregular, I'm sure.'

'I have a question to ask you, sir. Have you ever been to India?'

'That is entirely beside the point,' said Master Johnstone.

'If you have not been to India and are unfamiliar with life there, how can you make these statements with any degree of accuracy?'

'How dare you say such a thing!' Johnstone exclaimed, stomping his foot.

'You are incorrigible, Master Fubster,' said Master Knubby, grabbing his cane and getting to his feet. 'How many times must we tell you that things are right because *we said so*? Do you expect to tell your commanding officer, 'Sir, you are wrong'? The statements of your superiors must be accepted without question!'

'Not if they contradict the truth,' said Fubster firmly.

'The truth? The truth is whatever we say it is,' spat Knubby.

'But, sir, that's not the right philosophy. We are all under the authority of the truth. That's what my father taught me, and I believe him.'

The other students were watching this exchange as though mesmerised, scarcely daring to believe that someone was bold enough to challenge the schoolmasters. Even McAuliffe, who was treated as the favourite and granted all sorts of special privileges, was eagerly awaiting the outcome of this contest.

Master Knubby advanced toward Reginald with his cane raised.

'You will recant every last word you've just said or you'll receive the soundest thrashing you've ever had.'

'Thrash me then,' said Reginald.

Something about Reginald's cool determination unnerved Knubby. He was used to pupils he could bend easily to his will. As someone who had always done whatever was expedient with no thought for moral principles, he was cowed by those with firm convictions, especially those who were willing to suffer for their beliefs. He knew that he could beat Reginald's body, but he couldn't beat out the boy's determined resolve. This made him afraid.

He lowered his cane and tried to muster as much menace as he could in his voice, 'I'll deal with you after class, Mr Fubster. Don't you dare say another word.'

Reginald sat and listened without complaint to the rest of Master Johnstone's lecture. His mind was racing. What would Knubby do to him? When the clock struck five o'clock, the schoolmaster caught up to him before he could leave.

'Master Fubster, on account of your scandalous behaviour this afternoon, you will stay at your desk and compose a five-page paper apologising to Master Johnstone and myself and another five page paper explaining why Englishmen are superior to Indians. You are not permitted to leave until you're finished.'

Reginald sat back down at his desk and opened up his notebook, heaving a sigh of relief as he did so.

'May I write my essays in Latin, sir?' he asked.

'And why might you want to do that?'

'I imagine this would be an opportunity for me to improve my skills in the language which you said this morning were appallingly poor.'

'Damn you, Fubster! Write it in Latin. Write it in Greek for all I care. Just get started.'

Reginald proceeded to compose two essays, the first explaining why he did not apologise for his actions that morning and the second describing the reasons why Englishmen were not superior to the Indians. When he had finished, he turned them in at Master Knubby's desk.

Master Knubby looked them over, but didn't say anything.

'You may go,' he said at last.

Reginald struggled to conceal a smile as he walked out of the room.

His father's long-awaited reply arrived in the mail that next morning. He tore it open as soon as the postman handed it to him and read rapidly.

Dear Reginald,

Master Merriweather has been in correspondence with me about the appalling conditions of Messer's Knubby and Johnstone's Military School for Boys. I quite agree with him that you should be removed from the school. However, for your own good, I recommend that you stay on until the end of the term to get your marks. I know the place is odious to you, but there are only a few weeks remaining, and if you depart now, the entire term would go to waste. Master Merriweather will ensure that you are speedily enrolled in a new institution. Not much has changed at home, except our friend Major Hawke has been promoted to district commissioner.

Your mother misses you very much and sends her love.

Yours affectionately,
Captain Wilfred Fubster,
His Majesty's Thirty-Third Infantry

P.S. I received the letter from Master Knubby regarding your altercation with Master McAuliffe. I am sure the young rascal deserved everything he got and probably a great deal more...

Reginald gazed at the letter despondently. Three more weeks! How could he possibly survive Messer's Knubby and Johnstone's Military Academy for three more weeks? If this was a terrible disappointment, several much more bitter misfortunes lay in store for him.

# Ill Tidings

EARLY ONE TUESDAY morning, two weeks after the arrival of Wilfred's letter, Reginald was awoken early in the morning by a tapping on the door.

'Come in,' Reginald said, hurriedly pulling on his clothes.

The innkeeper entered, clutching a letter in one of his hands. 'I received this urgent note a few moments ago. The gentleman who brought it is waiting below for your answer.'

Reginald took it and read:

> Dear Mr Fubster,
>
> It is my unpleasant duty to inform you of the passing of your great-uncle Merriweather Fubster in his sleep yesterday evening. You are summoned to Fubster Manor to hear a reading of his will and to be present at his funeral, which will take place this afternoon at St George's Parish. My associate waits below for your conveyance.
>
> Yours respectfully,
> Mr Charles J. Howe, Esq. Attorney
> at Law, St Ives, London

'What is it, sahib?' asked Narendi Ram, seeing Reginald's face turn ashen.

'It's my great-uncle,' Reginald whispered, tears forming in his eyes. 'He's dead.'

The innkeeper respectfully removed his cap and regarded Reginald with a look of utmost sympathy.

'He had a good soul,' said Narendi Ram reverently. 'I am sure he is in heaven now.'

'Could you please tell the gentleman below that I need a moment to collect myself and will be down presently?' Reginald asked the innkeeper.

The innkeeper bowed and departed. Reginald brushed the tears out of his eyes and dressed himself in his best clothes. The news was so unexpected that he could scarcely believe it was real. Certainly, it was some kind of mistake. The jolly man he had seen just a few days ago couldn't be dead. Holding on to the railing to steady himself, he descended the staircase with Narendi Ram to meet Mr Howe's associate.

'We will be going to Fubster Manor for the reading of the will,' the lawyer informed him curtly.

They took a carriage to the station and boarded the train. Mr Howe's associate did not say a single word throughout the journey, busying himself instead in looking over some documents. When the train lurched into the village, he rose silently and conveyed Reginald and Narendi into a waiting carriage. Half an hour later, the familiar outline of Fubster Manor appeared ahead of them. The associate led them into Master Merriweather's study where another lawyer, Mr Charles Howe, was seated at Merriweather's desk. Natalie was there also, her eyes swollen from crying. She gave Reginald a weak smile as he sat down beside her.

'Good day, Mr Fubster,' said Mr Howe. 'It is my duty to read to you Mr Merriweather's will as you were formerly under his care.' He put on his spectacles and cleared his throat. 'The last will and testament of Mr Merriweather Fubster. All of my possessions are to be left to the British Crown in the hope that they will be used to enhance the glory of the Empire. My dependent, Miss Natalie Prim, is to be entrusted to the care of her relations the MacFinns of Ireland. My other dependent, Mr Reginald Fubster, is to be returned to the care of his father. It is my desire that I should be buried in the churchyard of St George's Parish beside my ancestors. Signed, Merriweather Fubster, in witness thereof Mr Finnegan McAuliffe.'

Mr Howe removed his spectacles and looked up.

'There must be some mistake, sir,' said Reginald. 'That can't be my uncle's will.'

'As you can clearly see, it is made out in his handwriting, and this is his signature and seal at the bottom.' Mr Howe showed him the document.

'Impossible. This house has been in the family for generations. There is no way he would have left it to the Crown unless he'd been forced to.'

'Are you disputing the legality of this document?' asked Mr Howe, his eyes flashing.

'I am, sir.'

'Don't waste your time. The will is legally binding. Now you two had better get a move on. The carriage leaves for St George's in half an hour.'

With an air of finality, he rose to his feet and swept past them.

When they were left alone, Natalie buried her head in her hands and sobbed.

'Natalie, I'm so sorry!' Reginald exclaimed. He took hold of her hands. 'We'll have time to mourn for Merriweather. But I'm afraid there is something sinister going on here, and if we don't act fast, I don't know what's going to happen.'

She brushed away her tears and regarded him bravely.

'Did you notice any sudden decline in Merriweather's health?' he asked.

'No. He was perfectly normal up until yesterday.'

'What did they say was the cause of death?'

'The doctor said he died from a stroke. He said Merriweather was in very poor health because of his eating habits and could have died any time.'

'He didn't seem in poor health to me! He walked all over London with us, and he'd always have to wait for us to catch up!'

'The doctor said the exercise and cold air had brought on the stroke.'

'I think this doctor is a liar! No one ever got a stroke because of good exercise. Do you know this family, the MacFinns, who you are to be sent to?'

'I've never heard of them in my life.'

'Could they be distant relations?'

She shook her head. 'No, I don't think so. My family is English, not Irish, and as far as I'm aware, I'm the last one left.'

A chill ran down Reginald's spine. Events were moving too quickly. He was seized by a feeling of helplessness—he was letting Natalie down at the moment she needed him most.

'I don't have the money to hire an attorney. I'm useless! The only thing I can do is write to my father and urge him to come to England immediately.'

'What am I to do?' cried Natalie.

'I wish I knew. Oh, Natalie, why is this happening? You'll have to go to these people for now and write to me when you get there. I'm sorry!'

There was a sudden knock on the door, and Mr Howe entered.

'Come along now. The coach is ready to depart.'

Reginald squeezed Natalie's hand and got to his feet. They followed Mr Howe outside and into the coach. The vehicle bounced its way down a winding path that led into the forest. The little chapel of St George, a modest stone structure, lay in a valley beside a stream that trickled down through a coppice of oak and beech. A grove of ancient yew trees stood as sentinels over the tombs. It was a peaceful place which Reginald and Natalie had visited several times before on their rambles.

The coach stopped in front of the yews, and they got out to see another coach approaching. A sombre-looking gentleman wearing dark mourning clothes stepped out.

'I'm so sorry for your loss,' he said to Reginald and Natalie, then went on ahead into the church. Something about this statement seemed off.

'Who was that?' Reginald whispered.

'Finnegan McAuliffe, our neighbour,' replied Natalie.

*Jack McAuliffe's uncle*, Reginald thought.

Inside the little church, they recognised several other neighbours and village folk as well as the cook, maid, and old Mr Beech. They sat down in the front. The parson gave a brief eulogy in honour of Merriweather Fubster's life and a longer sermon on the resurrection of the just. The service over, they filed out of the church and watched in silence as Merriweather Fubster's coffin was lowered into the earth. Natalie cried, but Reginald was too agitated by conflicting emotions. He tried to make sense of these strange and sudden events, but his mind would not work. He could do nothing but stare at Natalie.

A rough hand grasped his shoulder.

'It's time for you to return to London,' said Mr Howe. 'If you leave now, you'll be there before nightfall.'

'But, sir, I can't abandon Natalie! What is she going to do?'

'She'll be in good hands, I assure you. Now let's go.'

'Can't I say goodbye, at least?'

'All right, but be quick about it.'

Reginald hurried over to Natalie and took hold of her hands.

'Write to me as soon as you get to your new home. When my father arrives, everything will be sorted out. I won't forget you, Natalie, or ever let you come to harm.'

'Oh, Reginald, I know you won't!' She sobbed.

He took one last look at her tear-stained face and turned for the carriage. He watched her out the window until the coach rounded a bend in the road and she was gone.

# The End of the Term

REGINALD WROTE AN urgent letter to his father the moment he arrived back at the Black Lion describing in minute detail the events surrounding his great-uncle's death. The more he tried to puzzle it out, the less it made sense. His father would know what to do. If only he was here now! One and a half weeks remained in the term. To make matters worse, Reginald's reserve of money was running dangerously low.

His final days at Master Knubby and Johnstone's Military Academy for Boys, if possible, passed more tortuously than ever. Reginald was so enveloped in the thick cloud of his misfortunes that he thought of nothing else all day. Even the mysterious absence of Jack McAuliffe escaped his attention. At last, the end arrived.

'I would like to congratulate all of you on making it to the end of the term,' announced Master Knubby. 'You may come forward to get your marks. That is, all of you except for Master Fubster.'

Reginald waited in his seat until the other students had all shook Master Knubby's hand and filed out of the classroom.

'Am I to receive my marks now, sir?' he asked.

'Come here, Master Fubster,' said Knubby.

Reginald stood and waited while he scratched a few lines on a piece of paper.

'I regret to inform you that by my judgement and Master Johnstone's, you have not demonstrated sufficient progress this term to be advanced to the next level. We recommend, in fact, that you enter school next term at the level *below* our own.'

He handed Reginald the piece of paper.

Reginald stared at him in amazement. 'I…I don't understand, sir.'

'Everything is laid out quite clearly in the document. I can help you read it if you'd like.'

The boy's body trembled all over.

'Why are you doing this to me?' he gasped. 'You know that I'm well ahead of the class.'

'I don't like your kind, *Master* Fubster,' sneered Knubby. 'Think you're better than everyone else, don't you? It's time you were brought down a notch.'

'That's not true!' Reginald cried.

Knubby waved him off dismissively. Reginald was seized with a fit of rage. He tore the document to shreds and threw it on the desk.

'This is what I think of you and your *school!*' he shouted. 'I denounce you, and I denounce this establishment! I pray to God that you will be brought to justice, if not in this life, then the next!'

He turned on his heels and stomped away, making sure he slammed the door on his way out.

His anger was still burning by the time he got back to the inn. But as he gazed around at his sparse surroundings, it was replaced by an even deeper feeling of melancholy. What on earth was he to do now?

Narendi Ram sat down across from him. Reginald tried to offer him a smile, but the effort was too much.

'What can I do, sahib?' he asked.

'Oh, Narendi, my entire life's come unravelled! Merriweather dead, Natalie gone, my schooling a complete waste… Now I'm running out of money. I've calculated the amount left, and it looks as if it will only be sufficient to keep us here for two weeks.'

Narendi Ram bowed his head. 'I will work.'

'Work?' said Reginald.

'To earn the money for us to stay here.'

Reginald almost laughed. Yes, it was that simple. Why hadn't he thought of it?

'Narendi, what would I do without you? Of course! But you needn't be the one to make the sacrifice. *I* will get a job.'

'I want to help,' said the servant.

Reginald reached out and took hold of Narendi's hand. 'Then we shall work together.'

Reginald went looking the very next day. His first stop was the candle factory that he passed every day on his way to and from school. Entering through the door, he was greeted by an ancient secretary who sat scribbling at his desk.

'Can I help you, young man?'

'Yes, please. I'm looking for employment. Are there any openings in this factory?'

'You'll want to speak to the owner. Right this way, please.'

The secretary led him down a hallway to a rather ornately furnished room where a man dressed in a neat black suit was inspecting a book of figures.

'What can I do for you, my boy?' the man asked, addressing Reginald.

'I'm looking to be hired,' replied Reginald.

'Then you've come to the right place. Have you ever worked at candle manufacturing before?'

Reginald shook his head.

'No matter. I'll start you on the lower floor for fifteen shillings a week. How does that sound?'

'Thank you, sir. I also have a friend who is also looking to be employed. Would you be able to hire him as well?'

'I could, but I won't pay him more than ten shillings.'

'That should do, sir.'

'Good. You and your friend are to arrive here tomorrow at six o'clock precisely. We will show you around the factory in the morning, and you will begin work in the afternoon.'

'Thank you, sir,' said Reginald.

When he got back to the inn, he happily told Narendi Ram about the morning's success.

'Am I to work too, sahib?' Narendi asked.

'Yes, if you're willing.'

'I am honoured,' replied Narendi, bowing his head.

# Jarreby's Candle Company

THEY WOKE EARLY the next morning and passed through the dark London streets to the candle factory. They were met inside by the ancient secretary. He led them into a large room where several machines were whirring loudly. A man was inspecting the machines and writing notes down on a piece of parchment.

'Mr Cooper, here are the new employees.'

The man turned and examined Reginald and Narendi as he would two new machines.

'Does he speak English?' Mr Cooper asked, inclining his head toward Narendi Ram.

'Yes, quite well.'

'He'll do. Come on, I'll show you around the place.'

The secretary took his leave as Mr Cooper gave them a tour of the factory floor. There were other workers about, occupied with their solitary tasks.

'These machines make the candles,' Mr Cooper said, giving them an affectionate look. 'The candles come out over here.' He pointed to a bin. 'Your job is to take the candles and put them in these packages. Each package must contain precisely two thousand four hundred and thirty-seven candles.'

*That's an odd number*, Reginald thought.

'Once the candles are packed, you will bring them over here.' He showed them to a set of tables where a few workers were waiting. 'These men will label the packages and load them into those wagons. The wagons are carted down to the Thames, the boxes are loaded onto a ship, and from there, sent out all over the world!'

Mr Cooper showed them back to the place where the candles issued out of the machine and demonstrated how to fit them into one of the packages. It looked simple enough.

'I'll leave you to it,' said Mr Cooper. 'If you have any questions, just ask.'

Reginald and Narendi Ram started at their task. They both packed the candles and took turns delivering the completed product to the men at the tables. They worked for several hours until Reginald's feet were sore from standing and his back ached from carrying the packages. At noon, they were given a half-hour break for lunch, but as neither had brought anything to eat, they sat in silence. At six o'clock, they took a half-hour break for dinner. Work continued until eight o'clock that evening.

'Looks like we'll have to shut down for the night,' said Mr Cooper with a slight air of melancholy. 'Good first day, gentlemen. I will see you tomorrow at six o'clock.'

Reginald and Narendi Ram staggered out of the factory and had to support themselves against each other to make it back to the Black Lion. They fell asleep as soon as they reached their beds.

The next day, the cycle repeated itself. They rose at six and made their way to the candle factory. They packed candles until lunch (which they had remembered this time), packed candles until dinner, and packed candles after dinner until eight o'clock in the evening.

'Another fine day gentlemen,' said Mr Cooper. 'I will see you tomorrow.'

Though there was no hint of it within the walls of Jarreby's Candle Company, the world at large was on the brink of a cataclysm. Neither Reginald nor Narendi Ram had any idea that these distant events were about to alter their destiny.

A new European country, moulded in the forge of war, had risen in Central Europe. It had humbled France in 1870, and since then, its power multiplied by the day. Though a late player in the colonial game, it managed to seize colonies in Africa and the Pacific and began the construction of a fleet of dreadnoughts to rival the Royal Navy. In response to this threat, Britain had signed the Triple Alliance with France and Russia. Germany, meanwhile (for this was the name of the new country), under its ruler Kaiser Wilhelm II, created the Triple Entente with the Austro-Hungarians and the Italians. Europe had become an armed camp; now it was only a matter of waiting for the spark to ignite the fire.

On June 28, 1914, Archduke Franz Ferdinand's cab driver took a wrong turn in the city of Sarajevo, and the archduke was assassinated by Gavrilo Princip, a Serbian nationalist. Austria-Hungary issued an ultimatum to Serbia and, when refused, mobilised its army. This started a chain reaction. Russia declared war on Austria-Hungary to defend Serbia. Germany entered the war on the side of Austria-Hungary and France on the side of Russia.

The Germans feared fighting a two-front war and planned accordingly. They predicted (incorrectly as it turns out) that the Russians would take several weeks to mobilise, giving them enough time to drive to Paris and knock the French out of the war. The Schlieffen Plan, as it was called, required the German army to advance through neutral Belgium in order for the man on the far right to 'brush his sleeve on the English Channel.' The Belgians, to everyone's surprise, decided to resist the German intrusion on their national sovereignty, and even though their army was immediately overrun, they convinced the British to come to their aid. England declared war on Germany on August 4, 1914.

All of London was in an uproar. Newspaper boys were everywhere shouting about the recent events. Recruitment for a British expeditionary force to aid the French was launched immediately. Soon, the newly enlisted soldiers were marching proudly through the streets. A patriotic fervour swept the city, and there was so much excitement that the men could hardly concentrate on their work.

It was during this time that Reginald finally received a letter from his father.

Dearest Reginald,

It saddens me deeply to hear of Master Merriweather's passing. I quite agree with you that his will is very suspicious. I would like to speak with this Finnegan McAuliffe and get to the bottom of the whole matter. Naturally, I would have come to England as soon as I received your letter; however, there has been a terrible outbreak of cholera in Delhi and your mother is very sick. I cannot leave her side. You must find some means of supporting yourself until I can get there. I pray to God that I might see you soon.

Yours affectionately,
Captain Wilfred Fubster,
His Majesty's Thirty-Third Horse

Reginald's hand shook as he read. Now his mother was in danger! He'd have given anything just then to be back in India.

*I wish I'd never come here at all,* he thought, tears rolling down his cheeks.

His thoughts turned to Natalie, who his father hadn't even mentioned, though she'd been the chief subject of his last epistle. He had no news from her. She had to be settled down by now. Was somebody preventing her from writing? This fear gnawed in the back of his mind until he was certain that she was in danger and that if he didn't do something to help her, no one would.

The excitement created by the outbreak of war could not disrupt the routine of the candle factory. Every day was a repeat of the last. Reginald could feel his mind growing numb from the unspeakable boredom and drudgery. Though he tried to hide it, Narendi Ram was as miserable as he had ever been in his life. His gait became an awkward shuffle, and his eyes were glazed over with melancholy.

*He's dying,* Reginald thought. *We have to get out of here.*

Meanwhile, the Germans marched on Paris. Nothing could stop them. It would be a repeat of 1870. The British and French forces made a desperate, last-ditch stand along the Marne River on the fifth of September. The German legions were turned back by a surprise allied victory and forced to dig a series of trenches across Northern France to protect their lines. While England celebrated the Miracle of the Marne, Reginald was seriously considering running away to Ireland to try to search for Natalie. He sat up late at night brooding by the fireplace.

*I will wait for my father one more week*, he decided.

# 10

## *The Duke of Marlborough Military Academy*

AFTER A PARTICULARLY gruelling day of work, Reginald and Narendi Ram stumbled back to the Black Lion. There was no one about at that hour except for the innkeeper and a gentleman who sat reading the *Times*.

'We've won the race to the sea,' the man told the innkeeper. His voice sounded strangely familiar. 'The Germans won't take Paris now.'

The gentleman lowered the newspaper to reveal none other than Captain Wilfred Fubster himself.

'Father!' Reginald shouted, running to embrace him.

'Is that you, Reginald, my boy? I'll say, you've grown!'

'I've missed you so much!'

Tears dripped down Reginald's cheeks. He was so overcome with happiness that he forgot himself.

'I've missed you too, old boy. Let's go to your room and talk.'

Reginald led him up the stairs and pushed open the door.

'A cosy little nook,' remarked Wilfred, settling into the chair. 'Good to see you again, Narendi. Hope things are going well for you.'

'Thank you, sahib,' Narendi Ram replied.

'Now we have a lot to talk about. I think our first order of business is to have you enrolled in a new school.'

'But, Father, I promised Natalie that I would find her. I have to go looking for her!'

'Patience, old boy,' Wilfred said. 'We'll deal with Miss Natalie and Merriweather's will in due time. I've been transferred to the British Army, and I'm expected to join the regiment on Thursday. We sail for France on Monday. I won't be away for long. Everyone says that the war will be over by Christmas.'

Reginald was shocked. He'd waited for months, and now his father was going away again?

'What about Mother?' he asked. 'How is she? Please tell me she's recovered!'

Wilfred's face grimaced in pain. 'Son, your mother is in heaven now.'

He quietly described the circumstances of her passing. She had been infected with cholera during an outbreak in Delhi. Just when it looked like she would recover, she suddenly relapsed and died a couple of days later. That was simply the reality of life in India, where the hand of God struck down the young and healthy without discrimination.

Though he had been removed, Spartan-like, from his mother's bosom at the age of seven and trained to be an ideal soldier, Reginald had always longed for his mother's society and the gentleness of a domestic life. Now he found he missed it more than ever. The emotions he'd tried so hard to suppress since coming to England over-flowed, and tears spilled from his eyes.

Embarrassed, he tried to brush them away.

'There, there, old boy,' Wilfred said softly. 'It's all right.'

Reginald bit his lip so hard, it drew blood and managed to choke back the rest of his tears.

'I've inquired at the Duke of Marlborough Military Academy in Westminster and made an appointment for you to see the headmaster tomorrow. You'd better get some sleep now.'

He shook Reginald's hand. Then, with a nod good night to Narendi Ram, he closed the door behind him. Reginald crawled into his bed. He pulled the covers over his head and wept silently, so as not to disturb Narendi Ram, until he at last fell asleep.

The Duke of Marlborough Military Academy was beyond walking distance from the Black Lion, so Wilfred hired a carriage early the next morning. They entered the more fashionable West End of London and came to a halt before a stately building with marble columns. A secretary led Wilfred and his son past a couple of class-rooms to the headmaster's study.

The interior of the study was lavishly decorated. There were maps of battlefields, swords, shields, flags, and even a full suit of armour displayed on the walls. A pair of ornately carved bookshelves stacked with ancient manuscripts stood on either side. The head-master himself was seated at his desk perusing a map of the Battle of Hastings.

'Good day, Captain Fubster,' he said, looking up. He was just past middle age with grey hair, a moustache, and spectacles. He was dressed in the robes of an academic. 'Is this young Reginald?'

'It is indeed, sir. He is ready to sit for the entrance examination.'

'Very good,' replied the headmaster. 'I'll be half a moment.'

He rummaged through the pile of papers on his desk until he had produced a large stack of parchment.

'Here you are,' he said, handing the stack to Reginald along with a pen. 'You will have one hour to complete it.'

Reginald was nervous. His last term of study (as we've seen) had been an absolute waste and the candle factory had further dulled his intellect. Yet he felt an immense pressure to do well and make his father proud in return for all those years of training.

The first section of the exam tested his knowledge of Latin and Greek. His Latin was solid, and as he worked through a translation, some of the fog in his brain dissipated. The Greek section was much more difficult; some snatches of it from his time in Delhi came back, but he had always struggled with that particular language. He com-pleted the section in a reasonable amount of time. After that was his-tory, Reginald's favourite subject. He provided thorough answers to each of the essays. A quick glance up at the clock revealed that he had only half an hour left to complete the remainder of the examination.

Mathematics was the next subject. Here, Reginald found some of the problems to be too advanced for him to solve. He finished up the others and turned over to the last part of the examination: military strategy. He was in his element as he applied the tactics of the celebrated generals his father had taught him about as a child to the posited scenarios. He finished with a minute to spare and turned in the examination at the headmaster's desk.

'Now, if you wouldn't mind, could you please step out of the room while I do the marking? My secretary will provide tea for you.'

Wilfred escorted Reginald out the door and sat him down for tea.

'Well, how'd you do, my boy?' he asked.

'I'm not sure. My Greek has never been up to form, and I'm terrible at mathematics.'

Wilfred took a sip of tea. 'Your Latin's better than mine was at your age, and Master Merriweather told me that you were quite the reader. I'm sure you did all right.'

Reginald sat with his hand tapping on the table.

'Take a biscuit,' said Wilfred.

Reginald accepted it, but didn't eat it

'One lump or two in your tea?' Wilfred asked, picking up a spoon and the sugar cup.

'None, please,' replied Reginald. 'Father, can't you see I'm anxious?'

'Nothing calms the nerves like a cup of tea, old boy. Here you are. Drink this.'

Reginald took a sip and felt precisely the same.

'Here's the headmaster now,' Wilfred said calmly.

'Come in, please come in,' the headmaster said excitedly.

They re-entered and sat down.

'Let me congratulate you, son,' the headmaster began, grabbing hold of Reginald's arm and shaking it heartily. 'You did exceptionally well, especially for someone with so little formal education.'

Reginald looked over at his father, who concealed a smile.

The headmaster paged through the examination. 'Your Latin translation: flawless. Greek: four or five minor errors. Historical essays: concise, incisive, and enlightening. Mathematics: proficient. You failed to solve the advanced equations, but that's something we can teach you. Military tactics: a bold and insightful use of Frederick the Great's oblique tactics to the task at hand. In short, sir, congratulations. You have been accepted into the Duke of Marlborough Military Academy at Fifth Form. Four years of study here and you will be on the way to earning a prestigious commission and entering the army at the rank of lieutenant. Mr Secretary'—he clapped his hands—'show young Master Fubster to his new accommodations.'

Reginald heaved a deep sigh of relief. In spite of the wasted term, he was still on the right track. Knubby and Johnstone had certainly done their worst but ultimately failed.

The secretary led Reginald and his father up a grand staircase and down a broad hallway. They stopped at a door that had a number 5 carved above it and entered into an expansive common room. A few young scholars dressed in their school robes were seated at a table playing chess while a handful of others were sitting on the couches reading. The secretary led them to the far end of the room and up another flight of stairs.

'Your bedroom, sir,' said the secretary, opening a door.

There was one bed left open, at the far end near the window. Several pairs of dress robes were laid out on top of it, and there were a few books in the bookshelf by its side.

'I'll leave you to get settled in and meet your fellow pupils,' Wilfred said. 'I'll be back soon with Narendi Ram and your belongings.'

Reginald looked over his books and dressed himself in his new robes before cautiously descending into the common room. He took a seat next to the fellows who were playing chess, reflecting on the vast difference in atmosphere between this institution and the last. The boys all looked older than him.

'And who might you be?' asked one, who was stroking his blond hair.

'Reginald Fubster, sir. I'm a new student here.'

The boy laughed. 'You don't have to call me 'sir.' How old are you, friend?'

'Fifteen.'

'Really? How old would you say he is, lads?' he turned to the other boys. 'Twelve? Thirteen?'

'I look young, I guess,' said Reginald, turning red.

'I don't mean to offend,' said the blond boy. 'We're not used to having younger boys in Form Five. We're all sixteen, except Quincy here, he's seventeen. I thought there had been some mistake.'

'That's understandable,' Reginald said, though not quite comprehending how the ages of fifteen and sixteen were all that different. 'The headmaster put me here.'

The boy inspected him closely.

'What's your name?' Reginald asked.

'Waverley Nottingham.'

'After the hero of Sir Walter Scott's novel?'

The blond boy nodded.

'My father's Christian name is Wilfred, for Wilfred Ivanhoe. It's nice to meet you,'

Reginald shook Waverley's hand. The rest of the boys at the table introduced themselves, and they took up a conversation on the subjects that were taught at Form Five and what Reginald could expect from each of the professors. They had moved on to the topic of the dining arrangements when Wilfred and Narendi Ram entered the common room. Narendi was carrying all of Reginald's possessions on his back.

'Right up the stairs there,' Wilfred said, pointing. Then he pulled his son aside. 'Well, Reginald, my boy, I'm off to join the regiment. I'll make sure to write you from the Front, and I'll be back by Christmas. Best of luck to you, son. I'm sure you'll do well.'

'When you come back, do you promise to help me find Natalie?' Reginald asked.

The question had been burning in his mind the entire morning.

'I promise. But as you know, country comes first. Remember what I've taught you.'

'I will,' Reginald said and watched as his father strolled off to the door.

He had a sudden presentiment of fear and wanted to call out to him not to go but controlled himself. His father was off to do his duty; he would do his.

# A New Friend

'WHO'S THE FOREIGNER?' Waverley asked Reginald after Wilfred had gone.

'That is my servant, Narendi Ram.'

'How'd you meet him?'

Reginald blushed. 'Oh, that's a long story. It was on a tiger hunt, and well, I'll tell it some other time.'

'Tell it now,' urged Waverley.

The others boys got up and crowded around.

Reginald reluctantly narrated the adventure, after which the boys all looked at him with a new level of respect.

'I'd best go see he's settling in,' said Reginald. 'I will join you all for dinner.'

When the time came, Reginald followed the boys down to the wide lower hall. There were seven long tables spread about, one for each of the six forms and another for the headmaster and professors. There was an average of twenty students in each form in addition to a tutor. The tutor for Form Five was a Mr Lionel Quimpley. He made sure that Reginald was introduced to the other pupils. The supper proved a substantial improvement over the fare at Knubby and Johnstone's as did the conversation, by the fact there was any at all. Reginald retired to bed that night much happier than he had been in months, though the issue of Natalie still lurked in the back of his mind.

Classes began the next day, and their first subject was history. Reginald followed Mr Quimpley and the other Form Five students to a rather austere classroom where a rather austere man sat at his desk drumming his fingers.

'Let's have a little more promptness to class, Mr Quimpley,'

'I'm sorry, Professor Wicklow,' Quimpley replied breathlessly as the students took their seats.

The professor stayed at his desk and glared out at the students.

'New recruit, eh?' he said as his gaze rested on Reginald. 'What's your name?'

'Reginald Fubster, sir.'

'Fubster, eh? Your grandfather fought at Waterloo, didn't he?'

'Yes, sir.'

'And your great-grandfather fought in the Seven Years War, didn't he?'

'Yes, sir.'

'And your great-great-great-great-great-great-great-great-grand-father fought at Agincourt, didn't he?'

'I believe so, sir,' gasped the astonished Reginald.

'Yes, sir, I know your family history. Has your father gone to fight in our current war?'

'He has, sir. He left just yesterday.'

'Then I'm sure he'll distinguish himself in some way or another. The Fubsters have always made good soldiers. Anyway, today's lesson.'

Professor Wicklow began an account of the 1453 Ottoman conquest of Constantinople that was so gripping that Reginald imagined he was actually at the siege, hearing the roar of the cannons and the screams of the wounded men. The professor remained in his seat the entire class and did not once alter the tone of his voice. Yet his oratory was so absorbing that Reginald forgot to take notes and remained spellbound in his seat until he was prodded by Mr Quimpley.

'Master Fubster, it's time to go to the next subject.'

He took one last glance at Professor Wicklow on his way out to see him staring fiercely out of the window. The next subject was mathematics, and here, the professor was not quite so interesting. His name was Professor Clam, a short, portly gentleman who wore crooked spectacles. He gave a rather plodding explanation of Sir Isaac Newton's theory of calculus (the explanation was 'plodding,' not only on account of the boredom inherent to the subject, but also because the professor had to stop every five seconds to catch his breath).

After mathematics, the students convened for lunch and were given half an hour of free time. Reginald went to check on Narendi Ram.

'Have you eaten?' he asked.

'Yes, sahib. They have brought food for me here.' He pointed to some empty dishes. 'I like this place already. The headmaster promised me that he would introduce me to some other Indians who I might spend the day with.'

'That is excellent news. I think I like this place too.'

That afternoon, he had geography with Professor Anderson and military theory with Professor Dawkins, both of which he enjoyed immensely. Dinner that evening was once again excellent, and he went to sleep full and content.

The first week of classes rushed by. On Sunday, the Form Five boys went to the park to play cricket, accompanied, as always, by Mr Quimpley. It was a bright, clear day, and there were many people out. A couple of pretty girls sitting beside their governess had soon attracted the boys' attention. Mr Quimpley noticed the danger and attempted to relocate the game to the other end of the park. Somehow, though, the players kept drifting back toward the girls. It came time for Waverley's turn to bat, and he sent the ball sailing over the heads of all of the boys to land dangerously close to the young ladies' governess.

'I'll get it.' He volunteered and ran over to the girls. 'I beg your pardon, madam,' he said to the governess.

'Humph!' replied the governess, sticking up her nose. 'Girls, I suggest we move to some place where we are not in peril of being struck by flying objects.'

The girls rose obediently to their feet to follow her, but while her back was turned, one of them slipped Waverley a little scrap of paper. Waverley retrieved the ball and returned to the other boys as if nothing had happened. Mr Quimpley was none the wiser.

That evening after dinner, Waverley read the girl's note to an excited assembly of boys in the common room:

> Meet us at Cobbler's Street near St Dunstan's next Saturday at midnight. There are nineteen of us girls.

'One less than our number,' observed a boy.

'That's all right,' Reginald said. 'I'll stay behind.'

'What?' cried Waverley in astonishment. 'Don't you like girls?'

'I do, but there's something else. I don't really want to talk about it.'

He turned away from the quizzical faces of his fellow pupils and plodded up to bed. He'd been thinking about Natalie all week, lying awake late into the night, drawing up plans of how he would find her and unravel the mystery of Merriweather's death. That night, he couldn't sleep at all. The lack of news was the most unsettling thing; his active imagination dreamt up all sorts of possible scenarios, each more horrible than the last. In the long, dark hours before dawn, he formed the resolution that he must go after her to Ireland.

His father would not understand. Wilfred was not romantic except where duty to country was concerned. He could not believe that his son had fallen in love with a girl who he had seen only briefly and would willingly sacrifice his education and future career for her welfare. Here was the first serious rift in the relationship between father and son. Reginald was starting to think for himself. In his mind, fanatical loyalty to Britain was irrational. The nation was no more than a collection of individuals; some good (Merriweather, Natalie) and others bad (Master Knubby, Jack McAuliffe). It was his duty to defend the former from the latter. He was also animated by the words of Narendi Ram, who had encouraged him to prove his love. Yes, he would prove it!

Everyone would call him a fool, but his love for Natalie was true.

The Form Five boys appeared in unusually high spirits that next Saturday, and Mr Quimpley was at a loss to explain it. He inquired of Waverley, who replied that the boys were simply looking forward to another invigorating game of cricket that Sunday.

After dinner, the boys convened in the common room to discuss their strategy.

'I say we each leave five minutes apart. That way, if one of us gets caught, the others can still get away.'

'That's good thinking, Waverley. But how are we to get out? The back door's sure to be locked.'

'We'll have to use the front door.'

'And the guard?'

'He'll be asleep, like always.'

'And if he isn't?'

'Then the whole plan goes up in smoke,' Waverley conceded. 'But let's not worry about that. The girls want to meet us at midnight, so the first man should leave here around 11:30. Once he gets there, he should tell the girls that more are on the way. Now, does everyone know the way to Cobbler's Street?'

Most, but not all, of the boys nodded.

'Here then, let's draw a map. Commit this to memory,' he said as he passed the map around.

The parchment was then consigned to the flames, with the boys watching until it had turned to ashes.

'Who should go first?' one of the boys asked.

'Waverley, of course,' said another.

'No, I'll go last to make sure no one leaves early. Philip, you'll go first.'

Waverley's judgement as the *de facto* leader of the Form Fives was unquestioned. With these important tactical details decided, the boys waited in tense expectation for several hours until the clock struck 11:30.

'Go,' Waverley whispered, and Philip stole off down the hallway. Five minutes passed and the next boy was dispatched at Waverley's signal. So it went until 1:05 when Waverly was the last one remaining. Reginald had gone to bed early that night, but again had difficulty sleeping, so he got up and wandered into the common room. He found Waverly waiting there by the fire.

'You're still here?' said Reginald. 'I thought you were going to see the girls.'

'I'm just about to leave. There's still time for you to come if you'd like.'

'No, thank you.' Reginald sighed, sitting down on one of the couches.

Waverley regarded him curiously. 'Can't you tell me why, Reginald? I promise I won't breathe a word of it to any of the boys.'

Reginald looked him over closely. Could he trust Waverley? The boy's expression was earnest enough. With his father gone, Reginald had been feeling more isolated and lonelier than ever. He could use an ally.

'The truth is,' began Reginald, 'I'm already in love with someone. We've been separated. There was a will, and she has gone to stay with relatives in Ireland. She promised me she'd write, but I haven't heard anything from her. I don't know what to do.'

'Slow down, old boy,' said Waverley eagerly. 'Tell me the story from the beginning. Where did you meet her?'

And so Reginald described how he had first seen Natalie upon arriving at Fubster Manor and how he had confessed to his great-uncle Merriweather that he loved her. He told him about their first meeting and how over the next few weeks they had become the best of friends. He told him about her visits to him at the Black Lion during the weekends and what wonderful afternoons they had strolling through London.

But the subject he focused on the most was the last few hours he'd spent with her. He told Waverley about the mysterious death of his uncle, the confounding will which had abandoned the Fubster estate to the Crown and dispatched Natalie to live with dubious relations in Ireland. He confessed he was completely at a loss to the meaning of it all, but had determined to go after her at the earliest possible convenience.

Waverley had sat listening on the very edge of his chair. Initially, he was too excited and overcome with emotion to respond. The story had struck a romantic chord in his soul.

'Do you want to know what I think?' He finally managed to gasp.

'Of course!'

'I think it's all a vile plot!'

Reginald shuddered, the creeping, shadowy suspicions which tormented him taking on a more definite shape at these words.

'What do you mean?' he asked.

'Well, you told me Natalie is an heiress of a considerable fortune. Naturally, there would be other people interested in getting their share of it. But with your uncle Merriweather alive and in the position of her legal guardian, there was nothing that could be done. It must have appeared that Merriweather planned to have you and Natalie betrothed, keeping the fortune in the Fubster family. These MacFinns may very well be Natalie's relatives who believe they deserve their share and aren't afraid to resort to crime to get it.'

The enormity of the situation was rapidly dawning on Reginald. He'd forgotten about Natalie's fortune and never imagined that it might put her in danger. But what had Merriweather thought? The Fubsters were by no means wealthy, and a marriage between himself and an heiress would do much to improve the family's circumstances. Had this been the plan all along, the real reason he'd been sent to England?

He could scarcely comprehend the villainy which would murder a man and take captive an innocent young girl in the name of money. He prayed it wasn't true, that it had been, after all, a combination of unfortunate accidents. However, his intuition convinced him otherwise.

'I have to do something!' he wailed. 'I can't sit here while Natalie's in danger. I have to rescue her!'

'What can you do? Ireland may not be as big as England, but it's still a large country, especially if you don't have anything to go off of.'

Reginald couldn't dispute this. He sat and stared into the fire, engrossed by his thoughts.

The ticking of the grandfather clock finally arrested his attention. It read two-thirty.

'I'm sorry,' he said. 'I've made you miss your appointment with the young ladies.'

'I'd rather've heard your story than anything in the world!' replied Waverly. 'I want to help you if I can.'

'Thank you,' said Reginald, rising to his feet. 'I have much to think about, but we'll talk again, and I'll let you know what I decide.'

He stumbled back up to his room, leaving the spellbound Waverley to muse before the fire.

'Where were you, Waverley?' the boys asked as they were recounting their exploits with glowing faces the next day.

'I fell asleep,' Waverley lied.

'How could you?'

He shrugged.

'Well, it doesn't matter. They said they would see us again next week, same time, same place.'

'Good. I'm looking forward to it.'

Reginald received a letter from his father midway through the week, the postage indicating that it came from the Front.

Dear Reginald,

We have been forced to dig a series of trenches opposite the German lines all the way across the north of France. Any advance we make is cut down immediately by the enemy machine gunners, so there is little we can do but watch and wait. I made my first foray out into No Man's Land last night. It is an eerie place; I expected at any moment the Germans would open fire. Our trench lies a couple of miles from the Marne River. There are Scotch soldiers on our left and French on our right. So far, we have not been attacked, and I am longing for some action. I hate to say it, but I do not think the war will be over by Christmas. My request for leave over the holidays has been denied as the generals fear that the Germans are planning an offensive. I hope you are enjoying your studies at the Duke of Marlborough Military Academy, and I pray to God that I might see you soon.

Yours affectionately,
Captain Wilfred Fubster, Fifty-Fourth Infantry

Reginald read the letter twice and then composed a letter of his own.

Dear Father,

I am very happy at the Duke of Marlborough Military Academy. However, the promise I made to Natalie has been weighing heavily on me of late. I am heading for Dublin during my Christmas holiday, and I am going to find out where the MacFinns are keeping her. I pray to God for your safety in the war. Do not worry yourself on my account.

Yours affectionately,
Reginald Fubster

# Reginald Sets Out

THE CHRISTMAS HOLIDAY drew closer. Reginald enjoyed his classes, particularly Professor Wicklow's, but he struggled with an intense impatience to be on his way to Ireland. His mind was made up; he'd pondered the consequences and decided it was absolutely the right thing to do. He wrote a lengthy epistle to his father explaining everything and asking for his forgiveness. Now it remained to tell Waverley. One evening, he was sitting by himself in the common room when Waverley approached him.

'I've been thinking, Reginald,' he said. 'You won't have a place to stay over the holiday with your father off at war. I'll write to my parents and ask if you can spend Christmas with us.'

'That's very kind of you,' replied Reginald. 'But I am headed to Ireland over the holiday.'

'To search for the *girl?*' he gasped.

Reginald nodded.

'Let me go with you!'

'Impossible. If I don't find her during the holiday, I'm going to stay and keep looking for her.'

'I don't care. Please, Reginald!'

'I won't have you sacrifice your future happiness for me. This is my responsibility. I'm going alone.'

His tone had an air of finality. Waverley stared at him. Then he reached into his pockets.

'Take these at least,' he said, placing a couple of gold sovereigns in Reginald's hand. 'If that's the only way I can help you.'

'I can't...' Reginald protested, but Waverley turned and walked away.

Reginald sat staring at the coins for a long time afterward.

At last, the final day before the holiday arrived. Narendi Ram had already packed up all their things and scraped together the money they had saved from their time at the candle factory. He had been alerted to the plan and accepted it with his customary equanimity. In fact, he was as eager as Reginald to look for Natalie.

'Let's go,' Reginald said. 'The steamer leaves from Bristol tomorrow morning.'

They stepped out onto the London streets where a light snow was falling and hired a carriage to the train station. They caught the six o'clock train for Bristol.

'Sahib, what do you plan to do once we've found Miss Natalie?' Narendi Ram asked.

'I'm still working that part out,' Reginald replied.

Most of the ideas he had come up with so far involved storming a castle, sweeping Natalie out on a rope, and galloping away atop a noble steed.

The train chugged onward until one o'clock in the morning when it finally pulled into Bristol. Reginald found them a place at a nearby inn and tried to get some sleep with his mind still full of half-made plans.

'Wake up, sahib,' said Narendi Ram the next morning, prodding him gently.

Reginald turned over and looked at the clock.

'My god! It's nine o'clock! The steamer leaves in an hour! Why didn't you wake me sooner?'

'I only just woke up myself,' replied Narendi Ram.

'Come on, we haven't a moment to lose.'

Reginald threw on some clothes and stuffed the rest into his suitcase. He tossed some coins to the innkeeper and, not waiting to receive his change, rushed out onto the street. A carriage heading to the docks came around presently, and Reginald paid the driver an extra shilling in the hope that he would get them there faster. Soon enough, they could hear the cries of the gulls and could see the ships belching black smoke into the skies. They hopped out of the carriage and pushed their way through the crowd until they reached the Dublin steamer.

'Tickets please,' said the guard on the gangway.

Reginald produced them.

'Thank you. Enjoy your time in Dublin, and a merry Christmas to you.'

They had just reached their cabin when the ship sounded its horn, the gangway was pushed aside, and the engines roared to life. Some of the passengers were anxious to be afloat in U-boat–patrolled waters, but Reginald's trepidations were of an entirely different kind. He settled back and watched the shoreline recede out of the window. The ship ploughed on throughout the day and into the night, through the Bristol Channel and out into the cold, stormy waters of the Irish Sea. His mind worked feverishly throughout the voyage. He thought of every possibility and tried to plan accordingly. By the time the captain announced that they were approaching Dublin, he was in such a state of nervous unease that he was trembling all over.

It was the evening of the twenty-third of December when the steamer pulled into port. Reginald forced his way through the crowd that had gathered to greet the new arrivals and stood on the corner looking to hire a carriage. Two rattled past without stopping before a third pulled up beside him.

'Can I help ye, sir?' the driver asked. He was a tall, thin Irishman with dark hair and beard.

'Yes, sir, I am looking for an inn to spend the night.'

'Hop in then, I'll take ye. On second thought, what's yer name?'

'Why do you want to know?' asked Reginald.

'Climb inside, and I'll tell ye.'

'I will not get inside, sir, until you explain to me why you want to know my name.'

'Right then. There was a young miss, looked about yer age who passed this way a couple o' days ago,' said the Irishman. 'I don't think I'll ever forget her, beggin' yer pardon, sir, she being the most beautiful creature I ever laid me eye on. Golden hair, blue eyes, lovely red lips…' His eyes grew misty. 'Anyway, she told me that there might be a young lad about yer age named Regiold Foobster, or something like it, with a servant who might come lookin' for her. She had a message to give 'im, that's all. Seemed in an awful hurry 'bout it too. Wished she'd stayed longer…'

'Yes, I am Reginald Fubster! Do you still have the message?'

'It's here somewhere, if I can find it.' The Irishman reached into his pockets and produced a little scrap of paper. 'Here you go.'

Reginald unfolded it. There was one line, scrawled hurriedly, but unmistakably in Natalie's handwriting.

They have taken me to India.

'When's the next steamer for India?' Reginald cried.

'Not 'til after Christmas, I'd say,' replied the Irishman. 'One left tonight, but you know tomorrow's Christmas Eve and it's Christmas the day after.'

Reginald nodded. 'Then I guess I'll need a place to stay. Would you mind taking me to the inn?'

'Not at all. Hop in.'

The carriage rattled down a narrow winding road and stopped in front of a creaking sign painted with a lyre.

'That will be one shilling, sir,' said the Irishman, holding out his hand.

'Take three pounds,' said Reginald. 'And may God bless all of your future endeavours. You have done me more good than you could possibly imagine!'

Before the Irishman could protest, Reginald grabbed his suitcase and carried it into the inn, Narendi Ram following at his heels. They booked themselves a room on the ground floor and settled in.

'What did the note say, sahib?' Narendi Ram asked at last.

'"They have taken me to India,"' quoted Reginald.

'Who are "they"?'

'It doesn't say.' Reginald's brow furrowed. 'Why India? This doesn't make any sense.'

'What shall we do?'

'We'll go after her, of course,' said Reginald.

Narendi Ram's face broke into a wide smile.

'Why, that's that first time I've seen you smile in months,' said Reginald.

'That is because this is the first time I have been happy in months. I have missed my country most terribly. I do not like it here in Europe.'

'Nor do I,' Reginald agreed.

They sat together and had a merry conversation about their native country, its sights, smells, and sounds and all that they had missed while they were away. Though a light snow was falling outside of the windows, both of their minds had drifted away to the sun-washed streets of old Delhi, the baking plains and the steaming jungles of the land of India.

The next day, Reginald set out into Dublin to find the supplies they would need for their voyage. As it was Christmas Eve, most of the shops were closed, but he eventually found everything he needed. He even had time to buy Narendi Ram a few Christmas presents, which he had wrapped at one of the shops and hid under the bed when Narendi had his back turned. They enjoyed a delicious Christmas Eve banquet at the inn's dining hall along with the other guests.

Reginald woke up early on Christmas morning and pulled the presents out from under the bed. He waited silently until Narendi Ram began to stir.

'Merry Christmas, Narendi!' he announced.

'What are you doing with those gifts, sahib?' he asked.

'They're for you, of course. Come on and open them.'

'Me? But, sahib, I am not a Christian.'

Reginald laughed. 'You don't have to be a Christian to get Christmas presents. Come on!'

He grabbed Narendi by the hand and pulled him over to the presents. Narendi opened the smallest one first. It was a book on India full of colourful pictures.

'For you to read on the voyage,' said Reginald.

'Oh, I—'

'Open the other ones,' Reginald ordered.

The second present was a new blanket.

'It might get cold on the first part of our voyage, and you can use that to keep yourself warm.'

The third was an elaborately carved knife.

'It caught my fancy, so I bought it for you. Hopefully, you won't have to use it on our voyage.'

'Sahib, I—' Narendi Ram began.

Reginald waved his hand. 'That's actually much less than you deserve for all of your faithful service. A man couldn't ask for a more loyal follower. Thank you, my friend.'

Ignoring Narendi Ram's protestations, he sat down at the desk and wrote a quick letter to his father, informing him that he was following Natalie to India.

They spent the rest of Christmas Day making preparations for their journey. In the evening, they took a little stroll to take in the festivities. Snatches of carols drifted from every street corner and the ground sparkled with newly fallen snow. It was a magical atmosphere, and Reginald might have stayed out all night if he had not noticed Narendi Ram beginning to shiver.

That same day, the soldiers on the Western Front had laid aside their weapons and ventured out into No Man's Land. At first, they went only to bury their dead, but eventually, the soldiers from either side began to mingle together, sharing laughs and stories of life in the trenches. That afternoon, Captain Wilfred Fubster of the Fifty-Fourth Infantry participated in a game of football with French, Scottish, and German soldiers. The generals were furious when they found out and ordered their men to behave more aggressively in the future.

The next morning, Reginald and Narendi Ram hired a carriage to the docks and discovered that a steamer was bound for India that afternoon. Reginald purchased the tickets, and when the time came, they were ushered aboard. Once they reached their cabin, they tried their best to get settled in. This steamer would be their home for the next month. The clock struck four o'clock and the great ship churned out of port. After a disastrous year and a half abroad, Reginald Fubster was finally on his way back home.

# The Land of the Pharaohs

THE STEAMER MADE good time out of the harbour, rounding the Cape of Finisterre after a few days. They sailed along the coast of Portugal and made their first port of call at Gibraltar. The passengers had been confined to their cabins for the most part on account of the cold, but now, they began to congregate together on deck. There were a good number of young officers bound for India, as well as a dozen or so district commissioners and magistrates on their way back. The female society consisted of the wives of the aforesaid commissioners and magistrates and a few young ladies being escorted by their mothers or aunts. One or two of the latter proved of great interest to the young officers who devoted much of their time throughout the voyage to paying them court.

Reginald avoided this society. He went ashore at Gibraltar to have a look around, but aside from that, rarely ventured outside his cabin. He thought constantly about his father and whether he had done right in leaving England. But the image of Natalie's tear-stained face had so impressed itself on his mind that his internal struggles always resulted in him affirming his resolution. Fourteen days out of Dublin, the steamer arrived at Port Said in Egypt. The captain called all of the passengers on deck for an important announcement, and Reginald went grudgingly.

The announcement was given by a rather stern man in a drab army uniform.

'I'm afraid I have bad news to report. Army intelligence informed us yesterday that an army of Turks, being led and equipped by the Germans, is on the march to the Suez Canal. While the army prepares to defend the canal, we have been given orders to prevent any ships from passing this way. We apologise for the delay and will see to it that every passenger is given accommodation in Port Said until the canal can be reopened.'

As the officer finished his speech, an anxious murmur went up through the crowd.

'We will begin to disembark at once,' said the captain, stepping forward. 'Return to your cabins and collect any personal items. We will expect you back on deck in half an hour.'

Reginald hurried to tell Narendi Ram the news.

'How long will the canal be closed?' Narendi asked.

'I don't know. But it could be for a very long time. If the Turks capture it, it may never be reopened.'

'What are we going to do?'

'We won't let this stop us,' he cried. 'We are going to get to India even if we have to walk part of the way and swim the rest!'

They gathered up their belongings and returned to the deck. There they joined the pressing throng around the gangway. When they finally got ashore, they boarded a waiting carriage and were conveyed to the Port Said Hotel, an opulent building on the shore of the Mediterranean. In the hotel common room, there was a large map of Egypt displayed on the wall.

Reginald went over to study it.

'Excuse me, sir, what is the best way to get to Cairo?' he then asked the clerk.

'By rail, sir. The train usually leaves at eight o'clock in the morning, though it's best to arrive at the station a little earlier.'

'Where's the station?'

'There will be carriages waiting outside the hotel tomorrow morning to take you there.'

Reginald offered the clerk his thanks and went with Narendi Ram to their room.

'What is the plan now, sahib?'

'We'll take the train to Cairo tomorrow morning, and from there, we will go to Suez. Hopefully, we'll be able to find a ship bound for India.'

'Might it not be better to wait?' said Narendi Ram.

'Wait? Every minute we wait is another minute Natalie is in danger.'

'Yes, sahib. But we should not be foolish in our quest for her.'

Reginald did not understand the Indian's caution. His principle was to always act first and to confront every obstacle that he encountered head-on. He and Narendi Ram spent the rest of the evening talking about Natalie.

They got up early the next morning and found the carriages waiting for them just as the clerk had said. The railway station was only a short distance from the hotel, and they reached it in plenty of time. They bought their tickets from a British official and boarded the train. At nine o'clock, the steam locomotive chugged out of the station. Reginald sat back and looked out at the landscape passing by on either side of them. The Nile Delta was lush and green, sprinkled with villages beside cultivated fields and date palms. In more open country, however, sand dunes could be seen rising in the distance.

'I don't think I like the desert,' said Reginald. 'What about you, Narendi?'

'My people come from the desert. For me, it is home.'

Narendi Ram, as a rule, never said much of anything about his life before Reginald had saved him from the tiger. The only thing Reginald knew was that he was an orphan. Every time he was pressed to answer a question about his past, his eyes would glaze over with melancholy and he might not speak for a day afterward.

The train rattled along for the better part of the day. Toward sunset, they glimpsed those most famous of all ancient monuments, the pyramids, on the horizon for a brief moment until the mosques and minarets of Cairo obscured them. The station was bustling with people, many of them Arabs dressed in long white robes. Reginald and Narendi Ram struggled through the crowd to have a look at the time tables. A train for Suez was to depart at nine o'clock that evening. They decided to go and take a walk around the city to pass the time.

The streets were narrow and crowded. Arabs riding on donkeys passed on one side of the road while British officers in motorcars passed on the other. The heat soon proved too much for Reginald, and they found a shaded spot underneath a date palm in a little square that was enclosed by a wall and an enormous mosque made of mud-brick. Reginald took a drink from the fountain that babbled in the middle of the square and sat down beside Narendi Ram to watch the sunset. A muezzin climbed to the top of the mosque's minaret and called the faithful to prayer. Reginald watched Narendi Ram's face, but it remained unchanged. The servant seemed to have renounced his Mohammedan faith, but Reginald almost wished it would revive, as he knew that the Indian was of a more spiritual bent than he was.

Night stole across the sky and the stars began to shimmer in the heavens above the sprawling city of Cairo.

'We'd better get back to the station,' Reginald said.

The station was less crowded than before, but there were still many Arabs about, some of whom eyed Reginald contemptuously. They were forced to sit and wait for over an hour beside a particularly hostile-looking Arab with a long black beard, piercing eyes, and a dagger in his belt.

When the train arrived, Reginald discovered to his consternation that the Arab was getting on with them. Reginald selected a compartment near the back of the train where he hoped he would be as far from the man as possible. He had just settled into his seat when there was a knock at the compartment door.

'Come in,' he said reluctantly.

The door swung open to reveal the Arab.

'Do you mind if I join you, Englishman?' he asked in perfect English. 'All the other places are full.'

'I don't mind,' Reginald lied.

The fierce man sat down and fixed his eagle eyes on Narendi Ram.

'Are you a Gujarati, my friend?' he asked.

Narendi Ram nodded.

'I thought so. I trade with the men of Gujarat. I'm on my way to Surat after I get to Bombay.'

'You're going to Bombay!' Reginald exclaimed. 'How are you going to get there?'

'By boat, of course,' replied the Arab, smiling. 'How else?'

'Do you have extra room on board?'

'I do, as a matter of fact. But what do you want in India? Shouldn't you be with the other Englishmen defending the canal?'

'My business is no concern of yours.'

'So be it. I'll take you along for one hundred pounds.'

'That's outrageous!' Reginald cried.

'Come to think of it,' the Arab said, stroking his chin. 'I have need of an extra Gujarati translator once I reach India. Lend your servant to me for a month, and I will reduce your rate by one half.'

'I will not pay a shilling above twenty-five pounds,' said Reginald defiantly. 'And I go where my servant goes.'

The Arab revealed his perfect white teeth. 'You drive a hard bargain, Englishman. Twenty-five pounds it is. You will have to find lodging for yourself in Suez. We set sail in one week's time.'

When, several hours later, the train pulled into the station at Suez, the Arab wrote down a list of instructions and handed it to Reginald. Offering his salaams, he disappeared into the darkness.

'Do you trust this man, sahib?' Narendi asked.

'I'd trust anyone who offered to take us to India at this point.'

'What about a month in Gujarat? Can we afford the time?'

'We'll have to. We can start our search for Natalie there, though it's unlikely they'd take her to such a place.'

'Where would they take her?'

'Bombay, Madras, Calcutta, Delhi, maybe,' Reginald said, running through other options in his head.

Finding Natalie in the teeming vastness of India suddenly presented itself as a daunting task, especially as his reserve of money was already running low.

They were on their own to find supplies for the voyage. Reginald made several trips with Narendi Ram to the bazaar to purchase the necessities: a few pounds of flour, some oil, butter, tea, dried dates, and goat cheese. On the appointed day, they loaded their suitcases and provisions onto a donkey cart and set off for the harbour. The Arab (whose name was Niza Arish) met them there and showed them aboard his vessel, an ancient schooner with white sails.

They were introduced to the members of the crew, all of whom were dressed exactly like Niza Arish, and then taken to their rather cramped cabin.

Reginald and Narendi Ram unpacked their supplies and hurried back on deck to see the ship set off. The Arab crew members loosened the ropes as Niza Arish stood at the helm. A lively wind billowed the sails, and the schooner drifted off into the Red Sea. They were going places now, and it was only a matter of time before they would rescue Natalie.

## The Arab Council

REGINALD SPENT MOST of the day out on the deck. Of the crew, only Niza Arish could speak English. He encouraged Reginald to stand beside him as he pointed out all the different parts of the ship and explained what each of the crew members was doing. Reginald was sorry when Niza Arish retired to his cabin for a nap. He also tried to get some sleep, but finding himself too excited, he made his way back out after nightfall. The only sounds were the cool night breeze rustling the sails and the gentle creaking of the boat.

Life in England had dulled Reginald's spiritual senses, but now he was aware of the presence of a certain 'otherness' which existed in that clear night and yet beyond it at the same time.

'What are you doing about at this hour, Englishman?' asked a voice.

Reginald whirled around to see Niza Arish standing at the helm.

'Come here,' commanded the Arab.

Reginald returned to the place where he had been earlier in the day. The sky above them was perfectly clear and strewn with innumerable gem-like stars. They appeared closer than they ever had before, as though they were dancing all around them.

'What do you know about the heavens, Englishman?' Niza Arish asked.

'Nothing,' Reginald admitted.

'Do they not teach you in England?'

'No.'

'Then I shall.'

Reginald would not forget that night for as long as he lived. Niza Arish began to speak. He knew the name of seemingly every star and had a story to tell for each of them. Reginald half-listened and half-gave himself up to a feeling of wonder. The Arab talked on and on until the glow of dawn began to appear on the horizon.

'You had better get some sleep now, Englishman.'

Reginald yawned and, taking one last glance at the fading stars, returned to his cabin, rejoicing that he was back in the East, away from England.

The schooner sailed along at a rather quick pace. Soon, they were out of the Gulf of Suez and into the Red Sea proper. From there, they veered east toward the Arabian Peninsula.

'We will put into shore near Wejh for supplies,' Niza Arish explained.

A day or two later, the barren Arabian coast appeared on their left. After following it for a day more, Niza Arish steered the schooner into a sheltered natural harbour. A tiny village was nestled up against the cliffs.

'I have brethren further inland,' said Niza Arish. 'I will be gone a few days to see them. You may come with me if you like.'

'I would be honoured,' Reginald excitedly replied.

Reginald Fubster, Narendi Ram, Niza Arish. and two of the crew members rowed to shore on the schooner's lifeboat. The villagers greeted them hospitably, offering them dates, wild olives, and goat cheese. Niza Arish hired some baggage camels for them, and they set off for the interior. Near the coast, the land was relatively verdant, but the further they went, the more desolate and forbidding it became. They camped for the night in a *wahdi* beside a dry creek bed.

The next day, they emerged out of the coastal hills and crossed a furrowed plain whose only vegetation was thorny scrub bushes. When the Arabian sun had risen to its zenith, the landscape became a blazing furnace. Reginald's shirt was soaked through with sweat and his throat was horribly parched. Niza Arish and the other Arabs laughed and talked gaily, clearly more accustomed to this weather than he was. They climbed at last out of the plain and over a couple of enormous dunes.

'Can you see the oasis, Englishman?' Niza Arish asked.

Reginald craned his neck. There it was, glittering like an emerald through the haze. It was surrounded by date palm trees and the black tents of the Arabs.

'This is my tribe. You will meet my brothers. They have wives and herds of their own.'

The camels picked their way down the last dune. A procession of Arabs, led by a dark-bearded sheikh emerged from the tents to meet them. They exchanged greetings with Niza Arish, then turned to look in astonishment at Reginald.

'You will dine with us in our tent,' Niza Arish told Reginald and Narendi Ram.

He led them inside one of the larger tents, where a couple of slaves were busy preparing a meal. They sat on the lavish cushions and listened as the Arabs talked among themselves. The supper proved to be excellent, though if this was because of the actual quality of the food or because he was so famished, Reginald wasn't sure. The slaves cleared away the used dishes and brought a hookah which was passed around the circle. Reginald declined when offered, but Narendi Ram took a few puffs. Once the hookah had made it all the way around, the Arabs began a heated conversation accompanied by shouts and elaborate gesturing.

'What are they talking about?' Reginald whispered to Niza Arish.

'My brethren have decided to join Emir Faisal in his rebellion against the Turks. They are debating whether they should move south to join up with his forces or stay here to defend the oasis.'

One of the Arabs turned to address Reginald.

'He wants to know whether the English will help them,' Niza Arish translated.

'I don't know,' Reginald replied. 'I hope so.'

It was growing late, and the Arabs were preparing to turn in for the night.

'You are an infidel, and you will have to sleep outside. Narendi Ram may sleep inside with us.'

'I will sleep outside,' said Narendi Ram.

They laid two blankets on the desert sand and were so tired from the day's journey that they fell asleep the moment they closed their eyes.

Reginald woke the next morning just as the sun was rising over the dunes in the east. He walked down to the oasis for a drink and then sat for a while underneath the date palms. Not long after, he heard a sound like the marching of many feet and got up to see if they were being visited by another tribe. But no, the new arrivals were not Bedouins at all, but a column of soldiers. As they crested the sand dunes, the sun glinted off their rifles.

There was something about the way they approached that warned Reginald they had not come with peaceful intentions. He had to spread the alarm.

'Wake up, wake up!' he shouted, sprinting through the camp.

The Arabs emerged sleepily from their tents and, noticing the danger, took up the hue and cry. A few managed to get to their camels and load their weapons, but by that time, the soldiers were already in range. They formed a line and fired a volley. Several of the Arabs fell shrieking to the ground. Reginald caught sight of Niza Arish mounting his camel.

'Sahib, we must hide!' Narendi Ram said, grabbing hold of Reginald's shoulder.

'But Niza Arish and the ship—'

The soldiers fired again, and this time, a few of the bullets whistled directly over their heads. They took off at a run toward the oasis and threw themselves behind the trunk of one of the palms. A few Arabs were galloping away on camels, while the rest were trying to fight. Their swords and antiquated muskets proved no match for the soldiers' rifles. Some took off desperately toward the desert while the rest surrendered. A group of soldiers marched on the oasis. They spotted Reginald and Narendi Ram and barked at them in a strange tongue.

'Let's surrender ourselves,' Reginald whispered, getting up with his arms raised.

The soldiers looked at each other in surprise at the sight of an Englishman. They called for one of their officers who motioned for Reginald and Narendi Ram to follow him. The captured Arabs were being lined up. Reginald noticed that there were women and children among them. The commanding officer, who wore a turban, looked Reginald over from head to foot.

'English?' he asked.

Reginald nodded.

The officer turned and gave a few instructions to his men. They raised their rifles and aimed them at the crowd of prisoners.

'Stop!' Reginald shouted just as the rifles thundered.

He turned his face away, but he could not stop his ears. The pitiful cries of anguish echoed in his head and would do so for many days afterward. A heavy hand gave him a push forward. The commanding officer issued a few more orders, and the column began to march.

'Where are you taking us?' Reginald cried.

'Silence, Englishman!' barked the officer.

They marched south, over dunes and great stretches of barren, rocky land. Reginald and Narendi Ram were given one sip of water each that whole morning, and both were just about ready to collapse from thirst. Reginald was sure that he could not go another step when a city appeared ahead of them. It was dominated by several large mosques; the rest of the buildings were squat, drab, and inhospitable. The Red Sea shimmered in the west, and there were a great many fishing boats in the city's harbour.

The soldiers marched to their barracks while the commanding officer took Reginald and Narendi Ram to what looked like a government building, which was draped with flags of the Turkish crescent. The building was unassuming on the outside but sumptuously decorated with carpets within. They approached the desk of an important-looking Turkish official, who wore robes and a yellow turban.

The commanding officer addressed the official. The official listened and then stroked his beard.

'What were you doing with those rebels, Englishman?' he asked.

'Sir, the captain of the boat I was aboard was visiting some brethren inland and asked me to come with him. We were going to return in a few days to continue our voyage to India.'

'What all do you know about the rebels? Were they going to join up with Emir Faisal? Did they mention other tribes?'

'I don't know anything. I only stayed with them one night.'

'What are the English planning to do? Will they aid them?'

'I don't know, sir. I'm just an ordinary person on his way to India. Please let me go!'

'Our countries are at war, Englishman. I cannot release you. What if you returned to Cairo and told the English all about us?'

'You have my word of honour that I will not.'

'That is not good enough for my government,' he said as he scratched a few lines on a piece of paper. 'I am transferring you to Aqaba. You may be of some use to us there. You will depart tomorrow at dawn.'

He handed the officer the paper and gave a wave of his hand to dismiss them. Reginald and Narendi Ram were taken to the barracks and thrust inside a cramped room. The officer returned later that evening with a meal of unleavened bread and dates and a glass of water each. There were no beds, so Reginald and Narendi Ram laid out on the floor, musing on their misfortunes, thinking of Natalie, and wondering what Aqaba might have in store for them.

# Murad Pasha

THE DOOR TO the little cell was thrust open the next morning before dawn, and the officer ordered Reginald and Narendi Ram to their feet. They were given a sip of water and a date each and then shown to a waiting motorcar. Their driver was a stern Turk with a great drooping moustache. They were also accompanied by a soldier whose finger never left the trigger of his rifle. The motorcar sputtered down a dusty road that ran along the coast. For his part, Reginald much preferred travel by camel.

Around noon, they stopped at a military garrison and ate their lunch. The motorcar was refuelled, and they were on their way again. They drove for the rest of the day and stopped for the night at a fishing village. They slept inside a hut, with Reginald and Narendi Ram on one side, the driver on the other, and the soldier sitting in a chair with his gun pointed at the two prisoners.

The journey in the motorcar lasted for two more weary days. Finally, the coastal city of Aqaba lay ahead of them. They drove through an archway into the city's narrow streets. At the government building, the motorcar ground to a halt, and the soldier prodded Reginald and Narendi Ram with the barrel of his rifle. The stern driver led them before the governor.

This yellow-turbaned governor looked very similar to the one in Wejh.

'Murad Pasha!' he called.

A wizened Turk in a purple turban appeared and bowed to the governor.

'Take this Englishman and his servant to the barracks.'

Murad Pasha bowed again and motioned for them to follow him. Once they were out on the street, he turned to look back at them.

'You are English, aren't you?' he asked.

Reginald nodded.

'I'm delighted to meet you. I have read so many books about the English and their civilisation, it's hard to believe that I'm actually meeting one in person.'

They arrived at the barracks and passed through a mess hall where the soldiers were eating their lunch. Climbing a set of stairs, they arrived at a narrow, sparsely furnished room.

'Here you are. My room is down the corridor. Call me if you require anything.'

He closed the door behind them, and they heard the lock click. Reginald examined the room closely. There was a narrow window in the wall which looked out over the Gulf of Aqaba, impossible to squeeze through. The walls were solid rock. A bunk bed was pushed up against one wall and a bare desk against the other. Reginald collapsed on the bottom bunk.

'What are we going to do, sahib?' Narendi Ram asked.

'Escape, somehow. If I remember correctly, Aqaba is on the opposite side of the Sinai Peninsula from Cairo. We can cross it by keeping the Red Sea on our left the entire way.'

'But how do we get out?'

'I have no idea. Our jailor seems to have taken an interest in me. Maybe we can use that to our advantage.'

Narendi Ram climbed to the top bunk, and they lay there engrossed in their own melancholy reflections until evening. A knock sounded on the door, and their jailor entered, carrying a tray of food.

'I've brought you tea,' he said happily. 'I've read that the English like that. Is there anything else you would like? I'll write to the commander of the garrison and have him order it for you.'

'I can't think of anything right now,' replied Reginald, rather surprised by the Turk's friendliness. 'But I'll let you know if I do.'

The Turk laid the tray on the desk.

'Would you mind if I came in and sat for a while?' he asked.

'No,' answered Reginald.

He left the room and returned quickly with a chair. Reginald poured a cup of tea for Narendi Ram and divided the portions of salt meat, bread, and dates.

'Where are you from, my friend?' the Turk asked Narendi Ram.

'India,' replied Narendi.

'I should have guessed. How come you to Aqaba?'

'We were on our way to India aboard an Arab vessel when our captain stopped to see some of his brethren inland and brought us with him. Your people ambushed the encampment where we were staying, massacred the Arabs, and took us prisoner. They carried us first to Wejh, and then we were transferred here.'

'Why were you going to India?' asked the Turk.

'That's where I'm from as well. I was on my way back home from being educated in England.'

'I also wish to return home,' He sighed. 'I am not from here, you know. I am from the great mountains of Anatolia. Here, the weather is too hot and the people too rude. But tell me, sir, did you like your native country, England?'

'Somewhat.'

'Where did you live while you were there?'

'Kent and London.'

The Turk's face brightened at the mention of the latter. 'Oh yes! London. That is a very great city, is it not? They say it is the richest in the world. Could you please tell me what it is like?'

Reginald described it to him, focusing in particular on the smog-filled skies, the dirty buildings, and the vast, rambling factories.

The Turk shook his head in amazement. 'The English are truly a strange people. Do they not care for beauty?'

'They do, but I'd say they love money more.'

The Turk rose to his feet. 'I mustn't stay here longer. I hope I haven't bothered you with my questions.'

'No, not at all.'

'Would you mind if I came back tomorrow to talk to you some more?'

'Certainly not.'

The next morning, the Turk brought them tea and biscuits for breakfast and more tea and biscuits for lunch.

'Won't you stay a little bit?' Reginald asked as the Turk headed for the door.

'I would be honoured,' he replied with a bow. He came back soon with his chair.

'I don't think I remember your name,' said Reginald.

'Murad Pasha,' replied the Turk. 'And your names are Reginald Fubster and Narendi Ram, are they not?'

They nodded.

'I've been wanting to ask you, is Reginald a common name in England?'

'Fairly,' Reginald replied.

'I would also like to know how an island country with as few people as England came to control such a mighty empire.' The Turk looked at him excitedly.

'That I don't know,' said Reginald with a laugh. 'It might simply be because the weather on our island is so poor, we can't wait to head off somewhere else. We've always been an adventurous people, and we like nothing more than sailing the seas and exploring new places.'

'We Turks are also a people of adventure,' said Murad Pasha. 'We have expanded into many lands and conquered many peoples. But I also fear that we are a people whose best days were in the past.'

'What is your profession, Murad Pasha?' Reginald asked.

'My profession? I am an *ulama*, a scholar of the Quran and the Hadith. I was sent here to minister to the spiritual needs of the soldiers.'

'Could you teach me about your faith?' Reginald asked, his curiosity piqued by his night aboard the schooner with Niza Arish.

'I would be delighted to, as long as you will also teach me to understand the English God and some books that I have been reading.'

'It's a bargain,' said Reginald, extending his hand, though he thought he would have very little to offer on his end.

Murad Pasha hesitated for a moment and then reached out and shook it, a broad smile spreading across his face.

'Yes, it is good. I will first teach you the holy language.'

He rose a moment later and left the room.

'Why the sudden desire for instruction, sahib?' Narendi Ram asked.

'I don't know. I rather like the old fellow. Maybe he can teach us something we can use to get out of here.'

He laid back on his bunk and, for a lack of anything better to do, took a nap until late in the afternoon. Murad Pasha arrived with their dinner, identical to the one they had had the night before, and was soon back with his chair and two books.

'If you desire to learn of Allah, you must do so in the language he saw fit to communicate to mankind. That is, Arabic. Understand the language, and you will have a glimpse into the mind of God.'

He opened up an ancient, exquisitely decorated manuscript to the first page.

'Why don't you learn with us, Narendi?' offered Reginald.

'I already know how to read it, sahib.'

'You do? Why didn't you tell me before? You could have talked with those Arabs.'

'I cannot speak it, only read. I learned when I was a boy.'

'Then you can help teach me as well. Come on.'

Narendi Ram shifted his weight uncomfortably, then got up and sat down beside him.

Murad Pasha started on the Quran's famous opening line.

'In the name of Allah, the Most Gracious, the Most Merciful; Praise be to Allah, the Cherisher and Sustainer of Worlds; Most Gracious, Most Merciful, Master of the Day of Judgement.' Murad Pasha recited. 'That is it in English. A reasonable translation, but it does not capture its true beauty.'

'I don't understand any of the symbols,' said Reginald, looking at the text. One of the reasons he had so much difficulty mastering Greek was the fact that it didn't use the Latin alphabet.

'That is the first thing I will teach you,' replied Murad Pasha.

He drew out a piece of parchment and slowly copied the flowing Arabic script. Reginald was surprised to see him working from right to left across the page.

'You try now,' he said.

'But I don't know what I'm writing,' Reginald protested.

'Trust me. This is the way I learned from the *ulama* of my mosque and the way that I teach all of my pupils.'

Reginald took up the pen and did an unsatisfactory job of copying the script, smearing it with his hand.

'Try again,' said Murad Pasha.

Reginald did so with only slightly more success.

'I will leave the parchment with you. You can practise during the day. Now, it is your turn to speak.'

'Is that all you're going to teach me?' Reginald cried.

'Along with learning the language, you must also learn patience. It will be many days before you learn to the appreciate the beauty of the script and many more before you begin to comprehend its meaning.'

*Why all the waiting?* Reginald sighed. He feared this new endeavour would prove more trouble than it was worth. If only they could escape!

'Well?' asked the Turk, eagerly.

'What do you want to know?' said the exasperated Reginald.

'I want to know about your people's God.'

'That depends on who you ask. For some, it's country. For others, money or glory. But I don't know anything about it. I don't have a god.'

Or was Natalie his god?

'You mean you do not believe in Jesus the Christ?'

That name brought back faint memories of his childhood. His mother had read to him from the Bible on occasion, and they had attended church when the situation required it. Wilfred was more Deist than Christian and did not consider spiritual training as an important part of his son's education.

'Maybe I do and maybe I don't,' said Reginald. 'I don't know.'

'Think about it.' The Turk rose and departed.

Reginald crawled into bed burning with frustration. *What the hell am I even doing here?*

His mind drifted over the misfortunes he had undergone since he left India. He thought of Natalie and their separation and of his father fighting in the trenches in France. His mother's sweet face appeared before him and Master Merriweather's jolly one. He couldn't say why any of it had happened and he didn't know what he believed. A few tears ran down his cheeks before he mastered himself, turned over, and drifted into an uneasy sleep.

He awoke the next morning to find Narendi Ram seated at the desk, copying down the Arabic script.

'Would you like to take a turn, sahib?' he asked, offering him the pen.

Reginald sighed reluctantly and took it. As he scratched away at the paper, he discovered that the script flowed much more freely than it had the night before. He copied it three times, each one better than the last.

Murad Pasha entered with their breakfast and took a quick look at the piece of parchment.

'Well done! Sometimes the best thing to do is to try again in the morning. I realise I may have overwhelmed you last night. I've brought along a book. Maybe this will be easier to talk about.'

He held up a worn copy of *David Copperfield* by Charles Dickens. 'Are you familiar with this title?'

'Yes, but I haven't read it.'

'Read it then, and we will discuss it together.'

The Turk eagerly placed it in his hands and walked out of the room.

When he had gone, Reginald sat and stared out the window. His mind was churning.

*Natalie needs me. If I'd only waited for the canal to open…*

Vexation, coupled with the recognition of his impotence, mastered him and raged through the long day.

In the evening, Murad Pasha returned with their dinners, his chair, and his copy of the Quran. He recited the next lines of the Quran and copied them down on a new piece of parchment.

'Now it is your turn to try.'

'Could you please tell me what the symbols mean?' Reginald said, feeling his frustration returning.

'Patience,' the Turk said calmly. 'One thing I have noticed is that you always want things to happen at once. The joy is also in the process of learning, not only the end result. If you cannot appreciate the subtle beauty of the script, you will never learn the language nor will you know God.'

Reginald transcribed the lines, thinking all the while how much he hated this awkward script and the strange, barbarous culture that had created it. When he had finished, Murad Pasha shook his head in disappointment.

'You will have to spend more time practising tomorrow. Now, how far did you read in *David Copperfield*?'

'Half of the first chapter.'

'I will ask you again when you've made more progress.'

The Turk departed.

Reginald grudgingly read further the next day. He would have tossed it aside if another occupation had presented itself, but when the choice was between Copperfield and Arabic, he chose the former. The novel quickly became his exclusive focus. By concentrating on it from morning until night each day, he was done with it in a week.

'I've finished, by the way,' he said to Murad Pasha that evening.

'You did? And what do you think it *means*?'

Reginald was angered by this question.

'I'm not sure that it 'means' anything,' he replied. 'It's the story of a person's life and that's all.'

'But it must have *some* meaning. I will let you think about it and come back tomorrow.'

He took his copy of the Quran and left the room.

The next morning, Reginald woke to see Narendi Ram once again working at the script.

'Would you like to try?' he asked.

'No. In fact, I've decided to give up the whole business.'

'But, sahib,' Narendi Ram gasped, 'I've never known you to give up on anything before.'

Reginald stared out the window at the sea. 'It's all useless!'

Narendi continued with his patient effort. The sound of his writing had a soothing effect on Reginald's mind. After listening to it for a time, he stopped thinking about their situation and even put aside for a moment the plans for escape he'd been formulating.

He heaved a deep sigh and sat down beside Narendi Ram. Taking hold of the parchment, he scratched at it until his arm was sore. Looking back over his lines, he could detect an ever so slight improvement. Murad Pasha arrived with breakfast.

'Very good!' he exclaimed happily after inspecting Reginald and Narendi's work.

He left, and Reginald took his place by the window to think about what meaning there could possibly be in Charles Dickens's *David Copperfield*.

That evening, Murad Pasha recited the next lines of the Quran and copied them down, just as before. This time, however, Reginald reproduced the script without complaint.

'Excellent!' said the Turk, clapping his hands together. 'I think you are beginning to get the hang of it. Have you given any thought to *David Copperfield*?'

'I have. I'm not sure that I've discovered the meaning of the entire novel, but I think I can point out some of the themes.'

'Could you share them with me?'

'I think one of them is the importance of valuing the people in your life.'

'Yes, yes! I have thought that too! What else?'

'Things may look bad at the present time, but there's always a chance they will turn around.'

'Are you referring to when David was working in Murdstone and Grimbey's factory?' Murad Pasha asked.

Reginald nodded.

'Yes, yes! That is very well observed. You see, there is meaning to the book. Yes. There is meaning in everything. God always teaches us.'

He lifted his Quran and left the room with a broad smile on his face. Reginald had been thinking mostly of young David Copperfield's love for Little Em'ly and wondering how the story would be different if he had never given up on her. But he kept this to himself.

The following day was a Friday, and Murad Pasha was busy with his religious duties. A soldier served them their meals, and in the meantime, Reginald sat and copied the Arabic script until the entire piece of parchment was full.

'The commandant would like to see you today,' Murad Pasha said to Reginald as he arrived the next morning at breakfast.

When he had finished eating, Reginald followed the Turk out of the little room and down several flights of stairs. They arrived at an antechamber where a soldier was seated at a desk. Murad Pasha said something to him in Turkish, and he motioned for them to follow him. He pushed open a door to a broad chamber decorated with maps and crescent banners where the commandant, a fine specimen of a man with an enormous moustache, was waiting for them.

The commandant began a speech in Turkish, addressing his comments to Murad Pasha.

'The commandant wishes you to tell him everything you know about the British position in Egypt.'

Reginald decided to be as cooperative as possible. He told the commandant everything, which was not much.

'What are the British planning to do with the Arabs?' Murad Pasha translated.

'I don't know anything about that,' Reginald answered. 'Could you tell the commandant that I am not a combatant but an ordinary citizen who had the misfortune of being captured while on his way to India?'

The commandant examined Reginald closely before speaking.

'He says that you will meet with him once a week to discuss British military strategy, and in the meantime, you will help me to translate captured documents.'

The commandant gave a wave of his hand to dismiss them.

'Oh, bother,' Reginald muttered under his breath.

The next week passed in much the same manner as the first. Murad Pasha would enter the room in the afternoon to work out problems with his translation and then after dinner to recite the

Quran and discuss the English novel he was reading. Reginald was becoming quite adept at copying the Arabic script and discovered, in spite of himself, that he rather enjoyed doing it. With each passing day, he grew ever so slightly more patient. The language slowly, but surely, revealed itself to him and he began to fathom the depths of its beauty.

Days turned into weeks and weeks into months, and before he knew it, he had been in captivity in Aqaba for over a year. He grew to love the place: the view of the sea out of his window, the minarets rising above the dusty streets, even the barren sand dunes rising in the distance. He loved the Arabic language, which he could now speak and write with ease, and he loved Murad Pasha most of all.

Yet some days, he remembered Natalie and his father, and a strong yearning welled up within him to escape. He sat up late in the evenings thinking about it, long after the sun had set and the stars were shimmering in the night sky. At last, he decided that he would ask Murad Pasha for advice.

One night after dinner, Reginald laid aside his copy of the Quran and looked over at Murad Pasha.

'What is the matter, my son?' asked the Turk, sensing his unease.

'There's something I've been meaning to tell you for a long time. I can't stay here any longer. I made a promise to a girl I knew in England that I would find and rescue her. She's been taken to India, and I must go after her.'

'Ah. A girl. I understand. I was once young too.'

'But how can I get out of here?' asked Reginald.

'You would have to cross the Sinai,' mused the Turk.

'Is it possible?'

'Only a Bedu could make that journey. You will die of thirst or else fall into the sinking sands from which there is no escape.'

'What if I followed the coast?'

'The tribes will catch you and kill you as an infidel.'

'Then I will cover my face in a veil and say not a word to them.'

Murad Pasha sighed deeply. 'If your heart is set on going, I will not prevent you. However, I will ask you to first consider what you are doing in the larger scheme of things and ask yourself whether finding this young woman is worth possibly throwing your life away.'

'I have to keep my word. You would do the same, wouldn't you?'

'Perhaps. But is it the will of God or your will? As someone who loves you, I hope that you will listen to me. There is so much more that you can learn from me here. We have only just begun your education. Maybe you could be the one to solve the problems that have long plagued these troubled lands. You only have one life, my son, and it is your responsibility to use it for the benefit of mankind.'

'Don't talk to me as if you were my father!' Reginald snapped. He instantly repented. 'I'm sorry. I don't know what came over me.'

'You are right. I am not your father. But please take time to think this over,' urged the Turk, a slight melancholy in his voice.

'I will think of it all this week and give you my answer by Sunday.'

Murad Pasha rose and left the room quickly so that Reginald would not see the tears start in his eyes.

# First Day on the Somme

WHILE REGINALD WAS languishing in captivity, his father was in the thick of the action on the Western Front. Wilfred's exploits appear in the memoirs of several veterans of the Great War, all of whom express admiration for his courage and devotion to duty, which have been condensed into this narrative.

Wilfred Fubster served for most of 1915 in the trenches near the Marne River, seeing little action but nevertheless showing enough competence to be promoted to major. In the early weeks of 1916, the German High Command planned an offensive that they hoped would grind the Allies into submission and open up the way to Paris. They struck the French at Verdun, site of a famous fort and a symbol of national pride for all Frenchmen. The French rose to defend their country and managed to halt the German advance. Casualties mounted on both sides in this so-called 'mincing machine,' and the French, in particular, were starting to scrape the bottom of their barrel of manpower.

The Allied commanders Joseph Joffre and Douglas Haig meanwhile plotted a counteroffensive along the Somme River to relieve the pressure on Verdun. Major Fubster was transferred to the Fourth Army and stationed at Foucaucourt-on-the-Somme to prepare for the attack. In the East at this time, the Russian Army had regrouped from its earlier defeats and begun the Brusilov Offensive, a bold advance into Austrian territory. Haig and the other generals predicted that a victory at the Somme would sweep aside the German Army and clear the way for the British and the French to join the Russians in Berlin.

The artillery bombardment of the German lines began five days before the battle. The guns roared all day and all night while the infantry sat in the trenches and waited. The officers assured their men that the tangled webs of barbed wire would be destroyed by the shells and the German machine gunners blasted to pieces. It would be a matter of simply walking across No Man's Land to capture the enemy trenches. Wilfred, for his part, was not so sure. For as much as he despised the Germans, he admired them as soldiers.

'Mark my words, they'll be ready!' he told anyone who'd listen.

On the morning of July 1, 1916, the guns fell silent. The infantrymen huddled together nervously in the trenches waiting for the order to go over the top.

'Gentlemen,' Wilfred Fubster called down the line, 'today is the day that you prove yourselves worthy sons of the British Empire. We will not halt the advance until the German lines are ours. Fix bayonets.'

Wilfred drew his sword and, with a deep breath, pulled himself over the top of the trench. His body shook with excitement. This was the moment he had been waiting for since he was a boy, the crowning glory of his life's work. The only thing that lay ahead was immortality.

No Man's Land was completely silent except for the slog of the soldier's boots in the mud. A mist hovered above the German lines, obscuring them from view. They were now halfway across, and there still was no sound until suddenly, a terrible cry rose from the men. Entire columns were instantly mowed down by thundering machine guns. Wilfred called to the men to his right only to see every one of them fall screaming to the ground.

'Keep advancing!' he shouted over the roar of the bullets, but as he did so, all the men on his left were wiped out. Behind him the men were running back to the trenches.

'Where are you going?' he screamed, but no one could hear him.

Another wave of infantry climbed over the top, and Wilfred watched in horror as they walked calmly toward the machine guns. Feeling his instinct for self-preservation kick in, he dropped down into the mud and crawled back to the trench. A third group of infantry were waiting to attack.

'Fubster, what's going on up there?' said Colonel Kirkpatrick, his commanding officer.

'The artillery barrage failed, sir. The barbed wire is still intact, and the machine guns are cutting us all down,' he gasped.

'We'll have to send more men,' said the colonel.

'No, sir! It's useless. The defences here are too strong.'

'Nonsense, Fubster. A few regiments will have that line loosened up in no time.'

'They'll all die!' Wilfred cried.

'Pull yourself together, Major. This is war.'

The colonel gave a nod to one of his lieutenants.

'Fix bayonets!' the lieutenant ordered.

Wilfred watched as the men scrambled over the top to meet the waiting machine guns. He would never forget the looks on their faces.

'By the way, Fubster, they're having tea over at HQ. Why don't you go and take some? Might cheer you up a bit.'

'No, thank you, sir, I want to stay with my men,' Wilfred said quietly.

'Suit yourself then.'

The image of his machine-gunned comrades played over and over in Wilfred's mind. He was realising for the first time, alas, too late, that perhaps war was not the glorious enterprise he had conceived it to be. But he could not abandon his post. He had to follow orders and do his duty to the bitter end.

That evening, the demoralised soldiers crouched together in the trenches after the bloodiest day in British military history. Reports of casualties were still coming in, but it was estimated that they totalled nearly sixty thousand. Fubster's battalion had lost three quarters of its men. The survivors were too dazed to cry; they merely sat and stared, tormented by what they had seen. Wilfred was inspecting the lines when he found them in this sorry state. He felt the same way, but he had to cheer them.

'Gentlemen, do not despair. We may have lost this battle, but we shall win the war.'

The men looked up at him, their expressions unchanged.

'I suppose I am the one to blame for this disaster,' he said softly. 'I led you to certain death, and I accept full responsibility for every man who died today.'

'Major, it's not your fault,' said a sergeant, and there was a murmur of assent. 'You didn't know that the enemy lines were still intact.'

'It's Haig and the other generals,' said another. 'They lied to us and had us butchered for nothing!'

Wilfred waved his hand. 'Criticise me as much as you like, but do not speak ill of your generals. They want to win this war just as much as you do. Now, I would like to say one more thing to you. I have been an officer for more than thirty years, but I have never been more proud of my men than I am today. You have proven yourselves true sons of Britannia. No matter what happens, you can hold your heads high and say, "I fought at the Somme with the Forty-Second Infantry battalion," the bravest men there ever were.'

Wilfred wiped away a few tears from his eyes and walked away. A middle-aged lieutenant with grey hair and spectacles had heard Wilfred's speech and was moved to tears himself. His name was Silas Knubby.

# Sinai

REGINALD HAD STAYED up late into the night on Saturday evening, finally reaching a decision in the early hours before dawn. He rose as normal and started copying down a passage of the Quran.

'Are we going, sahib?' asked Narendi Ram.

At that moment, the door swung open, and Murad Pasha entered with their breakfast. He laid it out and sat down nervously.

'Murad Pasha,' Reginald began, 'I wanted to say first how grateful I am for everything you've done for us. You have been a second father to me. You've taught me how to see. I know Narendi feels the same way.'

The Indian bowed his head. 'You have restored my faith in God, Murad Pasha, sahib.'

'There's nothing we could ever do to repay your kindness,' Reginald continued.

The Turk smiled weakly. 'You've made your decision, then?'

'I've thought the matter over at length, and I'm sorry, but I'm convinced that we must try to escape at once.'

'I feared it would be so,' murmured the Turk. 'Nevertheless, it is all arranged.'

'What do you mean?' asked Reginald in astonishment.

'You will leave here this evening. I have asked the commandant for leave to take you on a walk to visit one of the mosques. We will meet one of my friends, an Arab named Bin Kabid, by the east well. He has provisions for your journey across Sinai.'

'But, *baba* (father), if they find out that you helped me escape, they'll kill you!'

'There is no danger. I will tell them that you overpowered me and ran off, and they will believe me.'

'Still—'

Murad Pasha raised a hand to quiet him.

'I am old and I do not fear death. It is the least I can do to make sure that you are safe.'

He rose and left the room.

Reginald and Narendi Ram spent the rest of the day sorting through their meagre possessions in preparation for the journey. Murad Pasha served them an early dinner and then they left the barracks for a stroll to the mosque. The Turk was dressed in his finest white robes and a yellow turban. His usually cheery face was clouded over with melancholy. They passed the mosque and reached the east well, where a few veiled women were drawing water. An Arab stepped out from the shadows of a mud-brick building.

'Salaam Murad Pasha,' he said. 'Are these the ones?'

The Turk nodded.

The Arab motioned for them to follow him.

'Put these on,' he said once they had reached the shadows between two of the buildings. He tossed them a pair of dark robes which were hooded in the manner of the Tuaregs of the Sahara.

'Do not speak to anyone,' he ordered. 'Follow me.'

'Let us say goodbye first,' Reginald protested.

'No. It will draw too much attention,' he said roughly. 'Let's go.'

Reginald turned to look one last time at Murad Pasha. The Turk stood in the same place and stared after them until they had passed out of sight.

Bin Kabid led them to the city walls where a Turkish soldier was standing in front of the gate.

'Halt,' he ordered. 'Who are you and where are you headed?'

'I am Bin Kabid of the Tarabin, and these are my nephews. We are going to visit our kinsmen.'

'The boy doesn't look like an Arab,' observed the soldier, his eyes flashing to Reginald's exposed hands.

'He was born with unusually pale skin,' said Bin Kabid.

'What are you saying, uncle?' Reginald asked in perfect Arabic. Bin Kabid and the soldier had been speaking in Turkish.

'We were talking about your skin colour. It is very light, isn't it?'

'Yes, it is. There are even some who have mistaken me for a European!' Reginald said, laughing.

The soldier looked at Reginald again and then stepped aside.

Once they were a good distance away from the city walls, they heaved a sigh of relief.

'That was good thinking on your part,' said Bin Kabid.

'What would you have done if he hadn't let us pass?'

The Arab pulled aside his cloak to reveal a revolver.

They approached an isolated grove of date palms where three laden camels were waiting.

'We will ride through the night. Murad Pasha will report that you are missing in the morning, and they will come looking for you.'

They mounted and set off at a brisk trot into the desert. Reginald was exhausted and had soon fallen asleep. At dawn, Bin Kabid steered the camels toward a rocky outcropping and dismounted.

'Wake up, sahib,' said Narendi Ram, giving Reginald a gentle prod.

'Drink this,' Bin Kabid ordered, tossing him a goatskin pouch.

Reginald gulped the water down as quickly as he could.

'We are only taking a short rest here for prayers, and we will be on our way again. I hope you are prepared for the heat, Englishman.'

The desert sun crept over the horizon and cast a red glow on the sand. Bin Kabid spread out his prayer rug, facing south (the direction of Mecca), and began the first of his five daily intercessions to the Divine. Narendi Ram found a carpet and did the same. When they were finished, Bin Kabid distributed a rather scanty breakfast among them.

'We'll eat as we ride,' he said, climbing onto his camel's back.

That morning, they passed through an incredibly harsh rocky country where the only things that grew were scrub bushes. The wind picked up, and the sand swirled all around them, blocking their view of the desert ahead. Around midday, they climbed a boulder-strewn slope and stood before a line of undulating dunes stretching as far as the eye could see. The sun was at its zenith, and Reginald had hardly felt so uncomfortable in his life. He had already taken off his hood and now was working to pull off his cloak.

'Leave that on,' Bin Kabid said. 'You'll feel worse without it.'

Reginald grumbled.

They kept to the ridges of the dunes, winding their way back and forth over the countryside.

'Look down there, Englishman,' said Bin Kabid, pointing into one of the valleys.

'Quicksand. The Sinai is filled with it.'

Reginald examined the ground closely and decided that it looked no different from any other patch of sand. *It's a good thing we didn't have to cross this by ourselves*, he thought.

The end of that miserable day finally drew near. A cool wind swept the desert and the shadows lengthened on the sand.

'How much further?' Reginald gasped to Bin Kabid, who was ahead of them.

'Not far now, Englishman.'

He pulled on his camel's reins and got down off its back. Reginald and Narendi Ram dismounted as well, grateful for a chance to stretch their cramped legs. Bin Kabid handed them a few dates and made sure that they each took a long draught of water. They rested for perhaps half an hour, prayed, and climbed back onto their camels. The temperature was actually quite pleasant now that the sun had gone down, and Reginald felt refreshed. The camels descended out of the dunes into a wide valley. Halfway across this, Reginald fell asleep.

'Wake up, Englishman.'

Reginald opened his eyes to see Bin Kabid staring down at him. He was lying in the sand. He pulled himself into a sitting position and noticed that Bin Kabid was still watching him expectedly.

'What is it?' he asked, somewhat irritated.

'Look!' the Arab said, pointing ahead.

A thin blue line snaked its way across the desert landscape.

'The canal!' Reginald shouted. 'We made it!'

Bin Kabid laughed as Reginald embraced Narendi Ram and cried a few tears of joy. They had their breakfast and made their way down to the canal.

'How are we going to get across?' Reginald asked.

'A ship will come along eventually,' replied the Arab.

Sure enough, a Royal Navy cruiser soon appeared on the horizon. It was good to see that the canal was still in British hands. They waved their arms and shouted frantically to get its attention. A boat was lowered, and they were brought aboard. The captain met them on deck.

'Who are you?' he asked.

'I am Reginald Fubster. This is my servant Narendi Ram and our guide Bin Kabid. We have just escaped from Turkish captivity in Aqaba.'

'We'll have you sent to Cairo at once to talk to the general staff,' said the captain, motioning to several of the members of his crew.

'Please, sir, I must be on my way to India at once.'

'All in good time. You have valuable information to give first. After that, I'll make sure personally that you are delivered to India at the expense of the Royal Navy.'

Reginald thanked him, and they were set down on the opposite shore accompanied by a lieutenant. There they waited along the road until two motorcars appeared and took them the rest of the way to Cairo. The vehicles ground to a halt in front of an ornate columned building which flew the Union Jack proudly.

'The general will see you,' said one of the drivers. 'Follow me.'

He led them inside where a crowd of British officers were milling about. They looked up in surprise at the sight of Reginald and his companions.

'Make way!' the driver said, and the crowd parted.

They climbed a marble staircase and reached a room that was being guarded by two soldiers. At a nod from the driver, they stepped aside and admitted them into a decorated chamber. One man in uniform sat at the desk reading a report while another in a suit reclined in a chair.

'General Murray,' the driver saluted, 'we found these three this morning at the canal. The boy is English, and he claims to have been held captive by the Turks in Aqaba.'

The general examined them closely.

'Please be seated,' he said.

The driver helped pull up some seats.

'Your names?' the general asked.

'Reginald Fubster, Narendi Ram, and Bin Kabid,' they replied.

The general scratched a few notes down on a piece of paper.

'How did you come to be captured by the Turks?'

Reginald told him the whole story.

'I see,' the general said quietly. 'I have much more to ask you, but I can see that you need to rest. Lieutenant,' he called to one of the men at the door, 'make sure that these three gentlemen are given a meal and a comfortable place to stay.'

'Sir, I have to be on my way to India at once,' said Reginald.

'I understand. I beg you to stay three days, and after that, we will pay for your voyage to India.'

They took their leave of the general and were shown to a set of lavish apartments.

'We'll bring tea up for you presently,' said the lieutenant.

Over the three days, they met with General Murray in the morning and the afternoon. He asked them about the defences of Aqaba and the habits of their Turkish captors. Reginald answered as truthfully as he could, but he left off telling the general too much about Murad Pasha. The information he provided proved to be one of the factors behind the capture of Aqaba by Lawrence of Arabia and the Arab League a year later, but of course, he did not know this at the time.

On the morning of the fourth day, Reginald and Narendi Ram took their leave of Bin Kabid, who was eager to return to the desert. A steamer for India was scheduled to leave that evening. They boarded at sunset and were shown to their first-class cabin where they were to spend the length of the voyage in comfort, at the expense of the

Royal Navy. The great ship's engines roared to life, and they churned their way through the Suez Canal. Reginald settled into his chair happily. After a hiatus of fourteen months, they were finally back on their way to India.

# Return to Delhi

AFTER A PLEASANT three-week voyage, the steamer pulled into the harbour at Bombay. Reginald and Narendi Ram hurried on deck to get a glimpse of their beloved country. There was a parade of Indian soldiers accompanied by a band marching past the Gateway of India. Further on were the thronging crowds of Indians and the bustling streets of the city.

'We made it!' Reginald cried, squeezing Narendi's hand. Yes, this was India. This was home.

It took a couple of hours for them to disembark with their luggage and join the rest of the new arrivals in the midst of the mob waiting to greet them. Hundreds of voices shouted at them from every direction, but they ignored them all and proceeded coolly toward the central square.

Overwhelmed by the mass of humanity in their way, Reginald had the suspicion that finding Natalie would be the equivalent of finding a single grain of sand on an endless shore.

'Where are we going, sahib?' asked Narendi Ram.

'To check the registry for Natalie,' he replied. 'Make sure you keep your eyes peeled for her. She could be anywhere.'

'I will, sahib,' replied the servant.

The inside of the Municipal Corporation Building (an elaborate mixture of Gothic and Indo-Saracenic architecture not far from the Victoria Railway Terminus) was brutally hot in spite of the employment of a small army of *punkah* coolies. Like everything in Bombay, it was vibrantly chaotic in spite of British efforts to impose order. Reginald and Narendi Ram waited for a long time as they were referred from one petty official to the next. Finally, a young clerk emerged with a ponderous volume and set it down in front of them.

'This is the best we can do,' he apologised. 'You see, people are always coming in and out of Bombay, and with the exception of the government and military establishment, it's hard to keep track of everyone.'

Reginald flipped through the dusty pages while Narendi Ram looked over his shoulder. Many of the names had been crossed out or amended. New arrivals were added in the margins, as were births and marriages. There were no MacFinns in Bombay. Reginald checked the last name Prim as well, though he thought it unlikely Natalie would be registered under it. This also failed.

He slammed the book shut and wiped the sweat from his forehead.

'It's hopeless, Narendi! Who knows where they might have gone in a year? They could be anywhere! We'll never find her!'

'Yes, we will, sahib,' said Narendi Ram serenely. 'You must never give up hope. It may be that we will find her in a place we do not expect.'

They stumbled out of the office to be greeted with a fresh wave of heat, dust, and noise. Reginald's head was pounding. He was at a loss. The only thing which made sense now was to return to Delhi. Accordingly, they purchased tickets for the five-o'clock express. Once aboard and in the privacy of their compartment, Reginald reviewed the plans that they had made during their voyage.

'We don't have much money left,' he said.

Murad Pasha had restored the minor sum they had been travelling with when captured, but this had dwindled down to almost nothing.

'I will ask Commissioner Hawke if he can help me find employment. He is a friend of my father's and hopefully will have mercy on me when I explain my situation. Meanwhile, we'll search Delhi and the surrounding countryside until we've saved up enough to make a thorough effort. I will also write to my father. I wonder how he's doing. From what I hear, the war with the Germans appears to be in a deadlock. I hope he's not worried about me.'

Narendi Ram expressed his satisfaction with the plan, and they both laid back to look out the window. They passed gigantic domed mosques and Hindu temples so ancient, they seemed part of the land itself. They skirted around mountains and steamed through jungles. As night fell, they crossed numerous dark crocodile-infested rivers. The country that Reginald remembered so fondly from his childhood as a friendly, home-like place had become suddenly vast and mysterious, brooding over the innumerable races of men who had lived and died here and whose secrets were buried with them.

The train rumbled onward through the night and pulled into the city of the Mughals early the next morning. Reginald hired a rickshaw that took them across to the cantonments. By the time they arrived, the soldiers were out on the field drilling, a reassuring sight for Reginald, who missed his time in the regiment. They made their way to the commissioner's building, a grand, imposing edifice in the very centre. A pair of turbaned Indian soldiers stood outside the door and stepped aside to let them pass.

The commissioner's office was on the second floor. It was a large room lined with bookshelves. Commissioner Hawke was seated at his desk, reading a report.

'What can I do for you?' he asked, looking up.

Reginald stepped forward, trembling. 'Do you remember me, sir?'

The commissioner took off his reading glasses and peered at him closely.

'You can't be Fubster's boy! My, my it's been a long time! You've grown a foot! Welcome back, sir, welcome back!' He got to his feet and gave Reginald's hand a vigorous shake. 'We've really missed your father here. Do you know how he's faring in the war?'

'I don't, sir.'

'Well, I'm sure he's up to something heroic,' said the commissioner. 'Anyway, I am so very sorry about your mother. The doctors did all they could, but it is a truly terrible disease. Your father wrote to me a while ago and told me you'd be coming 'round. He said you were searching for someone, a young lady if I remember correctly. You're welcome to take a look at all our records.'

'Thank you, sir,' replied Reginald.

'Is there anything else I can do for you?'

'Well, sir.' Reginald took a deep breath. 'I need to be employed. I've been thinking about joining the civil service here in Delhi, if that's at all possible.'

The commissioner raised his eyebrow. 'Are you sure?'

'Yes, sir, I'll do anything to earn an honest wage.'

'You're a Fubster, aren't you? I would've thought you'd want to join the army.'

Reginald's face fell. 'I would, sir, but I haven't finished my education.'

'Nonsense,' said the commissioner. 'I think your father educated you quite sufficiently. How old are you, my boy?'

'Seventeen, sir, eighteen next month.'

'Perfect age for your first assignment.'

The commissioner drew out a piece of parchment and wrote a few lines.

'Here's a letter of recommendation for Colonel Thornwood of His Majesty's Corps of Guides in Peshawar. The colonel is a good friend of mine. He sent me a telegram just the other week saying that he is looking for junior officers.'

'But, sir!' Reginald protested as the commissioner laid the letter in his hands. 'How…how can I ever thank you for this?'

'It's your father you should thank,' said the commissioner with a wink. 'Mr Richardson, see that Mr Fubster and his servant Narendi Ram get tickets for the first train to Peshawar.'

A civil servant with a drooping moustache, a monocle, and a rather pompous bearing appeared and motioned for Reginald to accompany him.

'Thank you again, sir!' Reginald called on his way out.

'Stop back anytime you please,' replied the commissioner, giving him a wave.

Mr Richardson escorted the happy lad to the ticket booth at the train station.

'Well, it looks like the train for Peshawar doesn't leave until four o'clock,' the civil servant said, handing Reginald the tickets. 'You'll have to find some way to amuse yourself until then.'

Reginald was bursting with excitement. He'd never dared hope for a commission after running away from the Duke of Marlborough. In normal times, he wouldn't, but his father's reputation and the fact that the entire world was at war opened the door for him.

He and Narendi Ram returned first to the commissioner's building to check the registry. This proved as futile an exercise as it had in Bombay. He also questioned Major Hawke, but there was no one in Delhi answering to Natalie's description. After this, they followed the familiar path through the banyan trees to the family bungalow. Underneath one of the trees was a grave where a few marigolds had recently been laid. He looked at it more closely and saw that it bore this inscription:

Elizabeth Maria Fubster, Beloved Wife and Mother, Born February 11, 1879; Died July 23, 1914

Reginald sank to his knees and allowed a few tears to trickle from his eyes, watering the ground in which his mother was buried. Narendi Ram knelt beside him and offered up a prayer.

'I never really knew her, Narendi. I was always with my father. He never had any time for females, and I didn't either. But she was always kind and gentle. If I could go back, I never would have left her. I should never have gone to England.'

'But then you would not have met Miss Natalie, sahib,' said the Indian.

'That's true.'

He wondered if his love for Natalie was a longing for something he'd never experienced, a lack he felt deep in his soul, a refuge from the hardness of the world and the constant striving for the things which remained ever out of reach.

'Want to see the old bungalow?' he said, brushing the tears out of his eyes.

'Of course, sahib.'

They walked on a little further together until they reached the front verandah of the structure which, apart from the memories it evoked, had nothing remarkable about it and was almost identical to all the other bungalows around. Yet this was the one place in the world that Reginald had called home.

They did not stay long. Life had moved on, and the childhood Reginald had missed was gone forever. They bid the old bungalow goodbye after a brief stay and headed over to the train station. They boarded the train and settled in for a journey to the fabled Northwest Frontier.

# Peshawar

EVERY BOY IN the British Empire has heard stories of the Afghan frontier. Reginald was no exception; in fact, he had listened a great deal more than most: many of his father's colleagues were veterans of the Second Afghan War, while the older rank and file had seen their first action during it. Soldiers are great storytellers, and the lore of the Frontier, passed on in their deep, husky voices, had lodged itself permanently in Reginald's imagination.

Cavagnari, Roberts, and Hamilton were his heroes, and the regiments who served—the Khyber Rifles, the Sind Frontier Force, and, especially, the Corps of Guides—had achieved through their exploits a mythical status. But the glorious dreams of his youth were tempered now with concern for Natalie. The Frontier was known to be a dangerous place and not one in which he was likely to find a young heiress to a considerable fortune.

The familiar countryside around Delhi rolled past, and they entered the fertile croplands of the Punjab (the Land of Five Rivers). This was the territory of the Sikhs, a religious faction who had risen in revolt against the Moslem rulers of Delhi. For a time, they had ruled their own empire until they were in turn conquered by the East India Company and incorporated into British India. Now they were among the Raj's most loyal subjects, with many of their number serving in the Indian Army. The centre of their faith was the Golden

Temple at Amritsar. Their distinctive brightly coloured turbans could clearly be seen as they worked in the fields.

Further on, they passed an increasing number of mosques, some of them constructed during the Mughal days, others even earlier. It was drawing on dusk when they crossed the bridge over the Sutlej River, the first of the five rivers of the Punjab. From there, it was a few hours more before they arrived in Lahore.

Lahore had, for centuries, been the cultural and political centre of the Punjab region. Founded originally by Hindus, it was conquered by the Sultans of Delhi and then by the Mughal ruler, Babur the Tiger. The Sikhs had made Lahore their capital after their successful rebellion, and now it was a major centre of British administration. The population of the city was mainly Moslem, but there were Sikhs, Hindus, and Englishmen who lived there as well.

They reached it a few hours after sunset. From what Reginald could see, the roads were still very crowded and lit by innumerable shimmering lights in the houses and shops. The train halted in the station to resupply. There was no time for them to get out and search; they would have to wait until Reginald went on leave. Narendi Ram drifted off to sleep. Reginald stayed awake for several hours more as the train rattled onward through the night, peering out the landscape rushing by in the moonlight. Eventually, he too fell asleep.

He was awoken the next morning by the call of an Indian servant pushing the breakfast trolley up and down the aisle. Once he had brushed the sleep out of his eyes, he resumed his position next to the window. They had entered a rugged country, not as fertile as the Punjab, yet still cultivated with plum, pear, and almond trees and dotted with villages whose mudbrick towers stood as sentinels over the fields. To the north lay the Vale of Kashmir, a valley justly celebrated for its beauty and serenity, and beyond that, just visible in the haze of the early morning were the Himalayas, 'the abode of eternal snow.'

As they went, the villages, once spread widely apart, began to cluster together and featured impressive mosques and the mausoleums of the mystic Sufi saints who had come down to preach from the hills of Afghanistan. An hour more and the gleaming domes and minarets of Peshawar appeared on the horizon.

Reginald and Narendi Ram disembarked from the train at the station with their scanty luggage and navigated through the crowd which, like everywhere else in India, had gathered around the arriving locomotive. The people here were far different in appearance from the Indians of the plains—they were tall and wiry with light skin and piercing grey eyes. These were the Pathans, as proud, independent, and warlike a race as has ever dwelt in the world.

Reginald spied a British military uniform somewhere in this mass and made his way toward it.

'Excuse me, sir,' he greeted the official who was trying to direct traffic. 'Which way is it to the cantonments?'

The man pointed and hurried away.

They finally succeeded in fighting their way out of the station and out onto the dusty road. A rickshaw driver was lounging in the shade of a tree, but he leapt quickly to his feet when Reginald drew a few shillings out of his pocketbook.

'Where to, sahib?'

'The cantonment, if you please.'

They boarded and the rickshaw driver took off as fast as he could.

'First time in Peshawar, sahib?' the driver asked, flashing Reginald a smile of perfect white teeth.

'Yes, is it obvious?'

The cantonments lay in a wide plain, with the rugged line of the frontier hills in the distance and the mosques and bazaars of the city of Peshawar rising to the east. The famed Khyber Pass, for centuries the route of invading armies, lay beyond the city. As his eyes swept the barren Afghan mountains, Reginald felt a slight shiver of foreboding. There was something about this place which could bring an unsettled feeling to even the calmest of minds.

'The cantonments, sahib,' said the driver proudly.

Reginald gave him a few extra shillings for his friendliness, and together with Narendi Ram approached the grandest building of the cantonment, the residence of both the commissioner of the

Northwest Provinces and the commandant of the Corps of Guides. Reginald spoke to a cheerful young secretary who directed him to the commandant's study. The secretary rapped on the door and was told to enter. Colonel Thornwood was seated at his desk talking to a young Pathan.

What is it, Henry?' he asked the secretary.

'Mr Reginald Fubster to see you, sir.'

'Oh yes. We will discuss this matter later, Ghalji Khan.'

The Pathan bowed and took his leave. His eyes flashed at Reginald on his way out.

'Please take a seat,' the colonel said, motioning in front of the desk.

Reginald sat and took a quick glance around the study to try to determine what sort of man he was dealing with. The bookshelves were stacked with ancient manuscripts written in a strange slanting hand, the walls were covered with sketches the colonel had made of the region's flora and fauna. Rare artefacts from antique knives and carpets to elaborately carved tiles filled every other available space. From this, it was plain that the colonel was not only a military man but a scholar—indeed, Colonel Thornwood was a true disciple of Commissioner Sir George Roos-Keppel, who, in addition to ensuring peace on the frontier, made it his duty to learn as much as he could about the Pathan tribesmen who lived in his district.

'Commissioner Hawke sent me a telegram. You have a letter for me, I assume?'

Reginald handed it to him, and he scanned it over quickly.

'You come highly recommended, which is unusual for a lad your age,' the colonel said as he stroked his moustache. 'Where were you educated?'

'The Duke of Marlborough Military Academy, sir.' Reginald hoped he wouldn't press him on this.

'Excellent school. Does Professor Wicklow still teach there?'

'Yes, he does, sir.'

'Wicklow's a good friend of mine. Brilliant mind. He was a captain in the Guides once. I don't suppose he told you that, did he?'

'No, sir.'

The colonel's eyes returned to the letter.

'How is your knowledge of languages?' he asked.

'I know Greek and Latin, sir, and I can speak fluent Arabic.'

'You'll be expected to learn Pashtu while you're stationed here. It's a must for all of the officers. Considering you've already mastered Arabic, you shouldn't have too much trouble. Wilfred Fubster's your father, is that right?'

Reginald nodded.

'I haven't met him in person, but as I'm sure you know, he has a spotless reputation.'

He perused the letter a while longer. Reginald trembled. So much depended on the colonel's decision.

'How old did you say you were?' he asked, looking him over again.

'Seventeen, sir, though I'll be eighteen in a couple days.'

'You look younger,' the colonel said and then sighed. 'It's not my usual practice to recruit officers without a diploma, but this war has stretched my ranks thin, especially among the juniors. I am commissioning you as an ensign in the third battalion of infantry. Captain Scott will be your commanding officer. You will report for duty tomorrow at dawn.'

'Thank you, sir!' cried Reginald joyfully.

'Henry!' the colonel called, and the secretary poked his head in. 'See that Ensign Fubster has a new uniform made and find him a place to stay.'

They went first to the tailor who took down his measurements and then Henry showed him to one of the nearby bungalows.

'Lieutenant Willoughby lives here, but he has a few rooms left over from Lieutenant Randall, who went to fight in France.'

Henry knocked on the door, and it was opened by an Indian servant.

'Is the lieutenant here?' he asked.

'No, sahib, he is out riding.'

'Would you please show Ensign Fubster to his rooms?'

The servant bowed and motioned for Reginald to follow. The bungalow was barely furnished, but this suited Reginald fine. His bedroom had a view across the cantonment to a row of grand palaces which he assumed were the residences of the leading European 'nabobs' of Peshawar. Beyond them, rising in the distance, were the wild hills of Afghanistan—eternal symbols of menace. Reginald and Narendi Ram unpacked their luggage and tried to settle in the best they could.

The next day, Reginald had the opportunity to meet his commanding officer, Captain James Scott, and the Third Regiment of His Majesty's Corps of Guides. The captain happened to be the cousin of the famous Antarctic explorer Robert Falcon Scott, who had perished while on his way back from the South Pole in 1912. Like his illustrious kinsman, the captain was a man of great stamina, resolve, and courage, qualities which, along with his fastidious personal habits, made him a model officer.

Reginald got along well with his bungalow mate Lawrence Willoughby, who served as a lieutenant in the regiment. The men themselves impressed Reginald as being a hardy, disciplined lot, well accustomed to the travails of border fighting and fiercely loyal to the Raj. The regiment gave Reginald the sense of belonging he had missed since first leaving India. In the evenings, after the day's training had been completed, he busied himself in the study of Pashtu or attended one of the lectures Colonel Thornwood gave on the subjects of botany, zoology, linguistics, archaeology, or any of the other subjects that struck the polymath's fancy. Several months passed, during which Reginald grew accustomed to the rigorous lifestyle while setting aside any extra money he earned to search for Natalie.

One evening, Reginald was sitting in his bedroom perusing a Pashtu manuscript when his eye was drawn to the glow of the sunset. The domes of Peshawar reflected back the amber colour of the fading sun, while the sky had turned a shade of ultramarine spread with glowing clouds. It was one of those famous Indian sunsets, the likes of which have never been seen here in the West, in which for a fleeting moment, heaven and earth are one.

As Reginald watched, he caught a glimpse of movement out of the corner of his eye in the garden of one of the palaces which rose on the edge of the cantonment. The garden had a stone wall surrounding it, but a girl, or rather a young lady, had climbed on top of it and was gazing up at the sky. Reginald watched her as she stared at the sunset. She was too far away for him to make out her features distinctly, but he got the impression at once that she was desperately lonely.

Unlike Western sunsets, which linger, the moment the Indian sun dipped below the horizon, the sky became immediately dark and the stars gleamed in the heavens above. The girl climbed down from the wall and vanished into the night.

Reginald's mind churned. The girl must've been about the same age as Natalie. Maybe it was her! The thought sent a shiver of excitement through his body, but it died down just as quickly. It couldn't be. Why would Natalie be here, in Peshawar, at the very edge of the known world? The girl was obviously the daughter of one of the nabobs. But why did she look so lonely? Had he imagined it? He had to find out for sure.

British soldiers were not permitted to leave the cantonments without written permission from their superior officers. The nabob palaces were particularly off-limits, falling under the jurisdiction of the civil magistrate. As many of the nabobs had amassed their fortunes through means questionable at best, they were eager to avoid interference from the governing authorities, especially the military. It would be highly irregular for Reginald to request Captain Scott's approval to inquire after this girl. But he could check the records of all British residents in Peshawar which were held in the Commissioner's Building on the cantonments.

He did this first thing in the morning. The registrar had no record of a girl named Natalie Prim in residence at Peshawar. Nor was there any mention of the MacFinn family. Reginald was not surprised. But before he gave up, he wanted a closer look.

He borrowed a pair of binoculars off Lieutenant Willoughby, ostensibly for hunting. That evening, he stole into his room and waited nervously for the girl to appear. Sure enough, as the sunset was reaching its way across the sky, he caught sight of a graceful figure climbing to the top of the wall. He raised the binoculars and brought her into focus. The distance was still great and her face was angled away from him, making it impossible to identify her for sure. He could not completely rule out the possibility that it was Natalie, but the odds were so great against it that it was useless to nourish that hope. Once again, though, he felt an overwhelming sense of this girl's loneliness and isolation. There was no logic behind it. She was the daughter of one of the wealthy nabobs, already well-off and not dependent on his help. Natalie needed him, and he would remain faithful to her. He lowered the binoculars and bowed his head. When he raised his eyes again, the sunset had passed, the stars were shining, and the girl had gone.

He tried to put the girl completely out of his thoughts. Yet he found himself attracted to the window the next day as the sun set. He couldn't explain why. Earlier in the day, he had returned the binoculars to Willoughby, determining never to look at the mysterious girl again.

Now he tried to compromise. He would not intrude on the girl. He gave himself permission to watch the sunset with her, maybe giving her a glance or two, but overall respecting her privacy and retaining his commitment to Natalie.

When she appeared, he felt a strange sense of relief, like he was afraid he wouldn't see her again. The sunset passed quickly, and she disappeared. What he allowed once, he allowed again, and it became a routine for him to watch the sunset with this girl. It was the most cherished part of his day, though he constantly reproached himself. Two more weeks and he would have a month's leave to search for Natalie. That would be his salvation from this distraction, and he looked forward to it with a burning eagerness.

# Journey Through India

REGINALD AND NARENDI Ram had prepared for how they would use their month's leave long in advance. Their goal was to cover as much of India as they could by rail, stopping at major population centres along the way to search for Natalie. They decided on a loop, starting off through Lahore, Bareilly, Lucknow, and reaching the holy city of Benares on the River Ganges. Reginald determined that Calcutta in Bengal would be too far for this trip; instead, they would turn back at Benares and visit Allahabad, Cawnpoor, and Agra before returning to Peshawar.

There was a persistent longing in Reginald to see the desert again. He had left part of his heart behind in Aqaba with Murad Pasha. However, the Great Indian (Thar) Desert was out of their way, being mostly located within the semiautonomous princely state of Rajputana, a hodgepodge of petty fiefdoms where many of the old ways still prevailed. It was rumoured that there some rajahs' wives practised *suttee* (self-immolation on their husband's funeral pyre), in spite of the long-standing British prohibition. Reginald would stick instead to those districts with a significant British presence, and he would have to slake his thirst for native splendour and the beauty of the sands some other time.

'How are you feeling, sahib?' asked Narendi Ram as they stood waiting at the railroad station in Peshawar. 'Do you think we will find Miss Natalie?'

'What do you think?' Reginald replied.

'I do not know. But we must not be discouraged. We must keep our faith, and God will reward us.'

Reginald had his doubts that even the power of God would be enough to overcome such odds. He made a morose companion on the journey to Lahore. While Narendi Ram went into the great Badshahi Mosque to pray, he lingered outside, kicking at the dirt, seemingly oblivious to the architectural masterpiece in front of him. He was thinking of the girl he'd seen in Peshawar and wondering why he was bound to such an impossible task. After the registry failed to record the presence of Natalie and the MacFinns, he drifted aimlessly through the civil lines before returning to the train station. There were English girls there, some quite pretty, but all with the haughty, self-satisfied air which contrasted so sharply with Natalie's modesty and the desperate loneliness of the Peshawar girl. The *memsahibs* (British women) of the Raj had a reputation for stuffy manners and a disdain for anything 'native.' This was one of the main reasons why Wilfred had removed his son from their society at such an early age.

The next stop on their route was the city of Bareilly, about one hundred and fifty miles northwest of Delhi. There was not much distinctive about the place, and they stayed only long enough to make their usual inquiries. The civil servants were a friendly lot, asking Reginald many questions about the Frontier, much more than he cared to answer. They were languishing in this peaceful backwater; any tidings of tensions on the border or the war in Europe would be discussed for days afterward. They regretted that neither Natalie Prim nor the MacFinns had been seen in the city or the surrounding countryside and promised to send a telegram to Peshawar if they should discover anything about them.

Their route descended into the teeming plain of the Holy Ganges, the spiritual heart of Hindustan. The river itself, considered a goddess by the Hindus, rose from glaciers in the Himalayas (or as the Hindus have it, the matted locks of Shiva's hair) before embarking on its long journey to the Bay of Bengal. A bath in the river would absolve a Hindu of all his sins. They saw many people wading in its water and the rising smoke from bodies cremated at the *ghats* along the bank, whose ashes would be carried down to the sea.

Though a Moslem, Narendi Ram could scarcely resist the allure of the river, whose significance was engraved on the hearts of all native Indians. He persuaded Reginald to walk down with him to the shore while they were waiting for a train. Narendi Ram's childish delight as he played in the shallows brought a smile to Reginald's face. He was otherwise unimpressed. The 'purifying' waters were beautiful in parts, but mostly dirty and foul smelling. There were too many people here, all poor and ignorant, all in need of saving. The Holy Ganges could not wash away these evils, and Reginald rather suspected that sins could be forgiven only at much higher price.

Whether he acknowledged it or not, his time in England had changed him. Though he still loved India, he could no longer look at it with innocent wonder. Now he saw much of the country as a problem to be fixed. The social contrasts which had once appeared natural were glaring inconsistencies. While he and Narendi Ram travelled in luxury and comfort in their own compartment, as did the other Englishmen and their servants, dozens of Indians squatted together in railway cars scarcely fit to transport beasts. The lean peasants they passed baked in the sun, going about their ceaseless labour as the days grew increasingly hot and oppressive.

Reginald wondered at the workings of fate. Why had he the fortune to be born an Englishman rather than one of these countless multitudes? And why, though he had every advantage of birth, was he so discontent and incapable of accepting his lot, when these Indians, who had nothing, did so with graceful equanimity? Was it they who needed his help in attaining the material blessings of Western civilisation, or he who needed theirs?

This sort of self-reflection quickly became oppressive, and he turned his thoughts elsewhere. He tried to imagine his father performing heroic deeds in France. This was hard to do, as everything he had heard about the war made the thought of fighting in it a nightmare. It had been two years since the eager recruits had departed for a war that would be over by Christmas. Millions had already perished, and there was no end in sight. If his father was with him, Reginald was sure that they would be able to find Natalie. But left to his own devices, there was little chance. He would nevertheless stay strong and do his duty as his father had taught him.

Reginald's spirits lifted slightly on their arrival in Lucknow, a bustling, thriving city which straddled the Gomti River, a tributary of the Ganges. Once part of the province of Oudh, Lucknow had been at the epicentre of the Great Indian Rebellion of 1857 when the Indians had nearly succeeded in throwing off the yoke of British rule. Reginald and Narendi Ram visited the old residency, which still bore the scars of rifle and cannon from Sir Henry Lawrence's heroic defence during the Siege of Lucknow. There were many other monuments, mosques, and temples to see. However, their search for Natalie once more proved to be in vain.

Two weeks of Reginald's leave had already passed. He was getting tired of sight-seeing and longed to be back with the Guides. Their next stop was the Holy City of Benares, inhabited since the days of the Vedas. Reginald was overwhelmed and appalled by what he saw. Here, the funeral pyres burned night and day; the ancient *ghats* swarmed with Hindu pilgrims, and the *sadhus* (Hindu holy men) bathed naked in the Ganges. Reginald had always felt more comfortable with India's Moslem population than with the Hindus; he found the latter's religion inscrutable and their customs remarkably strange. It was with relief that he turned back toward Peshawar after, to no surprise, learning that there were no MacFinns or Natalie Prim in the holy city.

'Well, Narendi, we have three more stops,' said Reginald as they settled into their private compartment on the train to Allahabad. 'I feel quite discouraged. How about yourself?'

Reginald knew that he would never offer an opinion unless asked.

'It is hard, sahib. But we must accept God's will.'

Narendi Ram was suffering, as Reginald could clearly see. He was every bit as invested in finding Natalie as Reginald was, and this long, fruitless journey was severely testing his faith.

They passed quickly through Allahabad and Cawnpore. In Agra, their last destination before their return, they went to see that most famous of India's monuments, the Taj Mahal (Crown of the Palace). It had been built by the Mughal Emperor Shah Jahan in the seventeenth century as a mausoleum for his favourite wife.

'If I had the money, I'd build something even grander for Natalie,' said Reginald as he gazed at the gleaming white marble. 'Would you help me, Narendi?'

'Yes, sahib,' replied Narendi Ram, whose expression showed that he was thinking along similar lines.

They stood and stared at it without another word. The sun sunk in the sky. First, the Taj Mahal glowed a slight pink, which darkened to red and then, as the sun neared the horizon, it turned suddenly a brilliant gold, like it had descended directly from heaven. Then the sun vanished, and the only light was the faint glimmer of a crescent moon. They might have stayed far longer, content to simply look at it, but they had a train to catch. So with many a backward glance, they hurried off to the station.

Reginald was relieved to be back in Peshawar with the Guides, where the rigorous training numbed the pain of his thoughts. There was always something useful to be done on the Frontier. The calm which prevailed for now over the Afghan mountains was liable to erupt into a storm with little warning. Only the unceasing efforts of the Guides kept the skies clear. For Reginald, there was another attraction to Peshawar which he blushed to acknowledge—the girl was still watching the sunset from the wall each evening.

The ineffable loneliness and desperation of the young lady slowly worked at Reginald's heart. He wondered what she was thinking of as she gazed at the glinting domes of Peshawar; for him, they had become so many Taj Mahals, symbols of an impossible love. As the days passed, his desire to declare himself to her reached a fever pitch. He hoped she wouldn't be offended by his concern. Once he had made contact and confirmed that there was nothing he could do to help her, this new obsession would lose its power over him, and he could return to pursuing Natalie.

But what would Natalie think of this lapse in his faithfulness?

While the battle raged in his mind, he remained at his post, watching the sunset. Then, one night, the girl did not appear at her usual spot on the wall. This was the first time she had missed. *She'll be back tomorrow*, Reginald thought, with a mournful sigh. But she was not there the next day or the day after that. *She must have fallen ill*, he decided. *But she'll recover and be back soon.*

Yet as days stretched into weeks with no sign of the girl, his mind imagined the worst. She must have moved, or maybe… The last thought was too horrible to imagine. A whole month crawled by, and Reginald was convinced that this girl, like Natalie, had disappeared forever, and his heart, which had begun to revive, would now be forever as barren and empty as the mountains of Afghanistan.

# The Victoria Cross

IT WAS THE twenty-fourth of September 1916 and the battle along the Somme had been raging for nearly three months. Wilfred had recently received a letter from Reginald and was proud that his son had been commissioned in the Corps of Guides. Not everything was well on the Western Front, however. The soldiers in Wilfred's battalion were exhausted and demoralised. A heavy downpour had recently flooded the trenches and the soldiers were forced to sit in the soaking mud. To make matters worse, they had just heard the news that they were going over the top the next morning.

Sometime after dark, Wilfred was making his way along the lines when he noticed one of the sentries had his head bowed in sleep. Wilfred cocked his pistol; 'Butcher' Haig had given the order that anyone who fell asleep on duty should be shot at once. This was an inhumane order, in Wilfred's opinion, but he was obliged to enforce it. He noticed that the man was an officer and lowered his gun.

'Terrible example to set for the men,' Wilfred muttered. 'He'll be court-martialed.'

He gave the man a rough shake.

As the man's eyes flew open, a look of abject terror spread across his face.

'What's your name, Lieutenant?' Wilfred asked.

'Knubby, sir,' he replied.

'Knubby, eh?' Wilfred looked the man up and down. He had thin grey hair, crooked spectacles, and the air of a pseudo-academic. He fit exactly the description Reginald had provided in his letters.

'Do you know who I am?' Wilfred asked.

Knubby shook his head. 'No, sir.'

'The name's Major *Fubster*. I believe you were acquainted with my son.'

The look on Knubby's face was one of utter dismay.

'Ah yes. I know all about you, *Master* Knubby. If I could only make you suffer as you made my boy! How does it feel now that *you're* the powerless one? By every right, I should blow your head off!'

He cocked his pistol.

'Please, sir!' Knubby begged. 'Please, I'll do anything!'

'You can't undo the past,' said Fubster. 'You must be held accountable for what you've done. But not by me. I'm not like you. I won't use my position to exact revenge. You will stand before the court-martial.'

Knubby groaned miserably.

'No, wait, I have a better idea. Since you failed so completely in your vocation as a school teacher, you should at least be given a chance to redeem yourself by serving your country. We are going over the top tomorrow, and you, my friend, are going to lead the charge for my battalion.'

'But, sir, I'm assigned under Major Wilson!'

'You've just been transferred. Come along now.'

'Sir, that's a death sentence,' Knubby protested.

'A death sentence!' thundered Fubster. 'Is that what this war is to you? Think about all the men who have already died for their country. Would you make a mockery of their sacrifice?'

Knubby wisely, from that moment on, kept his mouth shut.

The artillery bombardment for the next day's battle had begun. The guns bellowed and the night sky was alight. All kinds of weird and eerie shadows were cast across No Man's Land.

The soldiers imagined the Germans were advancing and began to panic.

'Steady, men,' Wilfred said calmly, though in reality he was as spooked as they were.

This war in the trenches had not been anywhere near the glorious affair he imagined it would be. In fact, he no longer wanted to have anything to do with it. But his country still demanded his loyalty.

'Try to get some sleep, men,' he urged the soldiers.

This was, of course, easier said than done because of the almost constant roar of the guns. When dawn finally arrived, the soldier's eyes were red and swollen, and they were barely able to stagger onto their feet.

Wilfred always carried a Union Jack with him wherever he went. He now took it out from its special place, unfolded it, and attached it to the end of a rifle.

'Lieutenant Knubby, come here,' he ordered. 'You are going to carry this standard into battle with you.'

Knubby accepted the pole, and the men watched as the flag fluttered in the light breeze.

'Gentlemen, we will not allow this standard to touch the ground. Once Lieutenant Knubby is killed, the next man will take it up and so on and so forth until it is planted in the very midst of the German trenches. Do you understand?'

There was a murmur of assent from the men.

'It is my prayer that as you look at this flag, you will reflect upon the majesty of our glorious empire. This is the reason that we fight and die. We are the sons of Great Britain and willingly give up our lives for her glory.'

A few of the soldiers removed their helmets as Wilfred spoke.

'Now please join me in "God Save the King."'

The rest of the soldiers took off their helmets and began to sing. With every line, their voices grew louder, with Wilfred Fubster's baritone sounding the loudest of all. The tune echoed along the British trenches and other battalions joined in as well. Their swelling voices carried out across No Man's Land and reached the enemy trenches where the Germans heard it and trembled.

'Fix bayonets, gentlemen,' Wilfred ordered.

There was a metallic ring all the way up and down the line. Wilfred nodded at Knubby. The old schoolmaster scrambled over the top with a determined look in his eye, stepped past the barbed wire, and took off across No Man's Land. Wilfred drew his sword and pointed it at the enemy lines, and the other soldiers surged after him.

As Knubby neared the enemy trenches, the machine guns started to roar. He was struck in the chest by a dozen bullets and collapsed to his knees, still holding the flag aloft. A soldier came up behind him and took it off him. The moment it left his hands, he died. The soldier with the flag was only able to take two steps forward before he too was killed, but by this time, a line of soldiers had appeared behind the flag and the next one took it up. In this way, the flag was carried step by step toward the enemy trenches. The German soldiers panicked and fired their rifles wildly at the advancing flag. Wilfred pulled out his pistol and dispatched two who lifted their heads too high.

It looked as though the flag would reach the trench when a machine gun snarled with all its fury and cut down the entire line of soldiers. Wilfred watched as the flag slipped out of the hands of the soldier who carried it and plummeted toward the ground. With a wild dash, he caught it a moment before it touched the ground and leapt into the German trench.

A German soldier fired his rifle and the bullet tore into Wilfred's chest. Ignoring the pain, Wilfred raised his pistol and shot him. To his right, the German machine gunners were desperately trying to turn their weapon around. Wilfred finished them off with two perfectly placed shots. Then he took up the weapon and, aiming it down the trench, unleashed a lethal stream of bullets. The Germans who were not killed took off running in terror. The other soldiers from Wilfred's battalion reached the trench and found their leader leaning up against the machine gun, blood rushing from his wound.

'Go back for a medic!' one of the soldiers shouted.

'No, it is too late now,' said Wilfred. 'Promise me that you will hold this trench.'

'We promise,' replied the men.

With his last bit of strength, Wilfred raised the flag pole and drove it into the ground. As he watched it, the flag faded away, and he thought only of his son who he was now leaving alone in the world.

'Oh, my dear boy!' he gasped.

Did he regret in that final moment his act of sacrifice and wish he'd raised his son with a different love than that which had claimed his life? It is impossible to know. And so Wilfred Fubster died.

When General Haig heard the story of Wilfred's bravery that day, he wrote to King George V recommending him for the Victoria Cross. The king agreed, and a week later, Wilfred was awarded the honour and a hero's funeral. Ultimately, Haig failed to follow up Wilfred's attack, and all the ground he had taken was subsequently lost and his soldiers killed to a man.

# A New Recruit

THE YEAR 1917 in Europe began with military deadlock between the Germans and the Allies. However, massive changes were afoot. On the Eastern Front, Brusilov's successful offensive had degenerated into a bitter rout for the Imperial Russian army. As the Russians withdrew across the vast front, losing hundreds of thousands of casualties to their merciless German pursuers, Russian society itself unravelled. An obscure radical named Vladimir Lenin who, ironically, had been shipped back to Russia by the Germans to stir up discontent, had gathered a fanatical band of followers. The Bolsheviks, as these revolutionaries were known, seduced the populace with their promises of peace, bread, and land. Soon enough, Lenin had seized control of Moscow, signed a humiliating peace treaty with the Germans, and executed Czar Nicholas II and his family.

In the West, the German U-boat blockade of Great Britain was beginning to provoke the ire of a country that had been making quite a pretty penny by selling arms to the warring nations. This country, which had spent its childhood in isolation, was eager to flex its newly developed muscles. The sinking of the passenger liner *Luisitania* was the final straw in a long series of grievances that convinced the United States of America to finally espouse the cause of the Allies. The European powers, blinded by their own sense of superiority,

135

grossly underestimated the vast power of the United States, which would ultimately turn the tide of the war.

The year 1917 was a troubling one for the Raj. The regiments were stretched thin with the war waging in Europe. Scattered pockets of discontent, which had been quiet during a period of general prosperity, were beginning to spread their influence. A diminutive Hindu named Mohandas Gandhi, who had been educated in England and spent time organising protests in South Africa, had returned to his native land with one goal in mind: dismantling the Raj. Preaching a gospel of nonviolence, Gandhi inspired tremendous devotion in his disciples and respect from his adversaries. British soldiers and civilians all through India were greeted with chants of 'Quit India,' though violent uprisings, due to Gandhi's moderating influence, were fortunately few.

On the Northwest Frontier, the situation remained tense. The Amir of Afghanistan, Habibullah Khan, had resisted the Sultan of Turkey's call for a *jihad* against the Allies. Always the pragmatist, however, he had allowed a Turkish embassy in Kabul in an attempt to play off the warring factions for the best deal. He also turned a blind eye to the Turkish agents who were fermenting rebellion among the border tribes. Despite a few violent clashes, the frontier was relatively stable, due in large part to the wisdom of Commissioner Sir George Roos-Keppel and the efforts of the Corps of Guides.

Reginald went about his days with a general listlessness caused by a gnawing guilt that he was failing Natalie. One evening, Reginald was about to retire early to bed when Lieutenant Willoughby, his bungalow mate, called his name.

'I'd like a word with you, Reginald,' he said.

The lieutenant was out on the verandah smoking his pipe, which was his usual occupation at that time of night.

Reginald took a seat beside him.

'What's been troubling you, old boy? You haven't been quite yourself lately.'

'Oh, I don't know. I'm feeling a bit lonely, I suppose.'

'Have you heard there's another ensign joining the regiment? He should be here in the next couple of days.'

'I hadn't, thank you,' said Reginald unenthusiastically.

Lieutenant Willoughby stroked his blond walrus moustache, which, it must be said, was the envy of the entire cantonment.

'You know what, old boy, I think I know what's bothering you. It's not good for a lad your age to spend all his time training and studying. You need to find yourself some female companionship.'

Reginald blushed.

'Why don't you go to the club? There's a few good-looking girls there.'

'No, thank you.'

The lieutenant raised an eyebrow. 'English girls not to your taste? I don't blame you. They're rather too demanding. It's the natives you want. That's more my style, too. Let me recommend some *kasbis* (courtesans) for you.'

'I'm not interested in girls.'

'Boys then? There's no shame in it. It's common among the Pathans.'

This suggestion was even more abhorrent than the idea of visiting a Peshawar courtesan. Reginald flushed angrily. Why couldn't Willoughby understand the simple principle of remaining true to one woman for life? Of course, Reginald had never told him about Natalie, and so this was an unfair reaction. The lieutenant was only trying to help.

'I'd prefer if we talked about something else,' said Reginald.

Willoughby nodded. 'All right, then. The captain and I are planning a hunting expedition up north during the hot weather. You're welcome to join us of course. Can we count you in?'

'Certainly,' Reginald said, gratefully shaking the lieutenant's hand. 'I'll look forward to it.'

'And, Reginald, if you need anything, just let me know.'

Reginald thanked him and retired to his room.

A handful of days later, while Reginald was out on the training grounds with the rest of the regiment, he caught sight of a figure approaching them out of the haze. It was a young man with blond hair and an exceptionally handsome face. Reginald was struck with the sudden feeling that he knew this person. Captain Scott ordered a halt to the drilling and went to meet the new recruit. Reginald followed a little further behind, his curiosity piqued. All at once, recognition dawned on him like a thunderclap.

'Glad to see you, Mr Nottingham,' said the captain, shaking his hand.

'Waverley!' Reginald cried.

Both Waverley and the captain looked up in surprise as Reginald came hurtling toward them. Before either could move, Reginald had wrapped his friend in a warm embrace. It took a moment for Waverley to realise just who was holding him, but once he did, he returned the embrace with equal ardour, tears of joy trickling down his cheeks.

By this time, the other officers had arrived and were regarding the scene with a mixture of surprise and amusement. Reginald was first to recover his dignity.

'Pardon me, sir,' he said to the captain, letting go of Waverley. 'This young man is my best friend. We last parted under very trying circumstances, and neither of us expected to see the other again.'

'No need to apologise,' replied the captain, who was a good-natured man. 'Perhaps it would be best if you two took some time to catch up. Mr Nottingham will officially join the regiment tomorrow.'

'Thank you, sir!' said Waverley.

Reginald led Waverley back to his bungalow and called for Narendi Ram.

'Narendi, look who it is!'

A smile of joy spread across the faithful servant's face as Waverley stepped inside.

'Waverley, sahib, it is wonderful to see you!'

'The pleasure's all mine,' said Waverley, shaking his hand.

'Bring us some tea, if you would,' requested Reginald, pulling out a chair for Waverley. 'Well, I must say, old boy, it's an absolute delight to see you again. This is the last place in the world I'd have expected to run into you. What brings you to the Frontier?'

'The truth is, Reginald, ever since I met you and heard your stories, I've had a burning desire to see India with my own eyes. My family is very well-connected, as you know, and as soon as I graduated, they were able to secure a commission for me in the Corps of Guides. Well, that's enough about me. I want to hear about your adventures. Have you found the girl?'

'I haven't.' Reginald sighed.

'I thought you said they'd taken her to Ireland. What brings you back to India?'

'Well, I did follow her to Ireland, but I received a message in Dublin saying that they had taken her to India. I followed, but in Egypt, we learned that the Turks were advancing on the Suez Canal and that it was closed to all ships for the foreseeable future. I couldn't wait, so I found a place on an Arab schooner that was sailing to India. Along the way, we stopped in Arabia, and I was captured by the Turks. They held me as a prisoner in Aqaba for nearly a year. Finally, I escaped and came here.'

'My god, Reginald!' cried Waverley in admiration. 'What an adventure you've had! You must tell me all about it!'

'All in good time,' said Reginald, waving his hand. 'The important thing is that we are reunited and Natalie is here somewhere in India. We will find her.'

'Where have you looked so far?'

'Bombay, Delhi, Lahore, Bareilly, Lucknow, Benares, Allahabad, Cawnpore, and Agra.'

'That's not a bad start. I'm a little rusty on my geography, it's been a while since Professor Wicklow's class. Where else could she be?'

'Well, there's the south, either Madras or the Malabar Coast. She could be somewhere in the Deccan, likely Hyderabad, and there's also Calcutta. We can search the hill stations like Shimla when we go hunting in Kashmir. There's much more, of course. It's a big country.'

'Tell me more about this girl. I'm afraid I've forgotten some of the details. She isn't related to you, is she?'

Reginald shook his head. 'Her parents died when she was very young. My great-uncle was looking after her. She's the heiress to a fortune which will be hers as soon as she comes of age.'

'Yes, that's right! Do you remember I suggested that they were trying to keep her hidden until she turned eighteen, when they could marry her off and gain control of her fortune?'

'My god! I remember it now! If that's true, it's going to be even harder to find her!'

He smacked himself in the head. All along, he'd been operating under the assumption that the MacFinns had legally registered her and that it would be a matter of time before they found the right place. But if they hadn't listed her in the registry, he couldn't rule out even the places they had already looked. His mind flooded with despair. There were all sorts of other possibilities. They might have gone to Ceylon or Burma or left the colonies entirely and returned to England.

'How old is she now?' asked Waverley, interrupting Reginald's frenzied thoughts.

'She's two years younger than I am, so sixteen, or at least she turned sixteen this spring.'

'Then we have two years before she's married. Will that be enough time?'

'Who knows?'

'We'll find her, Reginald. Don't you worry.'

They spent the remainder of the afternoon in eager conversation, Reginald elaborating on his adventures and Waverley describing his last year at the Duke of Marlborough military academy. Reginald informed his friend on what to expect from regimental life in Peshawar and the comparative virtues and vices of the other officers. He felt it would be silly to mention the girl he had seen watching the sunset.

Waverley had soon settled into life in the regiment. His natural good humour and affability made him a favourite of the officers and enlisted men alike. Waverley's company breathed new life into Reginald. His friend's open-eyed sense of wonder at the strange and fascinating land of India revived his own imagination and innate desire to explore and understand.

## *Journey to Kashmir*

THE HUNTING EXPEDITION mentioned by Lieutenant Willoughby came as a welcome break to the routine of study and drilling as the hot weather was beginning to set in. It also offered an opportunity to search for Natalie, though most of the trip would be through sparsely populated territory. The officer corps, including Narendi Ram, porters, and several Pathan guides, set out for a journey up the Indus River to Kashmir.

The Indus, in local parlance, the 'Father of Rivers,' was the cradle of an ancient civilisation whose relics could still be glimpsed along either bank, though most of its major cities had been located further south. The current inhabitants seemed scarcely to have altered the lifestyle of their primordial forbearers. Their villages were built on the edge of the water, and it was not uncommon during the monsoon season for the Indus to rise and sweep them away. But they were a hardy and resilient lot, well used to misfortune and starting anew.

One of the villages in which they stopped had been plagued by the presence of a man-eating mugger crocodile, notorious for seizing women as they came to the river to wash their clothes. Captain Scott promised the village elders that his men would rid them of the nuisance. Tracking the crocodile proved to be a difficult task; however, the monstrous brute avoided the bait they laid out for it and stopped making its customary attacks on the washing women.

One morning, Narendi Ram was up early saying his prayers in the direction of Mecca. The river was very calm, with scarcely a ripple disturbing its tranquil surface. Suddenly, Narendi noticed a gigantic creature lying sunning itself on a sandbank partway out. He hurried to wake up Reginald, who woke Waverley. The two friends slunk down to the riverbank with their rifles.

'Bless my soul, that's it!' Waverley whispered under his breath as Narendi pointed out the crocodile. He raised his rifle and took aim.

'It's too far of a shot,' Reginald said, lowering the gun. 'I'm afraid you'll shoot wide and it'll slip away. We need to get closer. Then we can finish it off for sure.'

They rolled up their trousers and waded out into the river. The water grew deep quickly before it levelled off into another sandbar. The crocodile turned its ugly head and watched as they approached.

'It sees us,' Waverley whispered. 'If we miss and it slips off into the water, it'll cut us off from the shore.'

Reginald took a quick look around and saw that Waverley was right. There was a deep channel between the shore and the sandbar where they stood ankle-deep, which the crocodile would certainly take once it entered the water.

'Don't worry about it,' he said. 'We won't miss.'

They raised their rifles and took careful aim. Both guns roared at once, and the crocodile let out a bellow as it dived into the water.

'Did we hit it?' Waverley cried.

'We must have,' said Reginald.

There was hardly a ripple in the water of the channel to indicate the presence of the crocodile. Reginald and Waverley reloaded their rifles and waited for a sign of movement. Suddenly, the crocodile launched itself out of the water at Waverley. Waverley barely escaped the reach of its jaws, but in backing up, he lost his footing. As the crocodile turned to seize him, Reginald fired his rifle at point-blank range right between its eyes. Releasing a blood-curdling roar, the crocodile thrashed about, knocking Reginald flying with a blow from its tail. Waverley recovered his feet and sent a bullet into the crocodile's mouth. This second well-placed shot was the monster's death knell. The mighty beast stopped thrashing and its eyes glazed over as its life blood seeped into the water.

'Are you all right, Reginald?' Waverley said, helping his friend onto his feet.

'Just bruised,' said Reginald. 'You?'

'I'm fine. That was a close call, wasn't it?'

'It sure was,' said Reginald, surveying the enormous bulk of the dead crocodile.

He'd underestimated the reptile's craftiness, and it had nearly cost them their lives.

Later in the day, the crocodile was paraded throughout the village, and Waverley and Reginald were given a hero's reception. The village elders treated them to a magnificent feast that lasted long into the night. They were even offered their choice of the most beautiful young maidens of the village to take as their wives. This boon was, to Waverley's regret, politely declined.

Passing on from there, the hunting party continued on its way up the bank of the great river. The villages stood further apart, and the land grew wilder as they proceeded north. Hills rose on either side of the river, some rugged and barren, others clad with pine and deodar forests, which filled the air with their aromatic scent. The hills grew in size until they were in turn dwarfed by the great snowy mountains. This was the India Reginald loved. Waverley was likewise fascinated with everything he saw and kept a sketchbook in which he included illustrations of all the birds, fish, mammals, and reptiles they had seen.

Finally, they reached their destination: the Vale of Kashmir. Verdant plains, planted with orderly rows of poplars between shining, mirror-like lakes stretched off to the horizon toward the jagged peaks of the Karakoram Mountains. It was the most beautiful place Reginald had ever seen. *Maybe one day, once I've found Natalie, I'll come back here and settle down*, Reginald thought.

The hunting was plentiful in the rhododendron-covered foothills. Waverley shot an Indian rhinoceros and a sloth bear, while Reginald took a full-grown gaur (a species of wild cattle) and a leopard. Once, while Reginald was picking his way through some elephant grass, he came face-to-face with an enormous Bengal tiger. They stood staring at each other for several tense moments before the tiger yawned and turned away, apparently deciding that the scrawny creature before it wasn't worth the effort.

All parties agreed that the hunting expedition had been a success. Reginald, Waverley, and Narendi Ram lingered on the way back to visit the popular hill stations where the officials of the Raj would retire while the hot weather roasted the plains. There were plenty of English girls and plenty of English gentlemen paying them court in an endless round of tea parties, tennis matches, and balls. This idle, self-indulgent life was an abomination to Reginald. They checked the registries out of habit, not expecting positive results. There was no hint of Natalie or the MacFinns at any of the hill stations. Waverley remained optimistic, Narendi Ram continued in his simple faith, while Reginald descended into an ever-deepening gloom.

# A Familiar Face

IT WAS AROUND this time that Reginald received the official telegram detailing his father's heroic death on the Somme. He was devastated, as can well be imagined, and wept as he never had before. This was his worst loss yet, as his father had been his rock and guide through life. For several weeks afterward, he scarcely had the strength to pull through the day. However, with the loving support of Waverley and Narendi Ram, as well as the comforting routine of the regiment, his heart slowly healed. Though the pain never went away completely, as the months passed, he could once again dutifully bear the weight of his day-to-day activities.

The inheritance he received was not large but sufficient for covering his needs for the foreseeable future. He made sure this sum was safely invested in the bank and paid his daily expenses out of his regimental salary.

In this way, the great and terrible year of 1917 came to an end. The year 1918 dawned with the Germans determined to break the stalemate on the Western Front. With a million soldiers freshly transferred from Russia, they executed a massive assault across the entire front. General Haig implored his soldiers to fight to the last man with their 'backs to the wall.' They only needed to hold out a short while longer before the Americans arrived.

It was in the spring of this year that Reginald found himself one evening drawn to watch the sunset from the window in his room. He had given up this habit long ago, but a strong feeling of nostalgia prompted him to do so on this particular evening, as he was reminded of the lonely girl he used to watch it with. Suddenly, to his astonishment, the very same girl mounted the wall and sat staring off toward the west.

Reginald had to pinch himself multiple times to make sure he wasn't dreaming. It didn't seem possible, yet there she was. Her desperate expression was unaltered; if anything, she was a more forlorn and romantic figure than before.

*I can't lose her again*, he decided. Forgetting Natalie and his duty, he rushed out of the bungalow and along the dusty path that led to the edge of the cantonment. Already, the Indian sunset was beginning to fade from the sky. Reginald increased his pace to a sprint, his heart in a knot as though his life depended on this. Just as he came within sight of the wall, he saw the girl's shadowy figure descending the other side. He stopped and wiped his face. He was too late!

The next twenty-four hours passed slowly. All of his thoughts centred on this strange girl, her beauty, and the haunting impression of need he got from her. He hated himself for becoming so quickly and easily obsessed. What would he do when he confirmed she wasn't Natalie? It had been four years since he'd last seen his beloved on the day of Merriweather's funeral. He wondered if he would even recognise her. It was awfully hard to stay true in such circumstances.

In the afternoon, he declined an invitation from Waverley to shoot blackbuck in the countryside and retired instead to his room to wait for the girl. The Pashtu manuscript he was holding was soon soaked with sweat from his hands as he stared at the place where, God willing, she would again appear.

Finally, he decided that he couldn't wait there any longer. He went out past the smoking Lieutenant Willoughby on the verandah, with an incoherent reply to the lieutenant's salutation. From there, he made his way furtively to the edge of the cantonment, trembling with each step. A little path ran along the edge of the wall which guarded the palaces of the nabobs, planted on either side with almond trees which, in that season, were in fragrant blossom. A quaking Reginald took his place underneath one of the trees to wait. It seemed a year before the Indian sun at last began to sink into the horizon, casting its multicoloured hues across the sky.

All at once, the girl appeared on top of the wall. Finally, he could see her face. If he had thought her beautiful from a distance, he was not prepared for the majesty of beholding her up close. She had golden hair which the sunlight tinged to amber, gentle blue eyes, and dimpled rosy cheeks. He was transfixed to the spot, forgetting what he had come to say. However, the shaking of his body against an almond tree alerted her to his presence.

She let out a gasp and turned quickly away.

'Wait!' Reginald cried.

She whirled around.

'Who are you?' she called.

He took a step forward.

'Here I am.'

Her face flushed.

'I…I just wanted to say,' he stammered. 'If you need anything, I am your most humble servant.'

He attempted a chivalrous bow with shaking knees.

When he had the courage to look up, he saw, to his utter astonishment, that she was gazing down at him with the most loving expression imaginable.

'Reginald, it's me!'

He stared at her blankly.

'Don't you recognise me?' she cried, her voice nearly breaking with emotion. 'It's Natalie!'

Reginald nearly fell over in a swoon.

'Natalie, I…' he rasped.

'You didn't think I was someone else?' Her eyes desperately searched his face. 'Oh, Reginald, you didn't give up on me, did you? I was so worried you'd forgotten all about me!'

'How could I?' he choked. 'You were so far away. I couldn't recognise you…I…I had to get closer.'

He could hardly stand to look at her. She knew that his faith had wavered. She burst into tears.

'But how is this possible?' he said finally. 'What are you doing here in Peshawar?'

'We haven't much time,' said Natalie, looking at the sky. 'Tomorrow, I will tell you everything.'

'Tomorrow! Let me come up there with you now,' Reginald said, starting to climb the wall.

'No, you cannot,' Natalie implored. 'I'm a prisoner here, and I'm being watched. The time is already late. I must be going.'

'Wait!' he cried, but she was already gone.

## Natalie's Story

REGINALD SPENT THE next day in a total daze. He performed so poorly at the drills that he was presumed ill and sent back to his bungalow.

'What's the matter with him?' Waverley asked.

'Who knows?' Lieutenant Willoughby replied.

Waverley paid a visit to his friend that afternoon, but he was dismissed on the excuse that Reginald was not up to seeing him. Reginald lay in his bed, his body shaking. Natalie here! And a prisoner!

*What a fool I am!* he thought. *She's been here all this time, under my very nose, and I did nothing! I didn't even recognise her! She must think I'm a faithless scoundrel. I hate myself!*

It was all too much for his already over-excited imagination to bear. At last, he managed to pull himself together enough to get out of bed and drink some tea to calm his nerves. When this failed, he turned to brandy, which, after several hearty swigs, succeeded in settling his mind to the point where he could think somewhat coherently. Did he have the courage to go and face her, knowing that he had let her down? He must do it, if he was ever to atone for his lapse.

'I'll go and wait for her,' he decided at last, though there were still some hours before sunset.

On his way out the door, he ran smack dab into Waverley, who was paying another visit to inquire after his health.

'I'm terribly sorry, old boy,' Reginald said, dusting him off.

'Are you all right, Reginald?' Waverley asked.

'Something's happened. I can't talk about it right now. I will tomorrow, perhaps.'

Reginald hurried away, with Waverley looking after him in bewilderment. He soon reached the wall and settled in beneath one of the almond trees. For a time, he amused himself by watching a couple of langur monkeys who were squabbling over some food. Then the monkeys were gone, and he was left alone to wait.

The moment the sun touched the horizon, Reginald heard a movement on the wall and Natalie appeared.

For a good while, the two simply stared at each other. Natalie had grown so much that Reginald understood why he had not recognised her. When they'd parted, she was but a girl; now, she was a woman. A great deal of sorrow and loneliness had been written on her face, but there was strength also, as if she refused to be bowed under the weight of circumstances, which suffused her features with sublime loveliness. Reginald was aware of her superiority to him in a spiritual sense and felt like an ordinary mortal encountering a divine being.

'Oh, Reginald,' she said at last, 'I can't even tell you how happy I am to see you! I've missed you so much.'

'I've missed you too!' he returned ardently. He steadied himself. 'Natalie, I'm sorry that I didn't come at once, I couldn't tell it was you, and I suspected it wasn't, Peshawar being the last place in India I expected you to be. Narendi Ram and I searched everywhere we could. I used to watch the sunset with you from my bungalow over there. I thought you needed help, but I was afraid it wasn't you. I…'

She held up her hand, and he stopped.

'Does it matter?' she said. 'God has brought us back together.'

He felt relieved. If Natalie could forgive him, he could forgive himself.

'How did you get here?' he asked.

'Oh, Reginald, it's a horrible plot!' she said, shuddering all over.

'What do you mean?' he gasped. Had Waverley been right all along?

'Your uncle Meriweather was murdered, his will was forged, and now I am to be married to a man I detest and into a family I hate so that they gain control of my entire fortune.'

Reginald cried aloud. So his worst fears were confirmed. He looked at her, hoping she would contradict herself.

'I'm sorry,' she said, brushing a few tears from her eyes. 'It's all true.'

'But who is this family? Who are you to be married to?'

'The McAuliffes. Jack McAuliffe is to be my husband.'

A blast from a cannon at close quarters would have had hardly a greater effect on Reginald than this terrible revelation. He collapsed to the ground, clutching at his heart. It was some time before he recovered himself enough to rise shakily to his feet again.

'I'll kill him!' he vowed.

'No, Reginald!' Natalie cried. 'You will not repay evil for evil. Let us trust in God to deliver us.'

Reginald shook his head. 'Natalie, I must.'

'You must not.'

Reginald was aware of a moral strength beyond his own.

'Promise me you will not lay a violent hand on him.'

Reginald looked up into her beautiful face and something softened inside of him. For himself, he could not, but for Natalie, he could do anything.

'I promise,' he said at last.

Her eyes shone with love.

'It is late,' she said. 'And I fear the McAuliffes will suspect me if I stay out too long. We will talk tomorrow night and the nights after. You will tell me what has happened to you since we parted.'

Just as quickly as she had appeared, she vanished again into the gathering twilight. Reginald plodded back to his bungalow with his mind in turmoil. The joy he had felt in Natalie's presence was overcome by anguish at the thought that she was to be married to his most bitter enemy. It couldn't be true! Yet it must be. Natalie was not a liar.

Never in a million years could Reginald have dreamt of such a fate. *Oh, wretched man that I am!* he thought as he crawled into his bed. *What have I ever done to deserve this? What has Natalie done?*

As he pondered this question, his mind drifted back over all of the misfortunes he had endured since he had left India for the first time: Johnstone and Knubby's Military Academy, toiling in the candle factory, the death of his mother and Merriweather Fubster and the loss of Natalie, being captured by the Turks, and the death of his father. Natalie's impending marriage to Jack McAuliffe was only the latest event in a long series of troubles which seemed to haunt his every step like a spectre.

*Suffering is my lot in life*, thought Reginald. *There is nothing for me but toil and trouble.* He thought of a phrase he had often heard Narendi Ram repeat: 'What is written is written.' Were his sufferings the result of the inscrutable universal decree over which he had no control? This was Eastern philosophy as he understood it, a surrender to and acceptance of whatever came to pass, be it good or evil.

But Reginald was no Easterner, he was an Englishman, and he came from a people who believed that it was possible to alter fate. How else had the English been capable of such wonders of exploration, invention, and conquest if they had not considered that their individual efforts were actually worth something and that they could, by force of will, rise above their circumstances? Reginald had often wondered at the aimless passivity of many of the Hindus and Mussulmans he met; they lacked the Englishman's power of action.

The more he thought about it, the more he convinced himself that no all-powerful will of God governed his destiny. He had faced adverse circumstances before and overcome them; there was no reason for him to believe he wouldn't be able to triumph again in the future. It was all well and good for Narendi Ram to say 'what is written is written,' but he, Reginald Archibald Fubster, was in command of his own fate. The tale of his life did indeed look bleak at the moment, but he would compose a new ending, which saw him and Natalie together forever after.

With this resolution reached, the confusion in Reginald's mind dissipated. He had a clear mission now, and he began to formulate a strategy for liberating Natalie from her captors.

## Waverley Meets Natalie

REGINALD HAD SO recovered his composure that he was able to resume his duties with the regiment. He had to fend off several questions from Waverley and Lieutenant Willoughby as to the nature of his supposed illness. He knew that he would have to tell Waverley and Narendi Ram eventually, but he decided to put it off until he had learned more about Natalie's situation.

When they met again that evening, Reginald began the tale of his adventures since they had parted, from the Duke of Marlborough Military Academy to his imprisonment in Aqaba with Murad Pasha and his return to India. Natalie was fascinated by his stories, her eyes flashing continuously with wonder and admiration. Reginald was so happy just to be in her presence that he forgot, for a time, the looming danger they faced. It took him nearly a week to finish the catalogue of his exploits, after which Natalie described her circumstances in more detail.

'You remember our neighbour Finnegan McAuliffe, don't you?' Natalie said.

'Yes, I do. He gave me a bad feeling, somehow.'

'He was in on the plot from the beginning. Once he learned that Merriweather had taken me in, a young heiress to a vast fortune, he knew that if he could have me married into his family, he would gain control of all of that wealth. Fortunately for him, he had a nephew of just the right age, your old enemy Jack McAuliffe. He didn't trust Jack to win my heart by fair means, especially with you around, Reginald, and decided instead on the use of subterfuge and deception. He hired his crooked associate, Charles Howe, to forge a will for Merriweather, surrendering all of his wealth to the Crown and entrusting me to the care of the MacFinn family (who were really the McAuliffes in disguise). Finally, when the time was right, he poisoned Merriweather and started all the awful machinery in motion.

'The day we parted after the funeral, Finnegan McAuliffe came up to me and informed me that he would be the one who made sure that I was safely conveyed to Ireland. We boarded a carriage and stopped first at McAuliffe manor where Jack McAuliffe joined us for the journey. It was then that Finnegan McAuliffe said something that sent a shudder down my spine. "You two had better get used to each other. You'll soon be spending a great deal of time together."

'That is when I first suspected what they were planning for me. I abhorred Jack with all of my soul, and for his part, he appeared initially contemptuous of me. He soon overcame his reticence, however, and quickly ensured that every moment of my waking life was a torment. We arrived in Ireland where I learned that this had merely been a detour to throw you off our track and that our real destination was India. I smuggled a message to one of the carriage drivers in Dublin and prayed to God that you would receive it.'

'I did!' Reginald cried. 'It was a miracle!'

'God heard me,' she said, her eyes shining. She offered a short prayer of gratitude before continuing. 'We sailed to India and came first to Bombay,' she continued. 'There we met Leopold McAuliffe, Jack's father, the mastermind of the whole scheme. It was decided that the family should avoid Delhi, in case you or your father were on their trail. They would return to their old residence in Peshawar, which was well-defended and off the beaten path. And so we did a couple of years ago. My only companion is a mute Indian maid, and I am allowed outside only once a day to watch the sunset. Jack McAuliffe is the bane of my existence. He lingers about idly, trying to get me alone so that he can touch me, though his father has forbidden it until we're married, for which I am grateful to him.'

'Natalie, have you been held in this palace all the time?' asked Reginald. 'I used to watch you as you were looking at the sunset, not knowing who you were of course, and there were several months when you did not appear.'

'Oh yes. I fell terribly ill not long ago with fever, and they kept me inside until I recovered. I didn't think I would make it. This country is so abominably hot. I feel as though I'm burning up every day.'

'Is Jack McAuliffe here now?' Reginald asked warily.

'Yes. He's always here. He waits for me to come back inside.' She shuddered.

'Come on, Natalie, let's make a run for it. We can be on a train for Bombay tonight, and from there, we can take a steamer back to England or America or anywhere!'

She shook her head sadly. 'We can't, Reginald. The McAuliffes have a servant watching the train station, and if I don't return to the house this evening, they'll suspect I tried to run away, and oh, the threats they've made! If they catch me...' Her voice trailed off as her body convulsed.

Reginald did not press her. If it was too horrible for her to contemplate, he didn't want to know it either.

'I don't have the courage for it. I'm not as brave as you are, Reginald.'

'I will find a way to get you out of here. You have my word. Give me some time to come up with a plan.'

The following evening, Reginald and Natalie met to discuss the several ideas of escape that he had formulated during his drills. They were in the middle of conversation when Reginald heard a slight rustling in the almond branches along the wall. He hoped it was only a jackal or hyena scavenging under the cover of twilight, but he figured he'd best make sure.

He approached the shadow of the wall from which he thought he heard the sound of heavy breathing.

'Who goes there?' he cried menacingly, cocking his revolver.

'Oh, Reginald, I'm sorry, old boy,' replied a familiar voice as Waverley emerged from the shadows. 'I wanted to find out what was bothering you, so I followed.'

Reginald was immediately relieved.

'I should've told you sooner,' he said, motioning for him to follow. 'Look, Waverley, I've found her! It's Natalie!'

Waverley gazed up at Natalie as she was silhouetted against the fading saffron sky. Whatever Waverley had imagined from Reginald's description of her proved woefully short of reality. She was by far the most beautiful woman he had ever seen. While always popular with the ladies, Waverley had never before fallen in love. A rush of unfamiliar sensations overwhelmed him.

'Natalie, this is Waverley, my best friend,' Reginald introduced them. 'Waverley, this is Natalie.'

'How do you do?' said Natalie with a graceful curtsey.

Waverley, who had never before been at a loss for words, could only stare up at her stupidly.

'It's growing dark,' Natalie said, with a fearful glance at the heavens. 'It was very nice meeting you, Waverley. I will see you both tomorrow night, I hope.'

She was gone in an instant.

'Come on, let's go back to my bungalow. I have a lot of explaining to do,' Reginald said, laying a hand on Waverley's shoulder.

Waverley emerged from his stupor. 'You aren't angry at me, are you, old boy?'

'Of course not. Why would I be?'

They made their way to the cantonment. Reginald called for Narendi Ram to bring them some brandy and to join them for their conference. He proceeded to tell them Natalie's story as she had relayed it to him, focusing in particular on the perfidy of the McAuliffes and the desperate situation in which Natalie now found herself.

'We must rescue her!' Waverley cried once Reginald had finished.

'I agree,' Reginald rejoined. 'Natalie will need some persuading to try to make a run for it, however. She considers it too dangerous, and she has strictly forbidden me to lay a violent hand on Jack McAuliffe.'

'I will write to my family,' said Waverley. 'We'll smuggle her out of India and back to England where we can provide sanctuary for her at our estate. My father knows many of the finest barristers in London, and I am certain that they will be able to restore Natalie's fortune to her and see that the McAuliffes pay dearly for their crimes.'

'What do you think, Narendi Ram?' asked Reginald.

The Indian had been sitting silently with his hands folded.

'Sahib, if you ask for my advice, I would advise you to wait.'

'Wait? Wait and do what?'

'Only wait.'

'You mean, do nothing!' Reginald exploded. 'Are you mad?'

'Let me explain, sahib. All that has happened has been the will of Allah. He has brought you and Natalie here to Peshawar for a purpose. You need only be patient, and he will reveal his plan. Remember what happened at the Suez when we tried to act in our own power.'

Reginald shook his head. 'So that is the celebrated wisdom of the East. Do you really think it is God's will for Natalie to be married to a man she abhors, to be plundered of her wealth and deprived of her liberty?'

'The will of Allah cannot be easily comprehended by us mortals,' Narendi replied.

'You must see the folly of your philosophy,' snapped Reginald. 'It's easy to be passive, do nothing, and attribute everything that happens to the will of God. But the important thing in this situation is our will to rescue her. God created us with minds to reason and bodies to act. And act we must.'

'That is true, sahib. But it is useless to act outside of God's timing. There may be a purpose to this which will only be revealed if we wait. If we take matters into our own hands, we might miss it.'

The old frustration welled up inside of Reginald. He had already waited four years. What good would it be to wait any longer, when every passing day brought Natalie closer to the catastrophe of marrying Jack McAuliffe? He was not the kind to stand by idly. His father had taught him to confront his problems head-on, and confront them he would.

Reginald's eye happened to glance over at the grandfather clock in the corner; it was nearly four in the morning.

'We'd all better get some sleep,' he said.

'So are we going to attempt the rescue?' asked Waverley.

'Of course we are,' said Reginald. 'That was never in doubt.'

# The Plan of Rescue

WAVERLEY COMPOSED A letter to his parents the very next day, detailing Natalie's unusual circumstances and asking permission for them to harbour the unfortunate girl at their estate in Nottingham. Waverley's love for Natalie exuded from every word, as he described her in the most glowing terms possible. He then delivered the letter to the telegraph office. With the telegraph lines now stretching across the majority of India, the relay of the message would take significantly less time than in the old days, but it would still be a week before he received a reply.

In the meantime, Reginald and Waverley formulated a plan. Narendi Ram, persuaded to support the cause out of loyalty, was dispatched to the train station to uncover the spy Natalie had spoken of. After a day or two of observation, his eyes alighted on a disgruntled-looking Pathan who lounged around the station all day, holding an antiquated *jezail* rifle. Narendi Ram engaged him in a conversation and soon discovered that the Pathan was a devout Mussulman like himself, and that he had a particular fondness for strongly brewed tea. They spent the afternoon in a tea shop that adjoined the train station, discussing the life of the Prophet and their interpretation of several difficult passages in the Hadith. Finally, they parted ways, with the Pathan citing his duties, but promising that they should meet again tomorrow at midday.

Reginald, meanwhile, bought a pair of Pathan robes in the Peshawar bazaar for Waverley and himself and a black *bourka* for Natalie. The plan was to travel as two Pathans and their sister to Delhi and then to Bombay, blending in with the polyglot crowds of natives and avoiding any notice that might be attracted by two British officers escorting a beautiful Englishwoman. They would meet Natalie at sunset, dress her quickly in the *bourka*, and head to the train station.

Narendi Ram was responsible for slipping a sleeping powder into the Pathan guard's tea.

Reginald wrote a long letter to Captain Scott explaining their actions, which he intended to leave with Lieutenant Willoughby the night of the rescue. Now all that remained was waiting for the reply from Waverley's parents and introducing the scheme to Natalie herself.

Reginald and Waverley went together to meet Natalie at the wall at sunset. She listened patiently as Reginald elaborated their plan of action.

'I'm not sure, Reginald,' she said at last. 'I don't want you to have to leave your regiment for my sake and give up your career.'

'This isn't about me, Natalie, it's about you!' cried Reginald in exasperation. 'We have to get you out of here!'

'I'm afraid,' she said, her slender body trembling.

There was a mysterious depth to her fear which Reginald could not understand. What had the McAuliffes threatened? They'd soon be out of that odious family's reach anyway, so why should she be so worried?

'Trust me, Natalie. Once we reach England, we'll have the law on our side. You won't have to marry Jack and your fortune will be safe. And I promise you that the McAuliffes will be brought to justice.'

Natalie's eyes swept the Afghan mountains, and she shivered.

'I trust you, Reginald, but I'm frightened, upon my soul I am.'

Reginald's heart ached with love for this girl, who had borne her head up so high through so many cruel twists of fate. She deserved to be a princess, and yet here she was in this foreign country as a prisoner.

'I'm sorry, Natalie' was all he could say. 'I'm sorry for everything. You will think about this, won't you?'

'I will,' she promised. 'I'm lucky I have two noble and gallant gentlemen to protect me.'

'Three,' corrected Reginald. 'Don't forget about Narendi Ram.'

Natalie smiled.

'Each of us would be happy to give our lives for you,' said a blushing Waverley.

'I know. That's what worries me.' She looked up at the darkening sky, said goodbye, and slipped away.

# The Rescue

WAVERLEY RECEIVED A reply from his parents a few days later. Waverley's father was of the romantic sort (a trait he passed on to his only son) and, like the hero of Cervantes's novel, had probably read one too many tales of chivalry. He fully endorsed the plan. Waverley's mother was more practically minded, but she too agreed, persuaded perhaps by the mention of Natalie's fortune and Waverley's obvious love for her. Natalie herself, when assured of the favourable reception of the Nottinghams, finally accepted the plan. A day was set, and the only thing that remained was putting their strategy into execution.

Lieutenant Willoughby was no fool. All of the conferences between Reginald and Waverley had not escaped his attention, and he knew something was afoot. The morning of the day of the rescue, he confronted Reginald about it over breakfast.

'So what are you and Waverley up to?'

'Up to?' said Reginald innocently. 'I don't know what you mean.'

'Come on, old boy, what do you take me for? I know you and Waverley are plotting something. I promise I won't tell a soul.'

'I meant to give you this anyway,' Reginald said, reaching into his pocket for the letter. 'Please don't open it until tomorrow morning. It explains everything.'

He put it in Willoughby's outstretched hand.

'You have my word of honour as a soldier,' he said, somewhat reluctantly. 'And good luck at whatever it is.'

The day passed with unbearable tedium. Reginald knew their plan was near-foolproof, yet he was still intensely anxious, mostly on account of Natalie's feelings. Narendi Ram made his way to the train station around midday with the sleeping powder. Once the drilling ended and the officers returned to their bungalows for tea, Reginald and Waverley tried on their disguises and practised speaking in Pashtu to each other.

'Well, old boy, do you think this is going to work?' Waverley asked.

'It should,' Reginald replied.

They waited until the long shadows were beginning to stretch across the ground and the sunlight was glinting off the domes of Peshawar before stealing out the back door of the bungalow. Reginald brought his revolver with him just in case, and he was also equipped with a long sharpened knife which every Pathan wore.

They waited, breathing heavily, underneath the almond trees, watching the top of the wall for a sign of Natalie. Finally, there was movement and Natalie appeared. This time, however, she was not alone.

'Must you always watch the sunset by yourself?' came a familiar mocking voice.

Reginald's blood turned to ice in his veins. It was McAuliffe!

'Let me stand here with you, Natalie. Or do you already have someone to keep you company?'

Reginald gasped. They were right above him, silhouetted against the sky. McAuliffe was touching her back while she regarded him defiantly.

'I admit that I've been spying on you,' continued McAuliffe with a harsh laugh. 'Either you really enjoy talking to yourself or there's someone who comes to you every night.'

He peered down among the trees, but Reginald and Waverley were well hidden.

'Oh, Jack, I never have anyone to talk to, so I talk to myself,' said Natalie, with incredible self-possession. 'Why don't you give me a companion, some young servant girl to be my friend? Why must I be a prisoner in solitary confinement? My heart will break of loneliness!'

'You have me, darling. It's your own fault you won't come near me or say a kind word to me every now and then.'

He continued to touch her, his hand getting incrementally lower on her back. It took all of Reginald's strength of will not to shoot him.

'You know that I detest you, Jack,' said Natalie.

McAuliffe appeared taken aback. 'But why? What have I done that you should hate me? You can't still be in love with that scrawny runt of a Fubster! Once you and I are married, you'll have everything your heart desires. Won't you be proud of me as your husband?'

His grasping fingers had reached the extremity of Natalie's lower back, and she whirled on him fiercely.

'Remember what your father said!' she warned. 'You can't touch me until we're married.'

'My father isn't here, and he doesn't have to know,' Jack said. 'You're in my power, Natalie. You might as well surrender and enjoy yourself.'

'Jack! For pity's sake! Give me five minutes alone! Then you may do what you like with me.'

'Five minutes, eh?' he grinned, pleased with her sudden capitulation. Then his eyes narrowed suspiciously. 'Are you sure you don't have a lover out there?'

'Where would he be?' said Natalie, gesturing to the open spaces between the wall and the cantonment.

'Five minutes, my dear.'

McAuliffe climbed down.

Reginald wiped the sweat off the hand that held the revolver. It had been shaking uncontrollably. He and Waverley waited until they heard the muffled sound of a door closing, then, in a moment, he climbed the wall, keeping his head down and out of sight of the house.

'Hurry, Natalie!' he said, taking hold of her hand.

Suddenly, the door to the house burst open, and McAuliffe reemerged. Reginald raised his head; his and McAuliffe's eyes met. In the twilight, Jack saw what looked like a Pathan grab hold of Natalie.

'What the devil!' Jack cried. 'Help, help! They're taking Natalie!'

'Oh, Reginald, what are we going to do?' Natalie gasped.

'Run for it!' he urged, grabbing hold of her hand. He helped her down from the wall to where Waverley was waiting below.

'We haven't much time,' he said to Waverley. 'You go ahead with Natalie, I'll cover our rear.'

They hurried along the path toward the cantonment, Waverley holding Natalie's hand and Reginald at their heels.

'Who goes there!' cried a harsh British voice from up ahead.

'Turn around, quickly!' Reginald ordered.

As they set off in the opposite direction, there was a commotion of voices.

'Where'd they go?' said one.

'This way, I'm sure of it,' replied a voice Reginald recognised as McAuliffe's.

'Waverley, take Natalie to the train station,' Reginald ordered. 'I'll stay here and hold them off.'

'No, I won't let you,' Natalie said. 'They'll kill you.' Reginald could see the silver shimmer of tears in her eyes. 'I'll give myself up. You two get away.'

Reginald's heart was torn. They couldn't stop now; they might never get this chance again. He didn't care if he died as long as Natalie escaped. Waverley would take care of her, and as long as he took McAuliffe with him, he would go in peace. Meanwhile, the voices of the pursuers, which were swelling to a tumult, drew closer.

'Please,' Natalie whispered.

He recognised the sacrifice she was willing to make because she loved him. He had to obey her.

With an almost imperceptible nod, he motioned to Waverley and they stole off into the shadows along the side of the road. McAuliffe and his servants arrived a moment later.

'Natalie, what happened?' he asked, seeing her lying on the road.

'Help! Help!' she cried hysterically.

'Tell me what happened!' McAuliffe demanded, shaking her roughly.

'A Path…' her voice broke.

'Why didn't you cry out? Did you want them to take you?'

Natalie tried to protest, but Jack wouldn't listen. He forced her to her feet and dragged her after him.

'Look for the Pathans,' he ordered the servants. 'Natalie and I are going inside, to *talk*.'

As he passed by their hiding spot, Reginald had a clear shot at him. Every moral fibre in his being demanded him to pull the trigger. This was his chance to execute justice. His finger touched the cold metal, but as he felt it, the promise he'd made to Natalie gripped his conscience.

He lowered the gun. A moment later, McAuliffe and Natalie rounded a bend and vanished into the night.

The would-be rescuers remained where they were, too shocked to move and too afraid to imagine what was happening to Natalie, until long after the moon had risen and the stars were shimmering in the heavens above. At last, Reginald turned to Waverley.

'Let's go home,' he said.

They plodded back to the bungalow in silence. Reginald collapsed in a chair while Waverley paced back and forth frantically.

'What are we going to do?' Waverley cried.

'Go back to your bungalow and get some rest. We'll talk in the morning.'

Waverley reluctantly took his leave. Before he also retired, Reginald took up the letter he had written to Lieutenant Willoughby, which the latter had left on the table, and held it up to a candle. As it turned to ashes, so did his hopes. He stayed up late into the night, cursing the strange twist of fate which had once again separated him from the woman he loved.

While gazing at the distant stars, he had an overwhelming sense of his powerlessness.

God was against him. And God's will would always triumph over his.

## Trouble for the Raj

LIEUTENANT WILLOUGHBY WAS quite surprised to find the next morning that the letter was gone and Reginald had resumed his usual routine. When he inquired into the reasons for this strange behaviour, he received a promise from Reginald that everything would be explained in due time. Narendi Ram, who had faithfully waited at the train station into the early hours of the morning, was eager to hear what had happened. Reginald gave him an abbreviated version and tasked him with finding out how the event was being interpreted by the nabobs and their servants.

Reginald heaved a sigh of relief when Narendi Ram reported that evening. The talk among the nabobs' retainers in the bazaar was that a couple of marauding Pathans, probably from beyond the border, who were wont to pillage during times of hardship, had tried to make off with the daughter of one of the nabobs. They had fled once their activities had been discovered.

There was nothing in this to implicate Reginald or Waverley or to even alert the McAuliffes to their presence in Peshawar, as long as they accepted this version of events. However, the failed attempt would certainly mean that Natalie would be guarded even more closely, and their sunset visits would be at an end. There was nothing to do now but be patient and wait for another opportunity.

We must explain what was going on in the world at large during this time. In Europe, a fragile peace had been restored. The ferocious German Spring Offensive of 1918 had ground to a halt without breaking through the Allied lines. Meanwhile, a million American soldiers, nicknamed 'doughboys' by the English and French for their plump and healthy appearance, had arrived ready to fight. This influx of soldiery, in addition to the handy invention of the armoured tank by Great Britain, finally broke the stalemate on the Western Front. As the Allied juggernaut rumbled toward Berlin, the German populace, driven to starvation rations by the Royal Navy's blockade, took to the streets demanding peace.

At last, the old warhorse Kaiser Wilhelm II, who had been preaching a doctrine of no surrender, was ousted from power, and the Germans signed an armistice on November 11, 1918, the eleventh minute of the eleventh hour of the eleventh day. The war to end all wars was over.

As the peace delegates gathered at the opulent Palace of Versailles, it soon became clear that negotiating the peace would be just as difficult as fighting the war. The British and French were eager to punish Germany for its aggression and divide up the conquered colonies among themselves. American president Woodrow Wilson, on the other hand, advocated for the self-determination of all oppressed peoples in order to make the world safe for democracy. His famed Fourteen Points included a provision for the establishment of a League of Nations to serve as an arbitrator between countries and thereby prevent the outbreak of another war. The Allies were none too pleased.

'God gave us Ten Commandments that we could not keep,' quipped French premier Georges Clemenceau. 'Now Wilson has given us fourteen.'

Wilson's idealistic dreams failed to materialise when his own country rejected the Treaty of Versailles and refused to join the League of Nations. Great Britain and France duly divided up the German colonies in Africa, reneged on their promise to liberate the Arabs and seized their land too, and humiliated Germany with the most scandalous treaty provisions ever devised. The seeds for another more terrible war were sown.

In the West, the Great War created a profound crisis of confidence. The technological advancements of the Industrial Revolution, which were meant to advance the cause of civilisation, had been used instead to create the weapons that had taken millions of lives. Disillusionment gave way to despair, and the Europeans, instead of examining themselves to discover the cause of the catastrophe in their own pride and greed, attacked instead the very ideas of truth, goodness, and beauty that they should have clung to. The past was rejected, and an entirely new course was set which was to rely on man's power alone. Western civilisation with its glorious history from Greece to Rome to the inestimable heritage of the Christian centuries, the Renaissance, and the Age of Enlightenment had morphed into something unrecognisable.

On paper, the British Empire was stronger than ever. It was still the 'empire on which the sun never set' with an even larger percent of the earth's surface under its flag and its bitterest enemies soundly defeated. Yet in many ways, the end of the Great War marked the end of the era of European ascendancy. The colonised peoples, used to viewing their white masters as something akin to gods, had seen them with their own eyes perish miserably in the trenches, fighting a pointless war. Once they returned home and were supposed to resume the mantle of subordination, they began to spread rumours that the white man, despite all of his technological wizardry, was no better than they were and had no right to rule them.

Celebrations swept India for the end of the war and the proud part that the Indians had played along with their British overlords. However, at the same time, many Indians, especially those who had received a Western education, were growing restive under the British yoke, and to top it all off, Gandhi was on the move. He had won a small but symbolically significant victory in his own state of Gujarat, lowering the tax burden on impoverished farmers. His next step was to try to consolidate support among his Muslim countrymen.

On the Frontier, the situation in early 1919 became volatile. The Amir of Afghanistan demanded a seat at Versailles and was condescendingly dismissed by the British viceroy. He did not have long to nurse his grievance, however, before he was assassinated in his tent by his own son. A bloody struggle for the throne ensued, pitting the Amir's murderer Amanullah against the Amir's brother, Nasrullah Khan. Amanullah eventually triumphed and had his uncle thrown into prison, demonstrating once again the extent of his familial piety. Alas, there were rumblings among the populace that he had seized power illegitimately. Amanullah promised reforms, and when these failed to appease his detractors, he decided that declaring war on British India would be the best way to unite his highly fractured country.

The tides of history have a way of sweeping up both great and small and carrying them along a course they would never have chosen for themselves. Such was the case with Reginald, Waverley, and Natalie as a war they had nothing to do with and did not want came suddenly crashing into their lives, adding another level of peril to an already tense situation.

# The Butcher of Amritsar

WE RESUME OUR narrative in the spring of 1919. Reginald was getting restless. It had been four months since their failed rescue attempt. Every day, he looked for a sign of Natalie, but she remained a prisoner. Waverley, for his part, was heartbroken. He regarded the hand which had held Natalie's as something sacred and would nearly burst into tears every time he studied it. Privately, Reginald concocted bold plans for a siege of the McAuliffe mansion and the liberation of the fair lady held there.

Storm clouds were gathering over the Afghan mountains. A sense of dread infused all of the soldiers of the Corps of Guides as their training took on a much more serious, urgent tone. As the news of the downfall of Habibullah trickled in from over the border, the officers knew that they were confronting a potential explosion. The tribesmen, who were rarely peaceable in the best of times, were in a state of agitation, and there were even riots among the Pathan inhabitants of Peshawar which had to be put down by force.

One evening, Colonel Thornwood called together all of the officers in the Corps of Guides to a meeting in his study.

'Gentlemen, I'm afraid we are on the threshold of another Afghan war.'

There was a great deal of murmuring and headshaking among the officers.

'Now, now, it's possible that this all might blow over. My greatest concern, however, is for our men. Are they loyal to us or to their tribes? You never know for certain. There were officers in '57 (the Sepoy Mutiny) who would have sworn on their lives that their men would never revolt.'

'What would you have us do?' Captain Scott asked.

'We all need to be vigilant,' replied the colonel. 'If you hear any whisper of disaffection, report it immediately. Captain Quebly, I want your regiment to take charge of fortifying the cantonment. We can't let rioting in the bazaars spill over into the civil lines.'

'Should we call for regiments from Rawalpindi and Mewar?' asked a grizzled lieutenant.

'They'll have their own problems to deal with,' replied the colonel. 'No, we'll have to trust in our own strength for the time being.'

A week later, the cantonment received a piece of shocking news. There had been a dreadful massacre in the Sikh holy city of Amritsar, and now protests were sweeping all of British India. Colonel Reginald Dyer had ordered his troops to fire into a crowd of unarmed men, women, and children who had gathered in a peaceful demonstration. The colonel purposefully directed the firing into where the crowd was thickest, with the intent to kill as many as possible. While Dyer justified his actions by claiming he had 'saved India,' many senior officials in the Raj, Colonel Thornwood included, were appalled. Gandhi himself paid a visit to the holy city to commemorate the martyrs of Amritsar.

Dyer's hard-fisted tactics had the opposite effect, and instead of quelling opposition to British rule, it increased it a hundredfold. Disaffection spread like wildfire across the Punjab, reaching the Frontier Provinces by early May. It became too dangerous for an Englishman to walk about in Peshawar without an armed guard. Drums beat in the city all day and all night, adding to the general unease. The commissioner of the Northwest Provinces, Sir George Roos-Keppel was finally forced to call all Europeans to withdraw within the safety of the fortified cantonment.

An assembly of all the British in Peshawar was called with Commissioner Roos-Keppel and Colonel Thornwood presiding.

Reginald attended with hopes of seeing Natalie somewhere in the crowd. He glanced eagerly around at the vast assemblage of people in the cavernous and ornately decorated *diwan* (meeting hall) of the commissioner's building, but there was no sign of her anywhere. He did, however, catch sight of a familiar face, albeit a hated one: Jack McAuliffe, seated with his father at the front.

'Now that we are all gathered, does anyone have any objections to the order to withdraw to the cantonment for the time being?'

'I have an objection, Your Honour,' sneered the elder McAuliffe, rising to his feet. 'I believe I speak for all of my colleagues.' He motioned to the pompous nabobs sitting around him. 'Our homes are outside of the fortifications. We demand that you post soldiers to defend them.'

'I appreciate your concerns, Mr McAuliffe,' replied the commissioner. 'But as of this moment, we do not have the soldiers to spare. I think in this instance, your lives must be considered more important than your property.'

'Ha! That's easy to say for someone whose interests lie entirely within the cantonment! What about my armament factory within the city and the assets of these other gentlemen?'

'I'm sorry that we cannot make a more comprehensive defence at the current time. I have sent a telegram to the Viceroy requesting aid, but he has been slow to reply.'

'Well then, if the government won't protect us, we'll protect ourselves,' said McAuliffe.

'Don't be foolish,' implored the commissioner. 'There's no guarantee of the loyalty of your Pathan militias. You'll be much safer in the cantonment. Please reconsider!'

Leopold, Jack, and the other nabobs stomped out of the room.

Reginald hurried back to his bungalow soon after and called a council of war with Waverley and Narendi Ram. This time, he decided to include Lieutenant Willoughby, whom he gave a brief overview of the situation.

'The McAuliffe palace is outside the cantonment and thus open to attack,' said Reginald. 'That means Natalie is in danger.'

'What should we do?' Waverley cried.

'We have to free her as soon as possible,' Reginald said with a determined glint in his eye.

'It's a risky business, old boy,' said Lieutenant Willoughby, stroking his moustache. 'Say all this hullabaloo fizzles out in the next couple of days. Then you're guilty of trespassing and carrying off a man's fiancée.'

'That's a risk we have to take,' replied Reginald.

'Yes!' exclaimed Waverley ardently. 'I would rather die than see her come to any harm!'

Reginald looked over at his servant who, once again, was sitting quietly with his hands folded.

'What do you think, Narendi Ram? Should I do nothing?'

'I advise you now, as before, to wait until the opportune time,' he said slowly. 'Remember what happened when you tried to force the issue.'

'I agree with Narendi,' said Willoughby. 'There's no sense in acting until you are absolutely sure Natalie is in danger.'

'Perhaps,' admitted Reginald. 'But how will we know? I'd say she's in enough danger now.'

'I will go into the bazaars and listen to the rumours,' said Narendi Ram.

'And we all will keep a watch out,' said Willoughby. He yawned. 'Now if you'll excuse me, gentlemen, I'd best be off to bed.'

Reginald retired that night frustrated and with a terrible feeling of foreboding. When he finally slipped off into an uneasy sleep, he saw a dreadful vision of McAuliffe mansion surrounded by a horde of wild Pathans, armed to the teeth. A flaming torch was thrust into an open window, and the mansion had soon become a blazing inferno. Natalie climbed out onto the roof and stood poised ready to jump. Reginald cried out in terror as she toppled through the air toward the waiting mob below…

His eyes flew open as she hit the ground. He was lying in a cold puddle of sweat, but was immensely relieved that the terrible scene he had just witnessed had been nothing more than a dream. Or had it? Glancing out the window, he saw that the stars were fading as the first light of dawn crept over the horizon. He rose, washed his face, and strapped his revolver to his belt.

India was calm that morning. The bright parrots sang in the trees and the langur monkeys chattered happily among themselves. A gentle breeze ruffled his hair as he set off down the road toward the McAuliffe mansion. Soon enough, the hot sun would be glowering down from above, signalling the travails of another Indian day, but for now, everything seemed right with the world.

He plodded along the little path covered with fragrant almond blossoms toward the familiar place on the wall where Natalie used to sit. He had just about reached it when a harsh voice cut through the morning stillness.

'Don't you take another step. I'm armed, you know!'

Reginald looked up in astonishment as a man stepped out from behind a tree a few paces ahead. The voice sounded strangely familiar. He thought for a moment and came suddenly to the realisation that it was the same voice that had accosted them on the night of the failed rescue attempt.

'Who are you and what are you doing here?' said the man. 'Be quick about it or I'll shoot!'

'I am a British officer in the Corps of Guides,' replied Reginald calmly.

'Oh! I'm sorry, sir!' the man replied, lowering his gun and attempting an awkward salute. 'I thought you was one of dem derned Pathans prowlin' 'bout.'

Reginald approached closer and got a good look at him. He was a short, squat man, of a corpulent build, with two great bushy sideburns framing either side of his baggy face. He spoke with a distinctive Cockney accent.

'What is your name, sir?' Reginald asked.

'Wilbur Dobbins, at your service.'

'Very good, Mr Dobbins. And who appointed you as sentry over this precinct?'

'Why, my master did, sir. He's the one who lives in the big house yonder.' He inclined his head toward the McAuliffe mansion.

'His name?'

'Leopold McAuliffe, sir.'

'Well, my friend, you can rest assured that you are not the only man who is concerned for the safety of that household. The Corps of Guides takes an interest in it as well. If you get word of any danger, I want you to inform me immediately.'

'How, sir?' Dobbins asked, genuinely convinced of Reginald's authority.

'Fire your rifle into the air thrice in quick succession. I will be waiting with my men to come to your aid. Don't tell anyone about this, either. It wouldn't do to have the commissioner get wind of it.'

The signal and secrecy agreed upon, they shook hands, the simple man's suspicions unaroused by what appeared to be a reasonable request. Reginald returned to his bungalow, relieved that he would at least be forewarned if Natalie was in peril.

## The Guides March

WITH THE ASCENT of the sun, the drums beat louder in the Peshawar bazaars. The noise of agitation and rioting extended to the cantonment itself. Captain Scott gathered together his officers and read them their orders:

'Colonel Thornwood commands us to make a show of strength in Peshawar City. We are to march out of the cantonment in full battle regalia and clear the streets in the bazaar. There we will present to the populace this proclamation which reads as follows: Citizens of Peshawar, the following laws are to be put into effect immediately. A curfew of 10:00 will be enforced. Anyone found out and about after this hour will be arrested. Gatherings of more than ten persons are prohibited. Anyone found guilty of violating this Statute will likewise be arrested. The city of Peshawar is now under martial law. Signed by Commissioner of the Northwest Provinces, Sir George Roos-Keppel, under the authority of the Lord Chelmsford, Viceroy of India. Are there any questions, men?'

'Are any relief regiments on their way?' asked Lieutenant Willoughby.

'We received word from Delhi this morning that two regiments are en route. However, it should be at least two weeks before they arrive. Anything else? No? Well then, get ready and have the men assembled to march out by eight o'clock precisely.'

Reginald and Waverley quickly returned to their bungalows and dressed themselves in their service uniforms. Reginald loaded his revolver and stuck it in his belt and strapped on a sabre that one of his favourite *sowars* (Indian cavalrymen) had presented to him when he was a boy in Delhi. He quivered with anticipation. Finally, after countless hours of drilling and mock battles, they were going to see some action.

He mounted a horse and took his position near the rear of the column of soldiers, with Waverley directly opposite. Like Reginald, Waverley was nearly overcome by nervous excitement. It gave him a primal thrill to be riding out to battle, a trait inherited from the countless generations of aristocratic forebears.

The regiment marched swiftly along the main road to Peshawar. Rickshaw drivers, full-bearded Mussulmen, and washing women in their vibrant *saris* stood aside to watch the Guides pass in respect. They had soon reached the university, a graceful Indo-Saracenic structure on the outskirts of the city. The cricketers on the front lawn took a break from their game to marvel at the display of force.

A moment later, they left behind the broad and orderly boulevards of the British quarter for the narrow and pungent streets of Peshawar City. Reginald noticed that there was an extraordinary number of people out that day, very few of whom seemed to be actually working.

Most were simply milling about, casting a spell of restiveness and anticipation over the city. Cries of 'Quit India' erupted from some of the bolder members of the rabble, while others jeered at the passing soldiers.

'The impudent rascals,' Willoughby muttered under his breath.

As they neared the bazaar, the crowds grew so thick, they were nearly impenetrable.

'Stand aside or we'll shoot!' ordered Captain Scott forcefully.

This was a tense moment. If the crowd did not part, there could be another Amritsar, and who knew when the violent reprisals would end. The crowd stood staring with their dark eyes and emotionless faces as the soldiers raised their rifles. All at once, somebody at the head of the crowd stepped aside, and the courage for continued resistance collapsed. The crowd had fully parted almost instantaneously afterward. There was a broad square at the centre of the bazaar, with two grand domed mosques at either end. Here, Captain Scott called a halt and read the proclamation from the commissioner. The throngs listened solemnly and then began to disperse.

This duty completed, Captain Scott divided up the regiment into squadrons with their own copies of the proclamation to post at various intervals around the city. The commissioner hoped that this display of authority would be enough to cow the populace into submission without the need to keep an armed guard over the city. The city police were vested with the authority to call for further military aid if they deemed it necessary. Fortunately, in this instance, the sight of the legendary Corps of Guides on the march had been enough to disperse the storm clouds for the time being.

Their mission fulfilled, the Guides returned to the cantonment for the night, and Reginald heaved a sigh of relief. Unfortunately, his relief was not to last long.

# The Declaration of War

BEYOND THE KHYBER Pass, in the inhospitable and barbarous country of Afghanistan, Amir Amanullah convened his chief ministers to inform them of his momentous decision. He was going to invade British India. Amanullah's reign from the start had been marred by controversy, and now, internal rebellion threatened to fracture an already divided country into a hundred pieces. The Amir's strategy was thus to unite the warring factions against a common external foe and offer for them as a prize the city of Peshawar, long claimed by Afghanistan.

On May 3, 1919, a day after the Guides' march, Afghan forces crossed the border and seized the town of Bagh on the Khyber Pass. News of this attack soon reached the commissioner's office via telegram, and an urgent message was relayed to the viceroy for assistance. The promised regiments from Delhi were still a week away from arriving, and who knew what tidings of the invasion might do to sway the loyalty of the Pathans against the British.

By midmorning, the news of the Afghan invasion had reached the Peshawar cantonment. Colonel Thornwood called all of his officers together and presented them with a new set of orders.

'Gentlemen, the Third Afghan War is upon us,' said the colonel, his eyes alight with a strange fire. 'I was but a lad when the previous conflict broke out, and I can remember clearly to this day the sight

179

of all my heroes, my father included, marching out to the Frontier. What a glorious day that was!' His eyes misted over momentarily in remembrance. 'Now, gentlemen, we face the same circumstances as our illustrious forebears. Will we, like them, rise to glory and immortality on the field of battle? The question is for us to decide.'

There was hardly a man among the officer corps who was not moved by this eloquent speech.

'The commissioner has given me the following orders,' continued the colonel. 'We must ensure that the city of Peshawar is not engulfed by riots before the regiments from Delhi arrive. Captain Quebly, your regiment is tasked with patrolling through the city today, while Captain Scott's regiment will remain to garrison the cantonment. Once the Delhi regiments have entered the city, the Guides will march to Jamrud to reinforce the Khyber Rifles. Do you understand your assignments, men?'

The officers nodded.

'Good! Now, we haven't a moment to lose!'

The drums had resumed their activity in the bazaars of the city. The residents of the Peshawar cantonment were warned to remain within their homes lest they become the victim of a Pathan sniper's bullet. Reginald was posted with a squadron of men on the far side of the cantonment, which faced an expanse of cultivated land and scattered mud-brick villages. From this distance, the drums were just a slight reverberation in the distance. As the burning Indian sun rose higher into the sky, Reginald began to sweat uncontrollably, so badly that his revolver continually slipped out of his hand and clattered onto the ground. He strained with all his might to hear a signal from Mr Dobbins. To his overexcited imagination, every distant sound he heard was that of gunfire, and every time he heard something, he gave a violent start. By the midafternoon, the sweat and strain finally proved too much for him, and he fainted clean away.

When he came to, he was lying in his bed in the bungalow. A concerned Waverley and Narendi Ram were seated by the bed while Lieutenant Willoughby was smoking his pipe in the corner.

'Reginald! Thank God you're all right!' cried Waverley.

'What happened to me?' Reginald asked.

'Heatstroke,' said Willoughby.

'My goodness! Well, I hope the cantonment wasn't attacked while I was unconscious.'

'It wasn't,' said Willoughby. 'Our regiment is to relieve Captain Quebly's men in Peshawar tomorrow at dawn. You, however, are to remain in bed and recover your strength.'

Before Reginald could protest, Willoughby handed him an order signed by Captain Scott.

'Tell the captain I'm actually feeling much better,' said Reginald, getting dizzily to his feet. He clutched onto the side of the bed to keep himself from toppling over.

'I don't think so,' said Willoughby. 'Narendi Ram, make sure he stays in bed tomorrow.'

He rose and went out to the verandah to finish smoking his pipe.

Reginald tossed the order aside in frustration.

'Don't worry about it, old boy,' said Waverley. 'It's only one day, and besides, you'll be closer to Natalie, in case anything happens.'

All of the anxiety Reginald had felt that day on Natalie's behalf came suddenly rushing back. He staggered and nearly fell. Waverley regarded him with great concern.

'Make sure you get some rest.'

He said goodbye and took his leave.

'Is there anything you need, sahib?' Narendi Ram asked.

'I don't think so, Narendi.'

Narendi bowed his head gracefully and departed. Reginald lay back down in his bed and tried to get to sleep. The drums in the bazaar were still beating, and every once in a while, there would be a distant shout or crack of gunfire. As can easily be imagined, falling asleep in these circumstances was extremely difficult. Reginald tossed and turned, trying to keep himself from thinking about Natalie. However, this only served to increase his anxiety to a fever pitch.

Finally, he got up and started pacing his room. This succeeded in allaying his frazzled nerves somewhat, but when he crawled back into bed, the fears returned. Thus, throughout all of the long watches of the night, he alternated between pacing and lying in bed. By the time the sun crept over the horizon, he had not slept a wink.

# The Siege of McAuliffe Manor

REGINALD ROSE AND splashed some water on his face. He surveyed his haggard and bloodshot appearance in the mirror with dismay.

*I'm a fright*, he thought. *Perhaps I should just stay in bed.*

The sound of a distant gunshot persuaded him otherwise. He struggled into his uniform, loaded his revolver, and even strapped his sabre to his belt for good measure. It was imperative that he spoke to Mr Dobbins and warn him of the danger that surely would be heading his way.

On his way out the door, Reginald was stopped by Narendi Ram.

'Where are you going, sahib?' asked the faithful servant.

'For a walk,' he replied simply.

'Sahib, Lieutenant Willoughby wanted me to make sure you stayed inside today.'

'Oh? And when did you start taking orders from Lieutenant Willoughby?'

'I want what is best for you, sahib, as he does.'

'Get out of my way!' Reginald snarled, pushing him aside.

He hurried to the edge of the cantonment where he discovered, to his chagrin, a battalion of soldiers was posted. Their commander, a grizzled lieutenant by the name of McSneed, saluted Reginald.

'Mornin', Fubster. Excellent day, wot?'

'Yes, excellent day,' replied Reginald sarcastically. 'I need to pay a visit to a friend in that house over there. Is that possible?'

'I'm afraid not, old boy, Colonel's orders, you know.'

Reginald gazed helplessly at the distant palace. With a sigh of resignation, he sat down underneath the spreading boughs of a deodar to wait. The sun was blazing in the sky like a furnace; sweat poured down from his face and soaked his clothes. Yet in spite of this discomfort, he felt extremely drowsy, so much so that he could barely keep his eyes open. Soon, he was dozing off.

'Sahib?' came a voice and a gentle prod on his shoulder.

Reginald's eyes flew open to see Narendi Ram standing above him.

'Narendi, what on earth are you doing here?' he said angrily.

Narendi Ram's reply was cut short by a cry from Lieutenant McSneed.

'Bless my soul! Look, men, there's a rabble headed our way!'

Reginald leapt to his feet and rushed to McSneed's side. Sure enough, a mob of Pathans was advancing along the path that led to the nabob mansions. Some were armed with modern rifles, others with *jezails*, and still, others with only knives or curved swords known as *tulwars*. Their purpose was clearly to loot the riches of the mansions as they would stand no chance against regular soldiers.

'Should I give the order to fire, sir?' asked McSneed's sergeant.

'No, wait to be fired upon first, I say. Don't want to be the aggressors, you know.'

As the rabble drew closer, a few of the Pathans took aim with their rifles at the watching soldiers.

'Get down, men!' McSneed ordered.

The bullets whizzed harmlessly over their heads.

'Take aim and let the beggars have it!' McSneed shouted.

A simultaneous volley exploded from the rifles of the defenders. A wide swathe of the rabble was cut down, and the rest scattered.

'That'll teach the beggars a lesson!' McSneed roared.

However, the mob soon regrouped and continued on its way to the mansions, this time out of range of the defenders.

'Hold your fire, men,' said McSneed.

'What are you doing? That mob will overrun those palaces!' said Reginald.

'My orders are to defend the cantonment,' replied McSneed. 'Those houses should've been evacuated already.'

Reginald paced up and down in a state of the utmost agitation imaginable as the rabble advanced on McAuliffe manor. Suddenly, he heard it, loud and unmistakable, the sound of a gun being fired three times in short succession, the signal from Mr Dobbins.

'Narendi, go get Waverley and Lieutenant Willoughby!' he ordered.

Before Narendi Ram could even open his mouth, Reginald took off at a dead sprint. He leapt over the barrier at the edge of the cantonment and toppled into the ditch that served as its moat. Picking himself up, he struggled to the top and took off toward the rabble.

'Fubster, what in damnation are you doing? Are you mad?' McSneed screamed. 'Come back here! Fubster! Fubster!'

Reginald was already too far away to hear him. As he ran, he drew his pistol from his belt. Up ahead, he could see Mr Dobbins and a group of servants holding out in front of the wall. They fired time and time again, but the mob surged irresistibly forward. Mr Dobbins tried to scramble over the wall and was grabbed from behind. A sword flashed and his head was severed cleanly from his shoulders. Reginald was still a hundred yards away as the Pathans mounted the wall and proceeded unimpeded toward the palace.

As he approached, Reginald changed his course, hoping to circle around to the far side of the mansion. Perhaps in the confusion of the attack, he would be able to slip in and out with Natalie. It was a faint chance no doubt, but it was the only course of action possible. Reginald's desperation gave extra strength to his legs, allowing him to reach the wall by the time the Pathans had begun their assault on the mansion. He scaled the wall in less than a heartbeat and paused on the top to survey the scene before him.

The mob had gathered around the front doors of the mansion, trying to force their way inside while defenders fired down on them from the upper windows. Part of the mob had split away from the main group and was heading straight for Reginald. Knowing he hadn't a moment to spare, he dropped from the wall and sprinted toward the house. Bullets whistled by him as a great shout went up from the Pathans.

He gained the palace wall and leapt with all his might for the high windowsill, just barely grasping it with his hand. The revolver slipped from his fingers as he struggled to pull himself up, bullets still exploding all around him. He drew his sabre, struck the window's pane of glass with the blunt end, and squeezed through into the house.

The room he entered was a sort of antechamber richly adorned and empty of inhabitants. He raced out into the hallway toward the grand staircase, all the while shouting Natalie's name at the top of his lungs. He passed several Indian maids and a terrified butler; he grabbed the latter and demanded to know where Natalie was, but the man, in his fear, had lost the ability to speak. He climbed the mansion's many staircases and threw open the door to seemingly every room until at last, on the topmost storey, he reached a locked door with a faint sound emanating from within.

A single powerful blow from Reginald's sabre was enough to force the door open. He burst into an elegant bedchamber, beautifully decorated and illuminated by sunlight streaming through several massive windows looking out over the city of Peshawar. In the centre of the room, in the midst of the four-poster bed, two people were struggling against each other. The one on top, a young man, was trying to kiss the young lady who lay beneath him while she was doing everything possible to evade him. Reginald realised to his horror that he was watching Jack McAuliffe and Natalie.

'Get your hands off her!' he screamed.

McAuliffe whirled around in astonishment and grabbed the revolver he had laid out beside the bed.

'Who are you?' he said, his hand shaking as he pointed the gun at Reginald.

'You don't recognise me?' Reginald said, stepping forward. 'I am Reginald Archibald Fubster, your sworn enemy and Natalie's protector!'

The expression of fear on McAuliffe's face instantly turned to one of gloating triumph.

'Fubster!' He lost himself in a fit of laughter. 'You're a little late to the party. Natalie is my wife now. We were married this morning. Sorry we didn't invite you. Oh well. Her fortune is mine by the way.'

Reginald felt as though his heart had been ripped from his body. He struggled to steady himself.

'All the money in the world won't do you any good if you don't get out of this house immediately,' he warned.

'What? You think I'm worried about that rabble outside? Those savages stand no chance against my men. Believe me, we're quite safe here.'

Reginald stared at him in amazement. Could he really be unaware of their impending destruction?

'You know what, Fubster, this couldn't be more perfect,' taunted McAuliffe with a grin from ear to ear. 'I'm so happy you're here to witness my victory. We stole Natalie from right under your nose. We knew you couldn't do anything, and your father was too busy charging at machine guns, patriotic fool that he was. Do you think you can stop me now? You swaggering, pompous little stooge! You're nothing! Your self-righteousness doesn't mean a thing. It's the strong who triumph in this world!'

Reginald looked from McAuliffe to Natalie, feeling more helpless than he ever had in his life. This was an absolute nightmare. It simply couldn't be true.

'Do you have anything to say for yourself? Do you admit defeat? No? Then I'm afraid it's goodbye. You're interrupting my honeymoon.'

He raised and cocked his revolver while Reginald could only stand there and brace himself.

'Fancy yourself a soldier? Time to die like one!'

Suddenly, Natalie lunged at McAuliffe, knocking him momentarily off balance. The revolver exploded, and the bullet whistled wide of Reginald, embedding itself in the door. McAuliffe struck Natalie with the butt end of the revolver and raised it again to shoot, but by that time, Reginald was upon him.

Grabbing McAuliffe by the scruff of the neck, he forced the revolver from his hand and administered several powerful blows to his face. McAuliffe, who was over a foot taller than Reginald and much more muscular, quickly regained the advantage. He tackled Reginald and beat his head into the ground until the blood was flowing freely, soaking Reginald's hair. Then he rolled off Reginald's prostrate body and reached for the revolver which had settled a short ways away.

Reginald drew his sabre from his belt and, his vision obscured by blood, swung it randomly. It connected with the revolver that McAuliffe had just raised to fire, catapulting it out of his hands and into the corner of the room. Reginald leapt to his feet in between McAuliffe and the gun and brandished his sabre threateningly.

'It's finished, McAuliffe,' he said. 'You take another step, and I'll cut you in two.'

McAuliffe gazed about wildly. His eyes alighted on the door, which was gaping wide open.

'This isn't over between us, Fubster!' he cried as he rushed into the hallway.

Unfortunately for McAuliffe, he escaped the frying pan to end up in the fire. The moment he rounded a bend, he came face-to-face with the howling mob of Pathans, who by now had breached the mansion and were scouring it for all the loot they could find. In a moment, he had been hacked to pieces.

Reginald could hear McAuliffe's screams and he knew that the Pathans were headed his way. He retrieved the revolver from the corner and gripped it in one hand while he held the sabre in the other. There was no time to see about a defence or to even help Natalie, who was lying in the bed, blood trickling from the place where McAuliffe had struck her.

The first Pathan came rushing into the room clutching a knife and heading straight for Natalie. Reginald dispatched him with a bullet. Three more entered, and Reginald felled them all with his revolver before realising to his immense agitation that he had only one bullet left.

Resolving to save it for when he had absolute need of it, he ran to the door with his sabre. Every time a Pathan stuck his head through the entranceway, Reginald slashed at him. In this way, he killed several more, causing the rest of the Pathans to lose heart and retreat down the hallway.

Scarcely pausing to recover his breath, Reginald dragged several dressers and chairs to the doorway to create a barrier that would allow him to attack the Pathans with his sabre while they tried to scramble into the room. This completed, he had just turned to care for Natalie when there was a fresh surge. These Pathans were equipped with *jezails*, and they sent a volley of bullets flying inaccurately into the room.

'Natalie, get beneath the bed!' Reginald shouted.

She made a tremendous effort to rise and crawl to safety. In the meantime, the Pathans drew their knives and started hacking at the furniture in their way. This provided the perfect opportunity for Reginald to thrust at them with his sabre. However, on one stroke, his sabre's blade collided with one of the Pathan tulwars and shattered, leaving Reginald with a useless hilt. Thinking quickly, he snatched up a jezail from one of the Pathans he had slain within the room and fired it. The bullet met its mark and the ferocious sound the gun had made scared the other Pathans off. Once again, they withdrew beyond the bend.

During this respite, Reginald replenished his arsenal with another *jezail* and an Afghan knife. He waited, blood and sweat pouring down his face, hoping desperately that the Pathans would not come again. For a long time, all he could hear was the distant sound of looting and shouting, then all at once a mighty clamour arose, as if an entire army was attacking. A volley of rifle fire split the air, followed by the deep bellow of a cannon. Reginald had just turned toward the window to observe the action below when he heard the sound he dreaded most, the harsh voices of Pathans heading his way.

The Pathans rushed forward, attacking Reginald's makeshift defences with their tulwars. Reginald shot one and stabbed another, but by that time, the others had broken through. One took a swipe at Reginald's head with his sword that Reginald barely ducked under. He slashed at the man's chest with his knife and wrested the sword out of his hand. Holding the sword out in defence, he retreated toward the bed, facing the three remaining Pathans.

One of the Pathans, seeing Reginald cornered, cocked his rifle and aimed. Before he could pull the trigger, however, Reginald hurled his sword and caught the man in his stomach; he fell with a hideous scream. This manoeuvre left Reginald unarmed except for the single-shot pistol in his belt. As one of the Pathans charged at him with his sword raised, he had no recourse but to shoot him. The other Pathan approached unimpeded, his knife pointed at Reginald's throat. He knew for certain he was going to die.

All of a sudden, out of nowhere, a British officer leapt into the room and, aiming his revolver, sent a bullet whistling into the back of the Pathan's neck just as he raised his knife above Reginald. The Afghan crumpled lifeless to the ground. Reginald staggered and would have fallen, had the officer not caught him up in his arms.

'Reginald! Thank goodness we got here in time!' cried Waverley, for it was Waverley indeed.

A moment later, Lieutenant Willoughby entered the room at the head of a squadron of soldiers.

'Looks like you've had your hands full, Fubster,' he said, surveying the bodies of the Pathans. 'It's a good thing we arrived when we did.'

'Natalie,' Reginald called hoarsely. 'Natalie, you can come out, we're safe!'

Natalie struggled out from underneath the bed and, with help from Reginald and Waverley, rose to her feet. Lieutenant Willoughby's jaw dropped open in astonishment.

'This is the girl?'

She attempted a curtsey, but her legs were so weak that they gave way.

'We need to get her to the hospital as soon as possible,' said Waverley.

'It looks like Reginald could use a visit too,' observed Willoughby. He turned to the soldiers. 'Go get some stretchers ready.'

Waverley and Lieutenant Willoughby made sure that Natalie was laid in a comfortable position on the bed. Reginald laid down beside her. She smiled at him and closed her eyes. In a moment, he too was fast asleep.

## The Court-Martial

REGINALD AWOKE SOMETIME late the following day to find himself lying in his own bed in the cantonments. His head was wrapped in bandages, and it ached abominably. He held it gingerly for a while before summoning up the strength to crawl out of bed. Waverley, Narendi Ram, and Lieutenant Willoughby were sitting around the table engaged in a sort of conference.

They looked up in surprise as Reginald entered.

'How are you?' Waverley asked.

'My head hurts, but besides that, I'm all right. Where's Natalie?'

'She is under the charge of Dr Mackenzie in the regimental hospital,' Lieutenant Willoughby replied.

Reginald gave a sigh of relief. Dr Mackenzie was renowned throughout the northwest provinces as a physician of consummate skill and professionalism. With him, Natalie was in good hands.

'May I go see her?' he asked.

'There will be time for that,' said Willoughby. 'But first, we have some serious business to discuss. Please sit down.'

He motioned to a seat that Waverley had pulled out for him. Reginald sat and looked at his friends with concern. What was this all about?

'Reginald, I'm sorry to say this, but Captain Scott was none too pleased to hear of your heroics yesterday. He is charging you with disobeying a direct order and commands you to stand before a court-martial that will be held tomorrow in Colonel Thornwood's office.'

A cold sweat broke out on Reginald's face. His bright prospects instantly evaporated.

'What can I do?' he gasped.

'Well, admittedly, the situation does not look good for you,' continued Willoughby. 'Your only hope, in my opinion, is to explain the entire situation from beginning to end and hope that the colonel, as a man of conscience, will have mercy on you.'

'What do you think the punishment will be?'

'You will almost certainly be stripped of your rank and dishonourably discharged from His Majesty's service. Beyond that, I have no idea.'

Reginald got to his feet. 'May I go and see Natalie now?'

'I'm sorry, old boy,' said Waverley. 'But I stopped by earlier, and the doctor told me that Natalie would not be able to receive any more visitors today.'

'How is she doing?'

'He said that she was healing quickly and that she should be out and about in a few days.'

'Thank goodness for that,' said Reginald, with a sigh of relief. 'Now, gentlemen, if you'll excuse me, I'm going out for a walk.'

He tried to say this calmly, but his voice was shaking.

The sun had just set over the city of Peshawar, and the stars were beginning to shimmer like diamonds in the vast expanse of the sky. So much had happened over the past few days. It was a confused and jumbled mess. How was he to make sense of it?

One idea that impressed his mind was that he had finally accomplished the goal for which he had directed all of his energy and passion for the past five years. Natalie had been found and rescued. McAuliffe, his archenemy, was dead. It seemed that his philosophy of life had been vindicated; it was his actions that had saved Natalie and rewritten their destinies. The cause of justice which had taken him through so many perplexing twists of fortune had finally been resolved.

At the same time, he was haunted by a sense of impending dread. There was the court-martial to worry about and, if he survived that, the war in Afghanistan. Who knew what other challenges and obstacles he and Natalie would have to face on their future journey toward happiness?

He realised that in his zeal for Natalie, he had intentionally broken the first rule of being a soldier: he had disobeyed an order. Hadn't his father warned him of this over and over in those early days of his education? Yet he had still done it, disgracing in one blow his father's name, his regiment, and his country. And in hindsight, he would do the same again.

When he had returned to his room, his thoughts took on an even gloomier mood, so that he fully expected to be condemned to death by the firing squad at the first light of dawn, having not slept a wink.

Narendi Ram entered the room and bid him good morning. He had come with some fresh bandages. Reginald suffered him to change them for his old ones, his mind embroiled all the while with feverish expectations.

'Sahib, I wanted to say that I will continue to be your servant and Miss Natalie's, no matter what the colonel decides,' said Narendi Ram.

Reginald looked closely at the dark-eyed Indian. He had the sudden thought that he was truly in debt to this young man. He had saved Narendi only once from a tiger, but Narendi Ram had encouraged him time and time again when his spirits were at their lowest ebb.

'Thank you! A man could not ask for a more faithful, kind-hearted friend than you, Narendi.'

Narendi helped him to his feet. Reginald dressed in his best uniform and went to join Waverley and Lieutenant Willoughby, who were already waiting for him on the verandah.

'Let's go,' said Willoughby.

They made their way along the path to the commissioner's building. Reginald's heart was mingled with gratitude for his friends and terror of his upcoming sentence. Colonel Thornwood's servant met them at the door and directed them to the colonel's office where an impressive assembly had already gathered. The colonel was seated at his desk examining a manuscript. Captain Scott stood nearby and the other officers in the Guides were seated against the wall. The colonel looked up when he saw Reginald enter. His stern visage cast a pall over Reginald's face.

'Ensign Fubster, please be seated here.' He motioned gravely to a chair in the centre of the room. 'You two gentlemen may take a seat with the rest of the officers.'

Waverley squeezed Reginald's hand and left to join the others. Reginald was acutely aware that every eye in the room was on him and thought he would perish of shame.

'Captain Scott, please present the charge against Ensign Fubster,' the colonel continued.

Captain Scott gravely stepped forward. 'I hereby charge Ensign Fubster with disobeying a direct order to stay in bed and rest himself signed by my own hand on the Fourth of May 1919 and delivered to him by Lieutenant Willoughby.'

'Lieutenant Willoughby, can you verify that the defendant received the said order?' asked the colonel.

'Yes, sir,' replied Willoughby, standing up. 'Ensign Nottingham, can you do the same?'

'Yes, sir,' replied Waverley weakly.

'It is alleged, Ensign Fubster,' continued the colonel, 'that instead of obeying this directive, you left your bungalow and mingled with the soldiers under the command of Lieutenant McSneed, imploring them to likewise ignore their express orders to remain within the cantonment in order to quell a mob of Pathans advancing on the mansions of the European community. It is also alleged that you departed from the safety of the cantonment fortifications to single-handedly charge at the mob, to the great hazard of life and limb and to the detriment of the morale of Lieutenant McSneed's troops. That you likewise enjoined your servant, one Narendi Ram, to invoke the aid of two of your fellow officers, Lieutenant Willoughby and Ensign Nottingham, who, in order to rescue you, were forced to draw their soldiers away from their strategic positions within Peshawar City.'

The colonel looked directly at Reginald. 'Those are the charges against you. How do you plead?'

'Guilty,' Reginald replied.

The onlookers shook their heads in disbelief.

'Now, I'm sure you know that these are serious charges and that the penalty will be severe. Do you have any words to say in your defence?'

'I do, sir. Though I don't expect to change anyone's mind or to soften the punishment I deserve. I know that what I did was wrong, and I apologise to everyone here for the disgrace I have caused.'

'Please proceed,' said the colonel.

'With your permission, Colonel, I need to call upon the witness of a young lady named Miss Natalie Prim. It was to save her from certain death that I disobeyed orders and committed all of the guilty actions for which I am charged.'

'Where is this young lady?'

'She is under the care of Dr Mackenzie at the regimental hospital.'

The colonel summoned his servant and charged him with bringing Natalie before the tribunal. In the meantime, the officers talked among themselves, and Reginald waited in agony, hoping that Natalie would be well enough to speak. He did not like his chances even so.

The door swung open, and Dr Mackenzie entered, leading Natalie by the hand. There was an audible gasp from the officers. Her face flushed as they stared at her. There was an ugly bruise on her forehead from where McAuliffe had struck her, but far from detracting from her beauty, it provided an added poignancy, reinforced by her gentle and long-suffering expression.

When she saw Reginald, she smiled with joy.

'Bring a chair for the young lady,' Colonel Thornwood ordered.

This was provided, and Natalie sat down beside Reginald. The colonel's face softened as he addressed her.

'Could you please tell us your name, miss?' he asked.

Natalie rose and gave a graceful curtsey to the assembly. 'My name is Natalie Prim, sir.'

The officers, to a man, were captivated by her. They stared in dumb astonishment.

Natalie caught sight of Waverley in the crowd and smiled at him.

'You have been brought here to serve as a witness for Ensign Fubster who has been charged with the serious offence of disregarding orders. We ask that you, to the best of your ability, affirm the truth of what Ensign Fubster is about to say. Do you understand?'

'Yes, I do, sir,' replied Natalie.

'You may begin, Ensign Fubster,' said the colonel, turning to Reginald.

'Thank you, sir,' Reginald replied and rose shakily to his feet. 'Gentlemen, if you will suffer me to describe my relationship with this young lady, I hope you will gain an insight into the motivation for my actions.'

He then began an account of the story that is recorded within these pages: his first meeting with Natalie at Fubster Manor, the perfidious scheme of the McAuliffes and their forced separation, his journey to find her and his captivity in Aqaba, his escape and return to India, his discovery of her in Peshawar, and finally his battle against McAuliffe and the Pathans. He had to pause several times to recover his composure. At intervals, Natalie was called upon to substantiate his claims, which she did with either a nod or a short 'yes, that is true.'

There was not an officer in the room who was not moved by the cumulative effect of the tale. The love between Reginald and Natalie was so obvious that it made them think of their own wives and sweethearts and ponder what lengths they would go to protect them. But the only man whose decision mattered was the colonel, and his emotions were concealed behind a blank face.

'Those are the reasons I felt compelled to come to Natalie's aid, even though it meant disobeying orders,' Reginald concluded. 'I submit myself to your judgement.'

The colonel called Captain Scott to his side and they held a brief conference in whispers.

'Why did you not bring this to our attention before?' asked the colonel aloud to Reginald. 'We are not men of stone here. We could have helped you. Leopold McAuliffe was a well-known scoundrel in these parts, and I'm sure there are not many mourning his death. It was his unfair business practices which sparked the riots of two days ago, during which the Pathans exacted a just revenge on the gun-smith and his family.'

He whispered some more with Captain Scott. Then he drew out a piece of paper and wrote for about five minutes. A tense, impatient silence hovered over the room. No one was more oppressed by it than Reginald, who assumed the colonel was writing out his death warrant.

'Ensign Fubster,' the colonel declared, as the atmosphere reached a breaking point, 'this court-martial finds you guilty of the charges as pled. Nevertheless, our judgement and the extent of punitive repercussions must take into account extenuating circumstances. In most every situation, disobeying orders is a serious crime and a breach of fundamental military law. How could we operate as an effective peace-keeping force if each officer simply did whatever he thought was best at the time? Order and discipline would immediately collapse. I hope you understand that, Mr Fubster. Actually, I'm sure you do, based on what you've said and the manner in which you were raised by your father.

'There are rare exceptions which do exist, however, that call for us to privilege our conscience over our duty when the two conflict. For example, an officer who is ordered by his superior to massacre civilians in clear violation of the laws of war and of humanity is justified in resisting that order. We must remember that we are not soldiers only, but men who serve a power even greater than that of country by upholding the dictates of divine commands.

'Again, I recommend caution in applying this principle, as it takes wisdom to discern when the earthly and the heavenly law are at odds. I do believe that Ensign Fubster wrestled with these thoughts and made a decision of conscience. To risk his life, reputation, and honour in what must have appeared a hopeless attempt to preserve the life of an innocent woman does not strike me as the flippant disregard for authority which is usually present in such cases. It is instead an act of valour or even of heroism.

'Therefore, as a result of the testimony, I am limiting the punishment inflicted on Ensign Fubster to a strong censure. He will not be removed from command. This is done in the expectation that he will be henceforth obedient to every order given and a loyal officer of the Indian Army. This court-martial is dismissed.'

Some of the old hands shook their heads, but most of the officers were pleased with the verdict. They came up to Reginald to congratulate him and pay their respects to Natalie, who curtseyed until she was quite worn out. Before every officer could take their turn, however, Dr Mackenzie decided that she had had quite enough stimulation for one day and advised her to return to the hospital to rest.

Reginald sought out Captain Scott, who had withdrawn from the others and had an unreadable expression on his face.

'Captain,' Reginald trembled, 'please forgive me.'

The captain waved his hand. 'If the colonel has absolved you, I do as well.'

Reginald could tell that the hurt lingered beneath the surface. He wished he could make it up and atone for the disappointment he had caused in a man he respected.

'That's enough socialising, men,' said the colonel to his officers. 'We've got a war to fight, if you'll remember. Return to your posts. Fubster, I'd like a word with you before you go.'

Reginald approached the colonel's desk.

'Yes, sir?' he asked.

'Take this and read over it carefully in private,' he said, putting the verdict of the court-martial in Reginald's hands.

'Thank you, sir. This is more than I deserved.'

'Don't let me down,' said the colonel sternly. 'This is the last warning I can give you.'

'I understand, sir.'

'Now we have some business to discuss. First, what is to become of the young lady?'

'I'm not sure, sir.'

The colonel stroked his moustache. 'From what I understand, it's a difficult situation. I'm having my orderly look into it. Her marriage to Jack McAuliffe is entered in the civil registry. But because he was killed that very day (as were his father and uncle) and the marriage was performed under compulsion, we may be able to strike it from the records. Now, there is also her fortune to consider. Is there a contact in England we can telegraph, a family attorney perhaps?'

'Not that I know of, sir.'

'Well, we'll figure something out. I'll schedule an appointment with Sir George Roos-Keppel (the commissioner) to talk the matter over, but in the meantime, the Guides will be moving into Afghanistan. I don't predict the fighting will last long, and after it's over, we'll turn our attention to the young lady's future.'

'Sir, thank you again,' said Reginald.

'It's the least I can do,' said the colonel.

He offered his hand, which Reginald shook, then they parted ways.

# Dr Mackenzie

IT NEEDS TO be mentioned that in the intervening period between Reginald's showdown with McAuliffe and the court-martial, the regiments from Delhi had arrived and restored order throughout Peshawar. The looting had been contained to two districts, one being of course the nabob mansions and the other a munitions factory within the city. The owner of the said factory, one Leopold McAuliffe, had been killed, but the factory had been saved by the timely intervention of the Guides. The Amir's plan of a general uprising in Peshawar as a prelude to his invasion had failed, and from now on, the initiative would be with the British.

All over India, regiments were being mustered and transported to the Frontier: Sikhs from the Punjab, Gurkhas from Nepal, Marathas from the Deccan, and Garhwalis from the Himalayas. Discontent among these legions was rife; many had been promised demobilisation at the end of the Great War and did not particularly relish the prospect of a hard-fought campaign in Afghanistan. Many of the frontier regiments, which were made up primarily of Pathans, had to be disbanded for fear of treachery. As a whole, however, the Raj's military council was convinced that they would be victorious and that the war would be of short duration.

The city of Peshawar was transformed into an armed camp. A strange and fascinating mixture of peoples had been assembled together.

Besides the polyglot Indian races, there were Englishmen from all over the Subcontinent, some old sahibs and others freshly arrived. Regiments of Scottish highlanders paraded by to the wailing of their bagpipes. Welsh infantrymen sang ditties they had learned in the trenches of France.

Equally intriguing was the mixture of weapons and equipment, ranging from the sleek and modern to the primordial. There were cavalry corps mounted on camels, field guns towed by elephants, and several fighter planes contributed by the Royal Air Force. The soldiers were equipped with lances, tulwars, khukuris (the signature knife of the Nepali Gurkhas), Enfield rifles, and machine guns.

Organising this mass of soldiery into an effective fighting force proved a nightmare for the British High Command. The Guides were forced to wait several days before they were issued definitive orders that they were to march to the Khyber Pass. Along with the Khyber Rifles, they would be serving as the vanguard of the assault into Afghanistan.

Reginald received this news with trepidation. Now that he had finally rescued Natalie, he was not anxious to leave her again so soon, especially for a dangerous expedition. The moment he heard the order, he hurried to the hospital to see her. The hospital was a handsome building, erected during the Second Afghan War to care for returning soldiers. Reginald entered and was greeted by a pretty nurse.

'I am here to see Miss Natalie Prim,' he said breathlessly.

'Oh yes. Right this way, please,' said the nurse.

She led him into a separate room, very nicely furnished and decorated. Natalie was sitting in bed, reading a book.

'A visitor to see you, Miss Natalie.'

She left and closed the door behind her.

Natalie looked up in joy as Reginald approached.

'How are you, Natalie?' he asked tenderly.

'Much better,' she replied. The bruise on her forehead had almost disappeared. 'I think the only reason they're keeping me here in the hospital is because I have nowhere else to go!'

Reginald sat beside her.

'How is your head?' Natalie asked.

'My head? Oh, it's fine. Hurts from time to time but nothing serious.'

She smiled.

'Natalie, I have some bad news. The Guides have been ordered to advance into Afghanistan. We leave at dawn.'

'I feared as much,' she said, a mournful look crossing her face. 'Fate always wants us apart, doesn't it?'

'I'm sorry, Natalie!' he cried. 'I can't believe I'm saying goodbye to you again. I promised I wouldn't let you go if I found you. But I don't know what to do. I'm a soldier, and I have to obey orders.'

Sensing the intensity of his inner struggle, she laid her hand on his arm. Her touch had an immediate soothing effect.

'Reginald, dearest, don't be troubled. I am safe here. You must do what is right. Your friends will look after you, and I will pray for you every day. It won't be long until we're together again. I promise.'

'Yes, and when I return...'

He proceeded to outline for her his plan of building a life for them both in the cool of the hills of Kashmir, describing in detail what their house would look like, what fruit trees they would plant, and which animals they would keep. They drifted back into the happy dreams of their youth which had sustained them through the long years of separation.

'Would you like that?' he asked when he had finished.

'Oh yes, Reginald, you know I would!' she said, her eyes shining.

Suddenly, however, a cloud passed over her face. She hid it a moment later with a smile, but there was something clearly bothering her.

'What is it?' he asked.

'It's nothing. Nothing important. Don't worry about it.'

The clock in the corner of the room tolled three o'clock, marking the end of visiting hours. The time had passed in a moment.

'Will you write to me?' he asked.

'I will write every day,' she said, then added, 'Wouldn't you like to kiss me before you go?'

'May I?' Reginald asked excitedly.

'I think you've earned it,' she said, laughing.

She presented her beautiful red lips, which he kissed quickly and blushed down to the roots of his hair. The years of suffering had been worth it for that moment. They embraced each other, and Reginald departed. On his way out of the hospital, he passed Dr Mackenzie, who was talking to a wounded British soldier.

'Ah, Mr Fubster?' he said, looking up. 'I'd like a word with you, if you don't mind.'

Reginald nodded.

'I'll talk to you later, Bert,' said the doctor to the soldier. 'Follow me if you would, Mr Fubster.'

Reginald followed the doctor into his office. The wall featured prominently a map of the United States of America and several paintings by the Hudson River School.

'Please have a seat,' said the doctor.

'Are you American, sir?' asked Reginald, noting the peculiar way in which the doctor spoke.

'I am. I was born and raised in New York City, where I studied medicine. Then I had a desire to see the world and India in particular, so I joined the Foreign Legion, and here I am.'

Reginald had always been curious about the American people from the stories he had read about life in the Wild West. Though Dr Mackenzie obviously did not fit his mental image of a coonskin cap–clad frontiersman, the doctor's manner nevertheless made a favourable impression on him. It was refreshing to meet someone who lacked the self-important snobbery ingrained in the British character.

'I wanted to talk to you about Miss Natalie. She is, on the whole, doing very well, but I would like to keep her in the hospital for a few days. There are a few examinations I need to perform since it's been so long since she's been seen by a physician. Overall, I will say that she has a remarkable strength of constitution and suppleness of mind. She's quite a gem, you know, the kind of girl you're lucky to meet once in a lifetime. In short, you needn't worry, we will do all we can for her and she'll be fine.'

'Thank you so much for all you've already done,' said Reginald, shaking the doctor's hand.

'I will write to you if there is any change in her condition,' said the doctor. 'Good luck to you.'

# 36

## *The Khyber Pass*

REGINALD SPENT THE rest of the afternoon and evening with Waverley and Lieutenant Willoughby preparing for the campaign. He tried on the new dun-coloured uniforms they would be wearing in Afghanistan. In his personal luggage, he made sure to include a few books on the Pashtu language, a concise history of Afghanistan, and copious writing materials for his letters to Natalie. Always a quick packer, Reginald was finished before either of his companions had reached the halfway mark.

Narendi Ram entered the room and sat down next to Reginald, who could tell by his face that something was troubling him.

'What is it?' he asked.

'Sahib, I will be going with you on this campaign, but I wish upon my soul that I was not.'

'Why?' asked Reginald, startled.

'I do not like these Pathans nor their country, and I would like to keep as far away from them as I can.'

'Aren't the Pathans Moslems, as you are?'

'That is true, sahib, but they are a disgrace to the faith of the Prophet. You will not find a more wicked and bloodthirsty race upon the face of the earth. It is truly said that they are the sons of Cain.'

Reginald looked at him quizzically.

Narendi explained an old legend that the biblical Cain, son of Adam, after killing his brother Abel, had journeyed east of the garden of Eden to Afghanistan and founded a city named Kabul. The Afghans were his descendants.

Reginald dismissed this as an old wives' tale but could not restrain an involuntary shudder at the thought of it. Everything he had seen so far of the land of Afghanistan and the people who lived there seemed to confirm this unfavourable appraisal.

'We will be quite all right, I promise you,' he said unconvincingly. 'The war won't take long, and we'll be back here before we know it.'

Narendi Ram sighed and went to gather his things.

Half an hour later, the four of them were out on the parade grounds where the regiment had been fully assembled and was ready to march. Reginald made sure that Narendi Ram was given a horse to ride before mounting his own and trotting briskly to the head of the column. As the Guides marched, they received hurrahs from the other regiments who thronged either side of the road to watch them pass. Reginald was filled with pride to be a part of this glorious assembly. He set his face toward the Afghan mountains with a determination that his men would be able to overcome anything the enemy might throw their way.

The Guides skirted the outskirts of Peshawar City by following a road that ran directly to the eastern terminus of the Khyber Pass. Situated in a broad valley ringed by furrowed and craggy hills, this outlet of the Khyber was controlled by the bastions of the massive Jamrud Fort. The Union Jack fluttered proudly from atop its lofty battlements. Here, the Guides reconnoitred, taking on an additional supply of rifles, ammunition, and field guns. The governor of the fort, Sir Ewart Winigan, met with the officers to inform them of the situation.

The fort at Landi Kotal on the opposite side of the Khyber Pass was in grave peril, its water supply severed when the Afghans had seized the nearby town of Bagh. To make matters worse, Landi Kotal was now being threatened by the Amir's marshal, Nadir Khan, and his army of Afghan regulars. The Guides were commanded to reinforce this garrison with all possible haste.

In order to reach it, however, the Guides would have to march through the length of the Khyber Pass, which was tribal territory.

'Let's move out, men,' Captain Scott ordered. 'We have a lot of ground to cover.'

They followed the road as it climbed up into the hills. It was a barren and desolate country. Scarcely a thornbush grew among the rocks, while gigantic boulders overhung the road, ready to give way at any moment. There was no sign of habitation in this part of the pass. For his part, Reginald considered it impossible for anyone to scrape a living out of such a wilderness.

Nevertheless, as they advanced deeper into the mountains, tribesmen could be seen watching them from atop the ridges, the sun gleaming off the barrels of their rifles.

Reginald glanced over at Captain Scott, who was riding beside him.

'Will they attack us?' he asked.

'I'd be surprised if they don't,' replied the captain. 'The men here will shoot someone for sport.'

Fortunately, these particular tribesmen seemed content to simply monitor the Guides' progress. After several hours of hard marching, they descended into a ravine which was carved out by a fast-flowing river. On the opposite bank, there was a mud-brick fort, constructed in ancient times, which commanded the stone bridge crossing this torrent. Reginald was relieved to see the Union Jack flying above it.

The soldiers pitched their tents along the valley, amid the plum and pear trees planted at intervals. The officers were invited inside the fort to have dinner with the governor, a vigorous Scottish major. They talked strategy until late in the night, to the point where Reginald was anxious to retire. A Pathan showed him and Narendi Ram to their accommodations, a rude bedroom with a straw mattress and an arrow-slit window, which opened to the chilly mountain air. Unable to sleep for the cold, Reginald took out his writing materials and wrote a long and detailed letter to Natalie, describing the events of the day and his various impressions of Afghanistan. At last, he was overcome by weariness and fell asleep, still holding his pen.

He was roused early the next morning and found himself on his horse and on the road deeper into the Land of Cain. They began to climb in earnest, up the steep sides of hills and in mighty bends around cascades of granite boulders and roaring waterfalls. In the distance reared the snowcapped peaks of the world's second highest mountain range, the Hindu Kush. Finally, around midday, the road levelled off and commenced a long descent. Here were signs of life. Deodar cedars clung to the upper slopes, filling the air with their aromatic scent. Mountain goats and markhors with great sweeping horns fled before the advancing army while gryphon vultures and golden eagles circled overhead. In the valleys, there were villages spread widely apart, each with its little plot of cultivated fields and fruit trees.

The tribesmen in this part of the Khyber were unfortunately more aggressive than their brethren further east. They perched above the road and sent bullets whining down into the midst of the marching soldiers. In this way, several Guides were killed and many more injured, but as soon as they raised their guns to retaliate, the tribesmen disappeared behind boulders. While this form of attack was little more than a nuisance in the eyes of the captain, the morale of the men was deteriorating rapidly. They gazed up continually in fear at the slopes, to the point where the march slowed to a crawl.

Captain Scott was at last forced to assemble a cohort of snipers to try to clear the road ahead of them. They had little success, and the tribesmen continued to molest the column until the late afternoon. At this point, the road snaked its way up the broad front of a gigantic hill, a spur of the Hindu Kush, whose broad top was crowned by decaying mud-brick ruins, erected by an unknown ancient civilisation. The Khyber Rifles were camped among the shadows.

'Good journey here?' asked Captain Norfield, the commander of the Rifles.

'Good enough,' Captain Scott replied.

The Guides sent up their tents besides the Rifles and settled down to rest after a wearisome day of marching. Reginald spent some time examining the view from the hilltop as it stretched off in all directions. To the east, he could see the road and the villages amid the brown hills, while to the north, jagged snowcapped peaks marched to the horizon, at once majestic and forbidding. There was nothing lovely or tame about this place nor was its wildness romantic. If any country deserved to be called evil, this was it.

All of these impressions of Afghanistan and others Reginald included in another epistle to Natalie. He was forced to conclude his letter after ten pages, realising that he would have to ration his remaining supply of paper if he wanted it to last him throughout the campaign.

Afterward, he amused himself playing whist with Waverley, Lieutenant Willoughby, and Narendi Ram. Narendi had had his horse shot out from under him by one of the tribesmen and had not quite recovered his nerves. As a result, he made a very poor card partner for Reginald, and they lost every game.

At the officers' meeting that night, Reginald learned that the Guides were to stay put until the Bengal Lancers, who were a day's march behind them, arrived. In the meantime, the Khyber Rifles would push ahead to the next strongpoint on the pass. One more day's journey would suffice to reach Landi Kotal where the fighting was expected to take place. Nadir Khan, the marshal of the regular Afghan forces, had been seen manoeuvring within striking distance of the fort.

'It's not Nadir Khan I'm worried about, but the tribesmen,' opined Captain Norfield.

'They're better soldiers anyway, and if they rise up, we'll be cut off.'

'That's true,' concurred Captain Scott. 'We'll just have to hope it doesn't happen. A war against the tribes would be a damned nuisance to fight.'

'I think we're lucky the Amir has such a weak hold on the throne,' said one of Norfield's officers. 'The tribesmen are about as likely to listen to him as they are to us.'

'I pray you're right,' said Captain Scott.

The next day passed uneventfully. After they had bid the Khyber Rifles goodbye, the Guides took full advantage of the opportunity to rest. Reginald led a company of soldiers out hunting for mountain goat, and they returned with several prize specimens which were roasted over the fire. The meat, however, proved to be unappetising, and most of the men discarded it in favour of their regular rations. Late in the evening, the Bengal Lancers arrived in camp. Most of them were mounted on camels, which they tethered amid the ancient ruins. The soldiers were much darker skinned than the Guides, having been recruited from Eastern India.

Their commander, Colonel Crummings, was a pompous old windbag. He took great pains in extolling the virtues of his Lancers while criticising the Guides for what he believed to be their lack of fighting spirit. Captain Scott grew increasingly angry with each word the colonel spoke.

'Yes, sir, we Lancers were there in the trenches when the Germans surrendered,' boasted Crummings. 'And what were the Guides doing? Sitting on their hands at Peshawar, that's what!'

'Pardon me, Colonel, but I don't think these comparisons are helpful for the situation at hand,' replied Captain Scott.

'Nonsense, Scotty,' said Crummings (one of his habits being to call people by nicknames of his own devising, the more condescending and demeaning the better). 'If the generals had any sense in them, they would have sent the Lancers in ahead of the Guides, not behind them.'

'I'm glad that you take such pride in your regiment,' said Captain Scott, 'but I will ask you one last time to stop insulting mine. We're fighting on the same side, after all.'

'Pooh!' said the Windbag. 'It's hard to talk of the Guides without insulting them, you know! But if you want to talk about something else, I would be happy to tell you and your boys my strategy for winning this war.'

'Boys?' exclaimed Captain Scott. 'I don't see any boys.'

'What about Shorty here,' said the Windbag, inclining his head towards Reginald. 'The Guides are starting to rob the nursery, I see.' He gave a great wheezing chortle.

Waverley jumped to his feet and was about to make a rush at the colonel, but Lieutenant Willoughby restrained him.

'That's enough, Waverley,' said Captain Scott, with a reproving glance. 'I wouldn't want you to stoop to the colonel's level. We can talk strategy tomorrow, hopefully when the colonel is more reasonable. Let's get some sleep, *men*.'

With that the officer corps of the Guides departed, leaving Colonel Crummings without an audience.

'A man like that should be immediately removed from command and sent to work in a coal mine,' said Captain Scott. 'Mark my words, he'll find some way to mess things up for us before this war is over.'

## News from Natalie

THE GUIDES CONTINUED their march the next morning. The heat was sweltering in the valleys and bitterly cold on the windswept hilltops. The alteration between the extremes of temperature was exhausting and uncomfortable for the soldiers. One moment, they were wiping the sweat off their brows, and the next, the sweat had frozen and shivers wracked their bodies. To make matters worse, bullets whistled into the ranks at intervals, launched from the guns of the nearly invisible tribesmen.

Everyone was immensely relieved when by midafternoon, they arrived at their destination, a village built on the bank of a slow, meandering river. The Guides had made good time, so they were awarded the several hours remaining before sunset to do as they pleased. Many of them stripped off their clothes and waded into the river, whose icy coldness was quite refreshing. Others laid down in the shade of the fruit trees and slept. The officers made their way into the village to speak with the British residents and the tribal Khan.

This particular village had a prosperous look about it. The buildings were well-built from deodar wood and the central square was graced by an enormous mosque, decorated with blue tiles. The women here appeared to have much more freedom than was common in this part of the world; they walked about unveiled in the streets, buying and selling with the men. They were a handsome race, light-skinned with grey eyes flecked with amber. Captain Scott had a hard time restraining his soldiers from acting improperly toward these women and ended up having to remove the camp several miles away from the village.

The Khan was eager to express his loyalty to Britain. He told them, in broken English, the story of how his father, at great risk to himself and his village, had sided with the British in the Second Afghan War and how his village owed its recent prosperity to British trade policies. The Khan finished his speech by promising to use his considerable influence among the tribes to foster cooperation against the Afghans.

*This tribesman is more loyal to Britain than I am*, thought Reginald. *I wonder if he would be so enthusiastic if he'd actually been to England and seen the smoke, the machines, and the factories. He's nothing more than a puppet being used by the British in their quest to dominate the world.*

As Reginald retired to his tent, he was struck by a sudden realisation. Was not he, Reginald Archibald Fubster, a pawn as well? There was something to be said for the fact that it was Afghanistan who had declared war, yet here he was, invading an independent country at the head of an army. Why was he doing it? For himself? Certainly not. For England? Yes, for England. For the country he despised and for all of the pompous and silly people of that little island a thousand miles away.

He was interrupted out of these melancholy thoughts when a soldier lifted up his tent flap.

'Lieutenant Fubster?'

'Yes, sir?'

'I have a letter for you here, sir.'

The soldier reached into his pack and pulled out an envelope. Reginald recognised Natalie's neat handwriting. He tore it open and read eagerly:

Dearest Reginald,

I hope this letter finds you well. I have something very important to tell you, and I pray that it will not cause you any undue alarm or distress. I wanted to tell you before, but I couldn't do it. Now I finally have the courage. Doctor Mackenzie was examining me yesterday and discovered that I am pregnant with child and should be giving birth within three months. The child is McAuliffe's, conceived, I'm afraid, on the night of your attempt to rescue me, when I was too weak to resist his advances. I'm sorry! (Here the lines were blurred.) On that account, I am very distressed, yet as I have always wanted a child, I have to see this, somehow, as a gift from God. I am anxious to hear back from you, Reginald, and to learn your thoughts. I do hope you will still love me even though you now know I am a fallen woman!

With all my heart,
Natalie

Natalie's tears had stained the paper. He added his own as he read this brief epistle to the point where the writing was no longer legible. McAuliffe's last words rang in his head: *This isn't over between us, Fubster!* Indeed, it was not over. It was possible that McAuliffe, his archenemy, could harm him and Natalie even from the grave!

His body shook with a sickening, useless fury. *If I'd only known, I'd've killed the bastard when I had the chance! How dare he touch her! I hate him! I always did, and I always will!*

The pieces were coming together in his mind. That's what Natalie had been so afraid of: Jack had threatened to deflower her if she tried to escape. Yet he (Reginald) had gone ahead with the rescue attempt anyway, completely oblivious of the consequences to Natalie. To his vehement loathing of McAuliffe was added a biting self-reproach.

*It's my fault too! I could have stopped it all, but I hesitated when I should have acted and rushed in when I should've waited. Narendi Ram was right. Oh, what a damned fool I am!*

He thought of Natalie. The pure, innocent girl! Even now, when everything had been taken from her, she still thanked God and saw the child as a gift! It was inexplicable. Surely Natalie must realise that God was the ultimate cause of her suffering. Everything that happened was God's will, and he had willed that she would be shamefully violated by a vicious brute.

Why should Natalie praise someone who had brought such evil upon her, who had demonstrated in his ordering of events that he hated her?

For a long time, he was too angry to move. The wick of his oil lamp burned out, and he did not relight it. Alone in the darkness, he wrestled with his thoughts until the cold hour right before dawn.

## *The Guides in Battle*

THE GUIDES WOKE and were back on the march. Twenty miles lay between them and Landi Kotal, twenty miles which proved to be the most difficult stretch of the entire pass. The road wound tortuously through the mountains, oftentimes on the edge of sheer cliffs where a false step would send a man plummeting to a horrendous death on the rocks a thousand feet below. Somehow, the tribesmen were able to find footholds on the slopes above the road and sent volleys of bullets snarling down at the marching soldiers. Captain Scott quickly assembled his team of snipers, who had much more success against this foe due to the lack of boulders for the tribesmen to hide behind. The tribesmen, when shot, fell screaming into the ranks. Others who tried to get away lost their footing amid the smooth stones and suffered the same fate. However, once one slope had been cleared, there was always another slope around the next bend with its own militia of tribesmen.

At last, the road began its descent into a broad valley in which the blue ribbon of the Kabul River threaded its way through orchards and croplands at the far end. The village of Landi Kotal and its strong fort were directly below them. The tribesmen fired a final salvo and then returned to lie in wait for the next regiment to pass that way.

The denizens of Landi Kotal were a devout and puritanical sect of Moslems. The women were in *purdah*, that is, strictly separated from the men, and when they did go about in the streets, which was rare, they were covered from head to toe by a heavy *bourka*. Reginald asked Narendi Ram whether he approved of such practices.

'I am happy to see that they take the faith of the Prophet seriously,' replied Narendi. 'But as for me, I do not think they need be so extreme.'

They passed quickly through the village, Reginald remarking on the beauty of the gleaming mosques, which stood out so incongruously next to the rude hovels of the citizens, and entered the fort. There they were met by their friend, Captain Norfield of the Khyber Rifles, who briefly explained the situation.

Afghan forces were in control of the town of Bagh on the far end of the valley. Part of the Kabul River was diverted from there to provide irrigation for Landi Kotal's fields via a series of canals. These canals also supplied the majority of the drinking water of the town. The Afghans had reduced the water flow into the canals to a mere trickle, making it impossible for the garrison at Landi Kotal to hold out much longer.

'We'll have to do something about this immediately,' said Captain Norfield.

'Do you have any orders?' asked Captain Scott.

'No. However, I received a telegram yesterday authorising me to command the forces in Landi Kotal until the arrival of Colonel Crummings.'

'Then we'd better move quickly. He'll be here tomorrow evening.'

The two captains held a brief private conference.

'We'll attack at dawn,' announced Norfield. 'Let's set up our artillery on that hill there'—he pointed to a mound topped by a Sufi mausoleum—'and bombard Bagh. In the meantime, a quarter of our force will advance on the left flank and free up the water supply. The remaining three quarters will swing to the right flank, skirting those fields there and hitting the flank. I don't expect much resistance. After a solid bombardment, the Afghans will retreat back up into the hills to join Nadir Khan near Kabul.'

'I trust your judgement,' said Captain Scott. 'Tomorrow at dawn it is.'

The officers dispersed to inform the soldiers of the situation. Rifles were cleaned, ammunition readied, and prayers said as the awful sense of expectancy that comes before a battle settled in over the camp. For some, this would be their first taste of action, for others their hundredth, but all alike felt, to one degree or another, that strange mixture of dread and excitement to which no soldier is immune.

Now was the time to write to Natalie. Reginald drew out his writing materials and, with a shaking hand, composed this letter:

> Dearest,
>
> We go into battle tomorrow. I received your last letter. All I can say is I'm sorry. I don't want you to spend a single moment worrying about the child. And don't think of yourself as a fallen woman. You are most certainly not fallen! You are the most virtuous person I know. Don't think you could ever lose my love; I have made a prom-ise that I will love you to the end of my days.
>
> With all my heart,
> Reginald

He read it over again and, trembling, attached it to the other letters he had written and delivered them to the regimental postman. *Let me finish fighting this war first*, he thought, *and then I'll deal with the child.*

Few men slept well that night, with Reginald himself achieving at most a light doze. He was up well before daylight getting his equip-ment in order. Captain Scott informed him that he and Waverley would be leading the attack on the Kabul River and two battalions of the Guides. This would be their chance to distinguish themselves in action and for Reginald to atone for his lapse in obedience. The plan was simple. They would wait until the bombardment of Bagh had commenced, then advance along the line of the canal to the earthen fortifications of the Afghan garrison. For this task, they were granted antiquated field guns towed by an elephant.

The men assembled. The main battery of artillery was placed around the Sufi mausoleum while the Khyber Rifles formed ranks in preparation for their assault on Bagh. As Lieutenant Willoughby organised the Guides, Reginald went to speak to the mahouts of the elephant that would be towing their field piece.

'Looks like you've got a good beast here,' said Reginald, surveying the elephant's vigorous appearance.

'The best, sahib,' replied the mahouts.

'He won't panic with the sound of rifle fire?' Reginald asked.

'No, sahib. He is well-trained and fought many battles.'

Satisfied, Reginald was headed back to the front of the column when he was intercepted by Waverley.

'Well, this is it!' said Waverley, his body quivering with excitement. 'This is what we've been preparing our entire lives for. I can't believe it's finally happening.'

'I can't either,' said Reginald, though in truth, his mind was elsewhere even then.

The sun crept over the Afghan hills, and the artillery started to roar. Mounting his horse, Reginald galloped to the front with Waverley. Narendi Ram, who had no stomach for fighting, was watching from the battlements of the fort. Reginald saluted him and gave the command to march.

It is hard to appreciate the sheer multitude of sensations a soldier in battle is bombarded with at every moment. There is the thundering of the artillery, the Queen of the Battlefield, whose voice sends a tremor to the very soul. Then there is the sharp crack of the rifles, the screams of the dying, the shouted orders of the commanders, the frantic beating of one's own heart. That everything does not dissolve immediately into chaos is miraculous, for in the heat of combat, everything learned from drilling is instantly forgotten and men are carried along by pure emotion. The soldiers lose their individuality

in that moment and become part of something greater. It is a thrill-
ing, almost spiritual experience, and therein lies its eternal attraction.

The Guides marched beside the dry canal, past orchards and
pastures where the startled villagers out tending their flocks fled in
terror. They did not have to go far, three miles perhaps, until they
were within sight of the little mud-brick fort the Afghans had hastily
erected on the bank of the Kabul River. Reginald called a halt and
spread out the soldiers in an arc, just beyond the range of the fort's
defenders. They were ordered to load their rifles and wait. Meanwhile,
Waverley supervised the positioning of the elephant-drawn battery
upon a slight incline. The engineers manned the guns and, at the
signal from Waverley, began lobbing shells into the midst of the fort.

After a few had landed inside to devastating effect, the Afghans
streamed forth from their defences toward the waiting guns of the
Guides.

'Fire!' Reginald and Waverly cried simultaneously.

The rifles exploded all along the line. The Afghans who weren't
instantly killed took off running in the opposite direction.

'Forward!' Reginald ordered, and the line advanced until it had
reached the fort itself. A few Afghans had decided to stay and try
their luck behind the fortifications. These were quickly shot down or
hacked to death with knives. Reginald mounted the partially demol-
ished walls and observed the flight of the few Afghans who had managed to escape. They were heading for a ford further downstream to
join with the main body of soldiers at Bagh.

'Let them go,' he ordered. 'Our main force will mop them up.'

Waverley climbed up beside him and clasped him on the
shoulder.

'Well, that went better than I thought!' he exclaimed. 'If fighting is always that easy, I think I could get used to it!'

'Yes, but I have a feeling it won't.' Reginald sighed.

The Union Jack was hoisted over the fort, and the soldiers settled in to eat their lunch and watch the assault on Bagh as it unfolded
in front of them. The artillery bombardment had lifted and the combined forces of the Guides and the Khyber Rifles were advancing
toward the smoking village.

'There's Willoughby,' said Waverley, pointing out a man at the head of a column with his sword drawn.

Here, the Afghans offered much stiffer resistance. Some had taken up positions on the roofs and windows of the houses and had to be tracked down and eliminated door to door. Others who had barricaded themselves inside a mosque took a heavy toll on the attackers by shooting through cracks in the wall that were nearly invisible from the outside. At last, to the regret of the Moslems under British employ and all admirers of fine architecture, the mosque was shelled by the artillery and the caved-in roof extinguished the last pocket of resistance.

By noon, both objectives had been achieved, and the Union Jack flew across the breadth of the valley. The remaining Afghans fled, as Captain Norfield had predicted, in the direction of Kabul. A squadron of engineers ensured that the canal was reopened, and after installing a small garrison to protect it, Reginald and Waverley returned with the remainder of the soldiers to Landi Kotal. Captain Scott, who had watched the day's campaign from the battlements of the fort, was pleased with his junior officers' leadership.

'Good show, gentlemen, good show!' he said, shaking both of their hands. 'I can't wait to see the look on Crumming's face when he sees what we've done.'

# Crumming's Plan

REGINALD RETIRED TO his tent and spent the rest of the afternoon writing two reports of the day's activities, one for the War Department and the other for Natalie. He was just adding the finishing touches to the latter when he heard the bugle calls of the Bengal Lancers.

'The captain would like to see you, sahib,' said a sergeant, lifting up his tent flap.

'Thank you. I'll be there presently.'

He signed his name and carefully folded the epistle into an envelope. A few minutes later, he had joined the captain and the other officers in the fort's *diwan*, an elegantly decorated meeting hall with a tall vaulted ceiling. Colonel Crummings had called for a bottle of claret and was pouring himself a generous portion.

'I hear there was a skirmish today,' said the colonel. 'How'd it go?'

'Quite well,' replied Captain Scott. 'My junior officers, in particular, distinguished themselves in the attack on the canal.'

'I'm sure it was nothing my own troops couldn't have done with ease,' said the colonel with a dismissive wave of his hand. 'The important thing is that I am now in command here, at least until the twenty-third when the general arrives. I am confident that under my leadership, we will bring about a decisive end to this war. Here's my plan.'

One of his junior officers rather reluctantly unfurled a large map and laid it on the table.

'Here we are and here is Nadir Khan,' said the colonel, pointing out the positions with his cane. 'His goal is to keep his army between us and Kabul. However, he would also like to find a way of cutting us off from the Khyber Pass. I am convinced that if we make a show of advancing through this valley here, he will take the bait and swoop down to take Landi Kotal. We will double back and rout him in this very place.'

'Colonel,' said Captain Scott slowly, trying a reasoned approach, 'you do realise that Nadir Khan commands a force of nearly twenty-five thousand soldiers while we are scarcely five thousand.'

'Pooh! Everyone knows that one British soldier is equal to five savages at the very least. Numbers won't be an issue, I assure you.'

'I don't think it's wise to underestimate our enemy,' warned Scott. 'That's the mistake we made in the first Afghan War, and the Afghans have already proven themselves to be more than competent soldiers. Besides, they know the terrain better than we do and have better supply lines—'

'Have you no backbone, man?' asked Colonel Crummings. 'And besides, you're as daft as your brother who made that crazy Antarctic expedition! This plan will work, I guarantee it!'

'My cousin, you mean,' snapped Captain Scott.

'Brother, cousin, whatever,' replied the colonel.

Captain Scott's face was bright red. He seemed on the very brink of an outburst when Captain Norfield pulled him aside.

'It's not worth it, James,' he said.

'Not worth it! This man will make us lose the Khyber Pass!'

'Not if we can prevent it,' said Norfield.

'How? Disobey orders? We have to go along with his crackpot scheme.'

'We'll find a way.'

The two talked further in whispers.

Crummings was too engrossed by his claret to notice this conversation. Captain Scott eventually returned to his place.

'Well, looks like we're all finished here,' said the colonel. 'Make sure your *boys* get a good night's sleep.' He cast a glance toward Reginald and Waverley. 'We'll march out tomorrow.'

When Reginald returned to his tent, he found a letter from Natalie waiting for him. He opened and read as follows:

Dearest Reginald,

I hope you are safe and happy, wherever you are. This hot weather has really been bothering me. Every day, I think about England or some other place away from these horrid plains. I feel as though I am burning up inside. I don't mean to worry you, Reginald, but Dr Mackenzie thinks there may be some complications with my child—nothing serious of course, I just thought you should know. I very much enjoyed reading your letters. You have such a beautiful way of describing things; I felt like I was right there with you. What an incredible adventure you are having! Thank you for your kind words and for your love. I consider myself the luckiest woman in the entire world. I do hope that this war is over soon—I can hardly wait to see you again.

With love,
Natalie

Reginald tore out a piece of paper. *What am I doing here?* he thought. *I should be with her! Confound Afghanistan!*
He hurriedly scrawled a few lines.

Natalie,

Tell Dr Mackenzie that you need to go to the hills immediately. There is a hill station half an hour away by train. You should be much more comfortable there. Did the doctor tell you what kind of complications you would have? Please let me know as soon as you can!

Love,
Reginald

He gathered up his packet of letters and, placing this last epistle on top, hurried to the regimental postman. The postman was smoking his pipe and joking with a few of his comrades.

Reginald placed the package directly in his hands.

'Make sure that this is delivered to Peshawar with all possible haste,' he said, tossing the man a generous handful of gold sovereigns.

The postman saluted and carefully placed the letters within his satchel. Reginald went back to his tent and, exhausted by the day's exertions, fell asleep.

# Ambushed

EARLY THE NEXT day, the combined forces of the Guides, Rifles, and Lancers moved to put Colonel Crumming's ill-advised strategy into effect. A woefully small garrison was left behind at Landi Kotal to guard the pass. The Guides were the vanguard of the column, while the Lancers, unsurprisingly, brought up the rear. Following the course of the Kabul River as it wound through the valley, they had soon left Landi Kotal and the cultivated fields behind and entered once again into a rugged and desolate country. Here, there was evidence of a faith even older than that of the Prophet: the caves of Buddhist hermits riddled the hillsides, some of which in that advanced year of 1919 were still occupied.

By nightfall, they had covered twenty miles of this inhospitable countryside. They camped on the riverbank and waited for news from Colonel Crumming's scouts.

'Well, have they taken the bait?' Crummings asked.

'No, sir,' replied the chief scout, a wiry Pathan with a drooping moustache. 'Nadir Khan is staying put.'

'Damn the old fool,' Crummings muttered. 'Why won't he do what I think he'll do? Oh well. Another day's march will persuade him.'

Unfortunately, Colonel Crumming's prophecy, like the overwhelming majority of predictions he had made in his life, failed to come to pass. They had advanced another day's march into the heart of Afghanistan, and yet Nadir Khan remained stubbornly put between them and Kabul.

'I say we give it up and turn back,' suggested Captain Scott.

'I second the motion,' said Captain Norfield.

'One more day should get the rascal moving,' countered Crummings. 'We will press on tomorrow.'

'But, sir! Nadir Khan is two days from Landi Kotal!' cried Captain Scott. 'If we keep going, we won't be able to make it back in time if he does decide to attack!'

'What's that? Of course, I'm aware of that! We'll go half-a-day's march. We all know that British regiments make the best time of anyone in the world.'

The captain's further protests fell on wilfully deaf ears. He retired to his tent that night, shaking his head.

'I don't like the look of this at all,' he muttered under his breath. 'I hope my men don't come to harm.'

The next day, they left the river valley and advanced along a narrow defile hemmed in on either side by craggy hills. The going was slow as they had to pick their way over and around innumerable boulders while the Afghan sun beat down on them mercilessly. Near midday, Colonel Crummings called for a halt.

As the soldiers were resting, a scout came sprinting directly to where Crummings was seated eating his repast.

'Sir! Nadir Khan is advancing on Landi Kotal!' he cried.

At the same time, another runner appeared from the front of the column.

'Sir! Nadir Khan is upon us!'

'What? He can't be in two places at once!'

The sharp crack of rifle fire split the air.

'My god!' Crummings exclaimed. 'Are you sure that Nadir Khan is moving toward Landi Kotal?'

'Yes, sahib. I saw it with my own eyes.'

'Then who the deuce is attacking us now?'

The Guides were at the front of the column. They were taken completely by surprise when an army of Afghan regulars appeared over the crest of the hills but, under Captain Scott's cool direction, were beginning to mount a defence.

Colonel Crummings summoned his officers.

'We will retreat back to Landi Kotal,' he said. 'Inform the Khyber Rifles that they will be retreating with us.'

'What about the Guides?' asked one of the officers.

'They'll have to fend for themselves.'

'You can't do that, sir! You'll be court-martialed for sure!'

'Better that than lose the Khyber Pass,' said Crummings, whose dreams of glory were rapidly going up in smoke. 'Hurry now, we haven't a moment to lose!'

Meanwhile, the Guides found themselves in an unenviable situation. They were nearly encircled, with Afghan soldiers ringing the hills on either side and advancing against them through the defile. If the Afghan's rifles had been more accurate, the Guides would have suffered a dreadful amount of casualties. As it was, the British regiment managed to hold out long enough to assemble some sort of order.

'Reginald, Waverley!' Captain Scott shouted. 'Clear the men off that ridge now!'

'Follow me, men!' Reginald cried, drawing his sword and pointing it up the slope of the nearest hill.

The men followed him on a wild scramble through the boulders while the Afghan fired down upon them. At last, they gained the top and an accurate volley sent the Afghans into flight toward the main body of troops. Reginald quickly took stock of the situation. Their position on the ridge provided them an excellent perch from which to shoot at the Afghans attacking along the defile. He arranged his soldiers along the ridge, and they fired with devastating effect on the Afghans below.

Seeing the advantage this afforded the British, the Afghan commander (who incidentally in this case was not Nadir Khan) regrouped his men and sent them to retake their position. Even the legendary accuracy of the Guides was not enough to slow their irresistible advance, supported as it was by such a mass of soldiery.

Below them, the rest of the Guides were executing a strategic retreat toward a narrow section of the defile walled in by sheer cliffs, which would make encirclement impossible. The bugle called for Reginald's men to withdraw as well. Reginald directed one final salvo at the advancing Afghans and turned to lead the retreat. A stray bullet, almost certainly not intended for him, struck him just below the knee, and he crumpled. In doing so, he lost his balance on top of the ridge and toppled down the steep, rocky slope until his head collided directly with a boulder, and he was knocked immediately unconscious.

# 41

## *The Land of Cain*

IT WAS NIGHTTIME when Reginald came to. He was lying in the same place he had fallen, blood trickling out of the bullet wound in his leg and his head aching terribly. Once his mind cleared, he tore off one of his sleeves for a makeshift bandage and lashed it around his leg. When he was sufficiently convinced that this would stem the bleeding, he rose shakily to his feet, leaning on the boulder for support. The mountain wind chilled him to the bone, and what was worse, his throat was parched with thirst.

His first necessity was to find water—a difficult prospect at night in those barren hills, especially with a wounded leg. He tried to remember whether there had been a stream at the bottom of the defile, but nothing came to him; the day before merged into a blur. Deciding it was worth a try anyway, he picked his way down through the boulders, one faltering step at a time.

The stars danced above in their millions, and the Milky Way was clearly visible, gleaming like a necklace of pearls across the sky. Reginald was struck with a gut-wrenching feeling of insignificance. He was alone. Whether he lived or died held no consequence for the world; it would continue on without him. The only reality now was his solitary struggle for survival in the face of an indifferent God.

It was a mental as well as physical battle to reach the bottom of the valley, but each step forward strengthened his resolve. His ears continually strained for the sound of water, returning nothing but the cruel moaning of the wind. The only hope was to head back in the direction of the Kabul River. It was half a day's march away, and he estimated that he wouldn't reach it until a couple hours after dawn. Could he hold out that long?

As he went, he stumbled continually in the ruts left by dry watercourses. The blood started flowing again from his wound, and he had to stop to tie his bandage tighter. He cut a walking staff for himself from a scraggly pine; this helped him to make significantly better time.

Onward, he struggled, hour after hour, until the first light of dawn appeared over the rocky slopes of the hills in front of him. How much further? He covered more ground now that he could see the obstacles in front of him. Yet as the sun rose higher, its merciless rays accelerated his thirst to an unbearable torment. The path rose to a slight promontory. He gained the top and shaded his eyes against the sun. Yes! There it was, the blue ribbon of the Kabul River, shining in the distance! Or was it? He'd heard of mirages which played tricks on wanderers in the desert, but his mind wasn't as addled as that. He would go to it. But just as he started, he suddenly caught sight of something between him and the river: an Afghan soldier.

Reginald leapt behind a boulder. Fortunately, it appeared the man had not seen him. He appeared to be a scout of some sort who, pausing on his journey, had stopped to light his pipe. There was nothing for Reginald to do but wait until he moved on. The Afghan took a few puffs and then lifted his waterskin to refresh himself. At the sight of it, Reginald's throat burned with thirst. *If only I could have a drink*, he thought as his hand reached involuntarily for his revolver.

The Afghan scout returned his pipe and his waterskin to his pack and rose to his feet. To Reginald's consternation, the Afghan was walking directly toward where he was hiding. He cocked his revolver. The Afghan appeared to be in no particular hurry; he ambled along at an easy pace, armed only with an antique *jezail*. Reginald was torn. On one hand, here was an enemy who might be conveying vital information. On the other, this was a fellow human being. The Afghan continued forward, and it soon became obvious that he would pass by Reginald without seeing him. Reginald was about to let him go when his eyes focused once again on the waterskin, and he thought about how thirsty he was and how much further it was to the river…

The gun exploded in his hands. The Afghan screamed and crumpled to the ground.

Reginald gasped and, returning the revolver shakily to his belt, approached the dying man. The Afghan was coughing up blood. A wave of guilt washed over Reginald when he realised that the scout was only a lad, about the same age as himself.

'Have mercy!' the Afghan spluttered in Pashtu.

Reginald shuddered as he looked into the youth's terror-stricken eyes. He crouched to examine his wound. The bullet had ripped a hole in his chest and punctured one of his lungs. It was obviously fatal, and the Afghan had only a few minutes left before he passed on to the next life.

'My wife!' the Afghan cried in between coughs. 'My lovely wife! I shall never see her again!'

Reginald was moved by this spectacle. What had he done? Were he and this Afghan all that different? What if their fates had been switched? Why should he, Reginald Archibald Fubster, Englishman, live and this Pathan die?

'Forgive me,' pleaded Reginald in Pashtu.

The young man's eyes met Reginald's. 'Only God can forgive, Englishman.'

The Afghan called several more times for his wife, then his eyes closed forever.

Reginald's first instinct was to reach greedily for the waterskin, but he caught himself before he could raise it to his lips.

'I killed a man for this!' he cried and flung the waterskin away.

He despised himself. He had to get away from Afghanistan and return to a place where things made sense. Desperately, he rose and stumbled toward the river. It seemed so close, yet it was over a mile away at least, and as he limped forward, he began to wonder if he would make it. His parched throat had nearly closed and the wound to his leg was throbbing with excruciating pain. He tripped over a boulder and the bandage came undone; the bleeding, which had never been properly stemmed, started afresh.

*I haven't the time to fix that*, Reginald thought. *I have to reach the river soon or die.*

The Afghan sun contributed its share to Reginald's misery, turning the narrow defile through which he walked into a furnace. There was no shade anywhere from its merciless rays. As Reginald stared straight ahead, the river began to shimmer. Had he only imagined it was there? He wasn't sure.

Finally, his legs, which had been trembling terribly, gave out, and he collapsed like a dead man on the hard ground.

'I'm finished,' Reginald gasped. 'Oh, Natalie, I'm sorry! I failed you!'

A figure appeared ahead out of the haze. From that distance, the only thing Reginald could see was the person's golden hair.

'It's Natalie.' He sighed. 'Now I can die content.'

He closed his eyes.

## *The Wound*

THE NEXT THING Reginald felt was cold water trickling over his face. A voice commanded him to drink, and he opened his chapped lips wide. The first drops of water caused him to splutter, but after several applications, his throat opened, and he was able to swallow some of the reviving liquid. The haze dissipated from his mind.

'Who are you?' Reginald asked.

'Don't you recognise me, Reginald? Narendi's here too.'

Reginald shook his head, and his eyes focused. Waverley was bent over him with a concerned look on his face while Narendi Ram was busy replacing his bandage.

'You came back for me?'

'Of course we did, Reginald! As soon as we had the chance!'

'How…how is the regiment?'

'We're all right. The Afghans fell back.'

'What about the Khyber?'

'It's safe. We received intelligence this morning that Nadir Khan has moved east to put down a rebellion among his own people.'

'Thank goodness,' Reginald said.

'Now we'd better get you to a doctor, Reginald.'

'I don't think I can walk.'

'Don't worry, we have a camel,' Waverley said, motioning to the shaggy beast they had tethered several paces off. 'Bring him over here, Narendi, if you would.'

Narendi Ram, who had just finished tying Reginald's new bandage, escorted the camel over and forced it to kneel. It was of the Bactrian breed of camel, which, unlike the familiar dromedary of Arabia, has two humps on its back instead of one. Waverley helped Reginald get settled in between these protrusions, then started off the camel at a slow trot by applying a blow to its backside.

Reginald, who had not had a wink of sleep that night, soon found himself dozing off. It was late in the afternoon by the time they caught up with the rear guard of the Guides. Captain Scott ordered an immediate halt and went to greet them.

'Reginald, thank God they found you!'

'Thank you, sir,' Reginald said as Waverley helped him down off the camel's back.

The captain caught sight of the bandage around his leg.

'Are you hurt bad?' he asked, then turned to his orderly. 'Fetch the surgeon.'

They pitched a tent and laid Reginald down on a soft Persian carpet. The regimental surgeon, Corporal McMillan, untied the bandage to examine the wound.

'You've lost a great deal of blood,' he said. 'But lucky for you, the wound's not infected, so I won't have to amputate your leg. Let me get the bullet out of there and then we'll see what we have to do.'

The surgeon's assistant approached Reginald with brandy, which he politely refused. He grimaced as the surgeon's scalpel probed into his flesh. Narendi Ram, who could not stomach the sight of blood, turned away and covered his eyes. The surgeon had performed hundreds of operations just like this one and had soon located and extracted the misshapen lead bullet. He dropped it into Reginald's hand for a souvenir.

'How does everything look?' Captain Scott asked.

'Not good I'm afraid,' replied the surgeon. 'The bullet has severed the ligament that holds together his knee and his femur.'

'Can that heal?' Reginald asked anxiously.

'It's a long shot. I hate to say this, but I don't think you'll be able to walk on that leg again.'

'Damn Colonel Crummings!' Captain Scott exclaimed. 'I knew harm would come of his idiocy! I understand you now, my boy. I should've disobeyed his ridiculous orders!'

'Don't say that, Captain,' said Reginald. 'It's not your fault. It was an unlucky accident.'

'You're a good lad,' said Captain Scott.

'What am I to do?' Reginald asked after a long pause, a sliver of a tear running down his cheek.

'We'll send you back to Peshawar,' replied the corporal. 'Dr Mackenzie is more knowledgeable about these matters than I am, and he might be able to fix you up. Until then, don't put any weight on that leg.'

The surgeon reapplied bandages and presented Reginald with a set of crutches.

'Get some sleep now,' he advised.

Waverley had a couple of tears starting in his eyes.

'I'm sorry, Reginald,' he said. 'I wish it was me and not you.'

Lieutenant Willoughby likewise offered his sympathy. Reginald tried to smile and tell them he would be all right, but as soon as they left him, bitter tears cascaded from his eyes. This was the one thing he was not prepared for. What would Natalie say when he came back a cripple? How was he supposed to provide for her and protect her like he should when he wouldn't even be able to walk? And what of his military career? All of the preparation, study, and drilling rendered useless in a moment. The best he could do now was sit behind a desk, filing papers.

*Now I know for certain that God is against me*, he thought before he fell asleep.

He awoke not long after and was hoisted back up onto the camel. The Guides made good time that day, and by nightfall, they were within a day's march of Landi Kotal. Scouts from the Khyber Rifles visited in the evening to share information with Captain Scott.

One of them also bore a letter addressed to Reginald from Miss Natalie McAuliffe:

> Dear Reginald,
>
> The doctor has heeded your advice, and we have removed ourselves to the hills. It is much more pleasant here, and I am feeling better every day. In terms of the complications, the doctor was concerned that I may give birth prematurely. He still thinks it may happen, but he assures me no harm will come of it. The doctor's wife, Clara, is staying with us as well; we have become very good friends. She is an admirable woman, and I can't wait for you to meet her. They are good people, these Americans. In short, Reginald, I am doing very well, and you needn't worry yourself at all on my account. I do hope to see you soon!
>
> Love,
> Natalie

Reginald breathed a sigh of relief. However, when he drew out a piece of parchment to write a reply, he found he couldn't put the words together. After several false starts, he gave up, deciding anything he wrote would only alarm her. An oppressive darkness was descending on his mind, making it impossible for him to think. When Waverley and Lieutenant Willoughby stopped by to pay him a call at his tent, his replies to their questions were so confused that they departed quickly, urging him to get some sleep.

The next morning, he arose at sunrise. He watched it for a moment in peace before he felt a sharp pain in his leg and remembered his wound and the young Afghan he had killed. The gloom settled in, as it had the night before. It was too thick to dispel and tormented him with painful recollections.

The Guides arrived in Landi Kotal in the late afternoon. The entire valley had been transformed to a military base with the arrival of the general and several more regiments from Peshawar. An aeroplane of the Royal Air Force circled overhead, on its way home from a reconnaissance mission.

The general summoned the officer corps of the Guides to the fort of Landi Kotal for a council of war. Reginald was excused on account of his leg, but he learned later that one of the main topics of their discussion was the impending court-martial of Colonel Crummings. The war no longer concerned Reginald; his heart yearned to see Natalie. It was to his immense relief that he discovered he would be returning to British India the following morning in an armoured motorcar. He had had quite enough of Afghanistan and of fighting; now he was ready for Natalie and peace.

# The Hill Station

REGINALD SAID HIS goodbyes the following morning. Captain Scott expressed his deep regret and, once again, cursed Colonel Crummings.

'We'll miss you, Fubster,' he said, giving Reginald a firm handshake. 'You've proven yourself a fine soldier.'

After the captain came Lieutenant Willoughby.

'Don't be discouraged, old boy,' he said. 'You have a will strong enough to overcome anything. I wouldn't be surprised to see you walking by the time we return.'

Reginald gave him a weak smile and shook his hand. Last came Waverley.

'I don't know what to say,' Waverley gasped, tears running down his cheeks.

'Don't worry about me' was all Reginald could manage.

Waverley gave his friend a tight embrace. They stood looking at each other for a long moment before the captain called for Waverley. Reginald watched him until he had vanished into the crowd of soldiers.

'Ensign Fubster?'

Reginald turned around.

'My name is Sergeant Butterfield. I'm in charge of conveying you back to Peshawar. Are you ready?'

'One moment,' said Reginald. 'My servant should be here presently.'

A minute later, Narendi Ram arrived with all of Reginald's baggage. They loaded it into the motorcar and took their seats. Sergeant Butterfield proved to be a friendly chap, but neither Reginald nor Narendi Ram were inclined much to conversation, and so most of their journey was passed in silence. Order had been restored to the Khyber Pass in the intervening week. The tribesmen no longer shot at the passing soldiers. They rumbled past many marching regiments, in numbers so great that Reginald was convinced that the war could not last more than a month.

The scenery rushed by in a blur. Reginald no longer cared. In fact, the barren mountains and deep ravines seemed like reflections of evil thoughts. By nightfall, they had reached the little fort in the valley where Reginald had stayed the first night. He crutched into the fort and was shown to a side room which, in ancient times, must have served as an armoury. There he caught sight of a straw mattress lying in the corner and collapsed onto it. He fell asleep directly.

The next day, the motorcar wound its way out of the hills and down into the plain where the familiar domes and minarets of Peshawar gleamed ahead of them. Reginald was relieved beyond words to be back in British India. Butterfield drove them directly to the door of the hospital and helped them unload their baggage. He shook Reginald's hand, wished him luck, and sped away in a cloud of dust.

Reginald crutched inside where he was greeted by the same pretty nurse as when he came to visit Natalie.

'What can I do for you?' she asked, surveying him with concern.

'I need to see Dr Mackenzie. I was informed he had gone to the hills. Do you know exactly where he might be?'

'Of course,' replied the nurse. 'He is staying in Jakha. There is a train that leaves for there this afternoon if you'd like to take it.'

Reginald thanked her and went back outside to hire a rickshaw to the train station.

He and Narendi departed for Jakha at two thirty in the afternoon and reached it by five o'clock. The hill station was situated in the midst of a spur of the Afghan hills which crossed over the border, growing less steep and barren as they proceeded east. The locomotive steamed its way through lush forests of deodar and Himalayan pine. Up ahead, crowning the hill was the pure white spire of a church. It immediately struck Reginald as being out of place in this land, and he felt uncomfortable.

A fashionable crowd of ladies in white muslin dresses and gentlemen in suits and top hats met them at the platform. Reginald was at once relieved and invigorated by the cool air and, for the first time in the past days, felt his mind clearing a little. An Indian porter helped Narendi Ram unload the luggage and deposit it in a horse-drawn carriage.

'Where can I take you, sahib?' asked the driver in perfect English.

'I am looking for Dr Mackenzie, if you know where he lives,' replied Reginald.

'I do, sahib,' he said, cracking the reins.

The road was lined on either side by British-style half-timbered cottages. On top of the hill was the church, the Grand Hotel (an elegant Neoclassical structure built in 1895), the post office, and even a pub with a swaying sign. English elms and beeches were planted on the grassy lawns. Reginald thought he had suddenly been transported back to England. Certainly, this was the village of Cottebury-on-Lalley in Kent, and the house that they were approaching now belonged to his great-uncle Merriweather Fubster.

'This is the doctor's residence, sahib,' said the driver, interrupting his musings.

'Thank you,' Reginald mumbled.

He crutched to the door and gave a heavy knock. An Indian butler opened it for him.

'Whom do I have the pleasure of addressing?' asked the butler formally.

'Ensign Reginald Fubster. Is Dr Mackenzie at home?'

'He is not. He has gone out on his rounds.'

'Do you know when he'll be back?'

'This evening, sir.'

Reginald was about to turn away when he heard a lady's voice within.

'Who is that at the door, Sarji?'

'An officer by the name of Reginald Fubster.'

'Show him in, show him in!' cried the lady eagerly.

'Right this way, sir,' said the butler.

Reginald gave a signal to Narendi Ram to wait outside until he was finished.

The butler led him past the foyer into the main hall where the lady of the house was waiting expectantly. She was in her late thirties, but still very pretty with auburn hair and bright green eyes.

'Reginald Fubster,' she said in a distinctive American accent, 'it's so nice to meet you. My name is Clara Mackenzie. I'm the doctor's wife. Natalie's told us all about you, of course.' She noticed Reginald's crutches. 'My goodness, you're hurt! What happened?'

'Bullet wound,' he replied simply.

'You'd better sit down.'

She showed him into a comfortable armchair in the parlour.

'Sarji, bring Miss Natalie and send out a message to my husband to come home!'

The butler hurried to do her bidding. When Natalie entered, Reginald was as awestruck at her appearance as he had been the first time he saw her. She was wearing a simple blue dress, which perfectly complemented her shining eyes, and the sunlight streaming in through the parlour's wide windows turned her hair into pure gold. He had to wonder, once again, whether he was not in the presence of some heavenly being. Her face smiled with complete joy when she saw him, making her, if possible, even more beautiful.

'Reginald!' she cried and rushed to embrace him.

They pulled back a moment later to look at each other. She asked him about his wound, and he briefly narrated what had happened.

He noticed, with a shiver, that her time of pregnancy was almost up.

'Oh,' Natalie whispered, seeing his look. 'The doctor says I should be giving birth in another month or two. You may touch it if you like.'

How could he? It was the physical reminder of McAuliffe's villainy. Yet it was Natalie's child too. Could he hate it and still love her?

He nervously pressed his hand to her stomach. The child, it seemed, recoiled at his touch and leapt away from him.

'Oh, dear,' Natalie sighed. 'I need to sit down.'

She took a seat. Narendi Ram was called for, and the doctor arrived not long after.

'Mr Fubster, excellent to see you again,' he said, shaking his hand and eyeing his knee professionally. 'I see you'll be needing my services.'

'Yes, sir.'

'Where are you staying?'

'Nowhere yet. I was going to book a room in the hotel.'

'I won't hear of it,' said the doctor, waving his hand. 'You'll stay here with us. Sarji!'

The butler presented himself.

'Prepare rooms for Mr Fubster and his servant.'

The Indian hurried off.

'Now, I'd better wash up. Mr Fubster, I do hope you'll join us for supper. It shouldn't be long.'

'I would be honoured,' Reginald replied.

# The Mackenzies

SUPPER WAS HELD in an elegant dining room. On the wall was a portrait of the American Founding Father George Washington and a pretty painting of a lighthouse on a rocky coast. The Americans, Reginald observed, treated their servants almost like members of the family, something the British would never dream of doing. Sarji, the butler, who happened to be a Goan Christian, sat with them at the table and had soon engaged Narendi Ram in a theological discussion.

The doctor, for his part, was anxious to hear about the progress of the war and the role Reginald had played in it. Reginald did his best to recount his adventures, much to his own dismay but to the wonder of his listeners. They then told him what they had been up to, the doctor explaining that he was expected to return to Peshawar by October to resume his duties until spring, the end of his term, when he and his wife would be taking a steamer to London to report to his superior in the Foreign Service.

'Tomorrow's Sunday,' Clara Mackenzie noted. 'You will join us for church, won't you, Mr Fubster?'

Reginald looked over at Natalie, who nodded eagerly.

'I'd be happy to,' he said, though this was not the truth.

'Wonderful,' said Clara. 'Now I think we had all better turn in and get some rest.'

Reginald was directed to the guest bedroom where he fell asleep content.

One of the Mackenzies' servants woke him the next morning for church. Reginald rose and reluctantly donned his dress uniform.

'Are you coming with me?' he asked Narendi Ram jocularly.

'No, sahib. But I do hope you will keep an open mind.'

'Fat chance of that,' said Reginald.

He crutched into the main hallway where Natalie and the Mackenzies were waiting for him.

The doctor hailed a coach, and they climbed aboard. Reginald sat next to Natalie who smiled and squeezed his hand. After a short ride to the top of the hill, they disembarked in the churchyard and hurried inside to find their seats.

Reginald had not been inside a church since Merriweather Fubster's funeral. He had been raised as ostensibly a member of the Church of England by his father. However, as we know, Wilfred's true god had been Country. They had attended as a family when duty required it, but the real worship took place on the parade ground and battlefield. The metaphysical aspect of religion had been an unapproachable mystery to a practical man like Wilfred Fubster, and he was content to leave it be. Thus, the only spiritual instruction Reginald had received was from Murad Pasha. Islam was straightforward enough. But Christianity? He had never understood it.

The congregation stood to sing some hymns, accompanied by a choir and a pipe organ. The Mackenzies and Natalie knew every word, while Reginald moved his lips to make it look like he was singing. Then they sat down again, and the preacher or pastor, whatever his name was, stood at the pulpit and delivered his sermon.

The subject was forgiveness. Reginald was reminded of the Afghan soldier, but he shoved that thought out of his mind. He had soon lost interest and stared instead at Natalie's face. She was hanging on to every word, a tear at times shimmering in her eye. Once again, Reginald was aware of his spiritual inferiority to her.

*What's the matter with me?* he thought.

The sermon over, the congregation rose to take communion at the altar. Reginald stayed in his place and observed this peculiar ritual. Bread and wine as the body and blood of Christ?

'Codswallop,' he decided.

Everyone returned to their pews and rose for one last hymn. It was 'Amazing Grace.'

Reginald knew the words to this one, but he didn't sing. Mercifully, the service was then over. The congregants filed out of their pews and waited their turn to shake hands with the pastor.

'What's your name, son?' the pastor asked when it was Reginald's turn.

'Reginald Fubster, sir.'

'Nice to meet you,' said the pastor, giving him a firm handshake. 'God bless you.'

Natalie and Clara were chatting with some of their friends. Reginald watched Natalie for a while. It did his heart good to see her so happy after all she had suffered. He felt a hand on his shoulder and turned around. It was the doctor.

'We have a tradition of eating a picnic lunch on Sundays. Would you care to join us?'

'Yes, of course. Thank you.'

'Excellent! I'll see if I can corral the ladies.'

This task proved a formidable one, but the doctor was eventually able to coax his wife and Natalie to the carriage. They stopped at the house, where Sarji presented them with the picnic baskets and continued onward until they reached a sunny clearing amid the pines and deodars, which afforded them a view of the neighbouring hills and distant snowcapped peaks.

They sat and ate and talked of nothing in particular. The unbearable darkness that had infected Reginald's mind since Afghanistan was being dispelled in the light of Natalie's presence. He had a burning desire to talk to her in private, but for this moment, he was happy to just watch her. It was strange to think that his struggles were over and a lifetime of bliss awaited him.

The picnic ended; they returned to the house for a nap. Reginald requested a private interview with Natalie that evening after dinner.

'Of course, Reginald,' she said.

# 45

## *Plans for the Future*

THEY MET IN Natalie's room, which was filled with the grace she carried with her wherever she went. Reginald sat on the bed next to her. He was reminded at once of the first time they'd talked and how nervous he'd been.

'What do you want to talk about?' she asked.

'Us,' he replied simply.

'Yes?'

'Natalie.' He trembled. 'I might as well come out and say it. I love you. Will you marry me?'

She looked at him and, overcome by emotion, started to cry.

'Natalie, dearest,' said Reginald, squeezing her hand, 'what's the matter?'

'Look at me!' she said, motioning to her stomach. 'How can you love me after all that's happened? I'm a fallen woman. I'm deserving of your pity, not your love. Find someone else. Someone better.'

'You don't understand. I love you even more because of what's happened.'

'But the child?'

'The child is yours. Anything that belongs to you is sacred to me. I want to help you take care of it.'

'I don't deserve it,' said Natalie, tears spilling from her eyes.

'What!' he cried. 'It is I who is unworthy of you!' He sank to his knees. 'Even if I were the greatest man in the world, I would scarcely deserve to touch the ground you walk on! But as it is, I love you and want to marry you. Will you have me?'

Something changed in her. She continued to cry, but these were happy tears.

'Yes,' she said. 'Yes! I love you too.'

They embraced each other tenderly.

'Should we tell the doctor?' Natalie asked.

'I'll speak with him tomorrow.'

'I'm so confused about everything,' Natalie continued. 'Was I married to Jack McAuliffe? Can I remarry now, or do I have to wait? What about the child? Who does it belong to?'

'Colonel Thornwood promised me he would look into all this, but I'm afraid the war has gotten in the way. There's your money to think of, too.'

Natalie shuddered. 'Oh, I hate that money! It's the reason for all my misfortunes. It would've been better if I'd been born a pauper!'

Reginald thought this over. Natalie was right, of course. If she did not care for the money, why should he? Besides some vague ideas of reestablishing the Fubster property to its former glory, he had no pressing need for it. From what he had seen, wealth and property tended to weigh a person down, and he feared being roped to a place he did not like. He would put the matter aside for now and see how it resolved itself.

'Another question is where to raise the child,' he said.

He spoke to her again of Kashmir: a house by a lake, with a view of the great mountains, with the freshness of the hills to moderate the climate. They would be insulated there from the troubles of the wide world in a land which existed outside the march of progress, free to live together in peace. Natalie had said she would like this, but that was before she knew about the child.

Natalie wrung her hands. 'I'm sorry, Reginald! I know that India is your home, but I do not like this country. It's funny because I was so eager to come here after all you told me about it, but now, I find it too hot and foreign for someone who has lived their whole life in England. I have been pining for home for a long time now. What would you think of a quiet little place in the English countryside where we could raise the child?'

Reginald's face fell. India was his first love, but his affection for Natalie was, of course, greater. He understood why she must hate it; it had been the scene of her long and wretched captivity.

'I would go anywhere and do anything to make you happy,' he assured her. 'England it is then. I will put in a request to be transferred. We will stay here for the child to be born, won't we?'

'Yes, in fact, I was thinking that we could travel with the Mackenzies when they depart in the spring.'

'That sounds like a plan. I'll have to write to Waverley and Captain Scott and explain the situation. I'm sure the captain will understand, but I don't know about Waverley. He might want to come with us!'

Natalie smiled. 'He's a good friend, isn't he?'

'He is.'

'And will Narendi Ram come too?'

'I don't think it would be possible to separate us from him. He'd swim the ocean if he had to. Do you mind?'

'Not at all. I was hoping you'd say that. I like him immensely.'

From there, the conversation drifted into other matters which, to protect their privacy, we will refrain from recording. It was well after midnight by the time they parted ways to each enjoy happy dreams of the bright future spreading before them.

## The Doctor's Report

EARLY THE NEXT morning, Reginald was conveyed via carriage to the doctor's office in the centre of the little town.

'Good morning, Reginald,' said Doctor Mackenzie. 'Let's have a look at that leg.'

Reginald rolled up his pant leg and the doctor examined it with a critical eye.

'Corporal McMillan wrote that you had lacerated the ligament connecting the knee to the femur. I'm afraid he is gravely mistaken.'

Reginald shuddered.

'The ligament is torn, not lacerated,' explained the doctor, his eyes twinkling. 'You'll walk. It'll be months, but I can promise you that if your heart is in the recovery, you'll be on your own two feet again.'

'Thank you!' Reginald exclaimed. 'That's excellent news!'

'Now, you'll have to avoid putting any weight on it for a couple of weeks. After that, I have some exercises that you will have to do faithfully every day if you want to be completely better.'

'Of course,' Reginald said and shook the doctor's hand.

Upon his return, he happily conveyed this information to Natalie, who rejoiced with him. They spent the rest of the day together, talking of nothing in particular, each glorying in the other's presence. In the evening, a letter arrived from Waverley, which he read aloud. The British Army was advancing on every front with the Afghans cowering before them. Reginald composed a letter in reply to assure him that everything was well on his part.

'Why don't you add a few lines?' he asked Natalie.

'Me? Why?'

'I think he'd appreciate it. He's very fond of you.' Reginald said, giving her a wink.

'Oh,' she said, colouring slightly. 'I will then.'

She wrote a few sentences, which Reginald read over quickly.

'Perfect.' He signed and sealed it and had Narendi Ram deliver it to the postman.

Three weeks passed in a similar manner. Reginald and Natalie spent all of their time together, picking up where they left off at Fubster Manor. His leg healed quickly, and by the third week, he was already doing the exercises the doctor had prescribed. Waverley wrote of triumph after triumph from the front.

All of a sudden, the winds of fortune changed. Natalie fell ill for long stretches as the end of her pregnancy drew near. Reginald was still with her, but on most days, she was too weak to get out of bed. Doctor Mackenzie assured Reginald that this was normal, but he wasn't sure. Meanwhile, the news from the front went from bad to worse. As the summer months advanced, disease began to ravage the British ranks. They had advanced too far too fast and found themselves cut off from their supply lines and facing the bulk of the Afghan army, which seemed impervious to the brutal climate. Even Reginald's knee refused to make progress and grew worse instead.

One bright morning, Reginald was thinking about all of this, when Natalie interrupted him.

'You look sad, Reginald,' she said. 'Tell me what's the matter.'

'I'm worried about you and the baby. You've not been feeling well for a long time now.'

'You needn't be worried about me,' she said serenely.

'But I am!'

'Reginald,' she said, fixing him with a serious gaze. 'I have to ask you, dearest. What would you do if I wasn't here?'

'What are you talking about?' he cried, alarmed.

'If I were to go, would you still find life worth living?'

'Think about what you're saying!'

'Answer me please, Reginald.'

'You know I can't live without you! How could you even suggest that?'

She sighed. 'That's what I'm afraid of, Reginald. If I leave, I need you to stay and look after the child. Promise me you will.'

'Natalie, I—'

'Promise me.'

He looked into her face and saw that she meant it with all her soul.

'I will look after the child,' he said.

She took his hand and squeezed it. 'Thank you. Now let's talk about something else.'

As the days passed, Natalie recovered much of her strength. The doctor predicted that the child would be born in mid-August and the preparations were made to welcome it into the world. In Afghanistan, the stranded British Army was relieved by a remarkable forced march executed by none other than General Reginald Dyer, the Butcher of Amritsar. With the British forces united and their strength waxing every day, the fighting spirit of the Afghans collapsed. The Amir sued for peace, and on August 8, the Treaty of Rawalpindi was signed, reaffirming the *status quo*, a fitting end to a useless war.

Waverley wrote that the Guides were on their way back to Peshawar. He had been granted leave and planned on visiting in early September. Reginald wrote back that everything was going well and that he was excited to see him. He was further informed that they would both be receiving honours from the viceroy for their leadership during the First Battle of Bagh and was asked if he would like for Waverley to accept his medal *in absentia*.

His heart at ease on account of Waverley and the rest of the Guides, Reginald focused his attention entirely on caring for Natalie as her time drew near.

## *Childbirth*

NATALIE ENTERED LABOUR on August 12, 1919, a few days before Doctor Mackenzie's prediction. Reginald was by her side when it happened. He rushed to fetch the doctor and Clara, who was a nurse and midwife herself.

'You'd best stay outside,' the doctor said as he entered Natalie's room and shut the door behind him.

Reginald pulled up a chair in the hallway and listened to Natalie's agonised screams, each of which threatened to rend his soul. He wanted to run away and hide himself, but he remained transfixed to the spot. From time to time, the doctor stuck his head out of the door to ensure Reginald that everything was going fine.

The hours crawled by. Night fell, and yet there was no end to Natalie's suffering. For a long time, Doctor Mackenzie stayed within the room, leaving Reginald to fearfully imagine what was going on inside. He rose from his chair and paced the hallway; when that failed to satisfy his restless spirit, he collapsed to his knees and prayed fervently in a way he had never prayed before. To whom he was praying, he did not know nor did he understand the words that were issuing from his lips.

At last, near dawn, the door opened and the doctor emerged.

'You'd better come inside,' he said.

Reginald entered. The first thing he saw was Clara cradling a wailing child in her arms, and his heart swelled with emotion. Then he looked at Natalie, who was lying there still.

'Natalie, I—' he cried joyfully, rushing to her side.

He stopped. She was not moving. It couldn't be! Had her fears come true? Would he be left alone in the world to raise the child?

All at once, she opened her beautiful blue eyes and smiled at him.

# About the Author

GOEFFREY HALL IS a teacher of history, originally from Pittsburgh, Pennsylvania. He loves learning and reading classic literature. *The Extraordinary Life and Love of Reginald Fubster* is his first completed novel.

Printed in the USA
CPSIA information can be obtained
at www.ICGtesting.com
LVHW091532221024
794497LV00002B/170

9 798893 451825